Tally knew why the high and mighty Viscount Chelmsford had asked her to dance. It was not passion for her person, but amusement at her ineptitude.

Now the music had stopped, and Chelmsford bent to whisper in her ear, "Thank you for a most enjoyable dance, Lady Talitha." He pressed a warm, lingering kiss on her hand, then bowed his leave, as if it was all he could do to tear himself away.

Tally was left seething with fury. The viscount's mocking wit was well known—and now he was making a joke of her humiliation. How she would have loved to hate this insensitive boor . . . and how she hated to think of being in love with him . . .

ANNE BARBOUR developed an affection for the Regency period while living in England. She now lives in the Black Hills of South Dakota with her husband, a retired lieutenant colonel. She is the mother of six children, all grown, and she loves to boast of her five grandchildren.

A Talent
for Trouble

by

Anne Barbour

A SIGNET BOOK

SIGNET
Published by the Penguin Group
Penguin Books USA Inc., 375 Hudson Street,
New York, New York 10014, U.S.A.
Penguin Books Ltd, 27 Wrights Lane,
London W8 5TZ, England
Penguin Books Australia Ltd, Ringwood,
Victoria, Australia
Penguin Books Canada Ltd, 10 Alcorn Avenue,
Toronto, Ontario, Canada M4V 3B2
Penguin Books (N.Z.) Ltd, 182–190 Wairau Road,
Auckland 10, New Zealand

Penguin Books Ltd, Registered Offices:
Harmondsworth, Middlesex, England

First published by Signet,
an imprint of New American Library,
a division of Penguin Books USA Inc.

First Printing, August, 1992
10 9 8 7 6 5 4 3 2 1

 REGISTERED TRADEMARK—MARCA REGISTRADA

PRINTED IN THE UNITED STATES OF AMERICA

BOOKS ARE AVAILABLE AT QUANTITY DISCOUNTS WHEN USED TO PROMOTE PRODUCTS OR SERVICES. FOR INFORMATION PLEASE WRITE TO PREMIUM MARKETING DIVISION, PENGUIN BOOKS USA INC., 375 HUDSON STREET, NEW YORK, NEW YORK 10014.

For Bob, for everything.

NOTE:
The novel, *A Talent for Trouble*, discussed herein, is modeled loosely on a rollicking adventure story written by one Pierce Egan, entitled *Life in London*. From the day it was published in 1820, it was a smash hit, and it continued to entertain the English public for decades. Its graceless heroes, Tom and Jerry, have become part of the lexicon of the language.

Chapter One

The traveling coach lumbering sedately along the Cambridge Road was not built for speed, and its days as an equipage of fashionable elegance were long past. A faded crest could be seen outlined on its panels, and the postilions wore livery of dark green and a somewhat tarnished silver. As the coach made its ponderous way along an uphill stretch, a diminutive head popped from the window now and then to implore the coachman to "Put 'em along, can't you, Greavey? Spring 'em! Please?"

Her pleas were to no avail, and after a final attempt, Lady Talitha Burnside drew back into the carriage and sank back into her seat.

"Really, Addie," she cried in a despairing voice to the elderly woman seated opposite her, "we shall never get to Town at this rate."

Miss Theodora Adlestrop smiled indulgently. She had been Tally's governess for thirteen years, and well knew the wide-ranging enthusiasms that dwelled in that young woman's slight form. She surveyed her erstwhile charge with a fond eye. No one could call Lady Tally a beauty— she was too small, and altogether too brown—but there was a certain something about her. Charm was perhaps the best word to describe it. Miss Adlestrop sighed. It was unfortunate that Tally's reduced circumstances prohibited her from displaying that charm, and her wit and warmth to any but a very few intimates. She reached to pat Tally's hand.

"The delay at Bishop's Stortford was indeed unfortunate, but it takes time to mend a broken axle. Merciful Heavens, it's a wonder we weren't killed!"

"No thanks to Henry!" responded her young friend tartly. "This old lumberbus has been moldering away in our coach-house for years, and I don't suppose he had anyone look at it before we started out."

"Well, now my lady, London has been a-building for nearly two thousand years now, and I don't believe it will vanish by the time we arrive. See, we are approaching Islington Village, and will be drawing up before dear Catherine's door in less than an hour."

"Yes, but Addie, we were to have arrived hours ago!" wailed the young woman. "I must be in London by four o'clock. If I do not see Mr. Mapes today, I will have missed my opportunity, for he is leaving town tomorrow and won't be back for weeks!"

"Oh, that." Miss Adlestrop fidgeted. "Lady Tally, you cannot mean you are actually going through with this . . . this foolishness. What will Lord Bamfield say?"

"Foolishness!" Tally's eyes widened in an indignant stare. "Henry has nothing to say to this! Of course, I told him that I'm on the hunt for an eligible *parti* . . . but I have come to the city to . . . to Launch My Career!"

Miss Adlestrop uttered a sound that was perilously close to a snort.

"Career, indeed. My dear, you are a lady of quality. What Lord Bamfield—the late earl, that is—would have thought to see his daughter scheming to earn her own way . . . ! And as a . . . scribbler of . . . obscene pictures!"

Tally stiffened, causing the bonnet which she had hastily tied over her thick chestnut hair to tilt even further askew.

"And just where is it written," she asked with asperity, "that a lady must starve on a wretched pittance, when she has the ability to earn her own bread? And I do *not* scribble obscene pictures." She drew herself up, lifting her already short, uptilted nose. "I am a caricaturist!"

"But you do not have to live on a pittance. Your brother has made it more than clear that you are welcome to make your home at Summerhill Park. You've always loved the Park, even more than your brother, I've often thought."

Tally's great brown eyes misted. Summerhill. Memories of endless tumbles through sunlit meadows spun in her mind—and companionable gallops with her father, flying over hedgerows and down leafy lanes. It was still hard to realize that she would never again enjoy a comfortable ramble beside the person she had loved the most in the world. Since the earl's death in a hunting accident over a year ago, she had not been able to think of those days without tears. So, she would not think of them at all.

"I have no desire to stay at Summerhill," she asserted. "Henry and I would simply live at daggers drawn. Besides, if I remained at the Park, I should decline rapidly into the status of 'dear Aunt Talitha.' " She pursed her lips in a scandalously accurate imitation of her sister-in-law's rather sour countenance.

" 'Children, you are giving me such a headache, why don't you all go up to the nursery for a game of spillikins with dear Aunt Talitha?' Or, 'It would be ever so accommodating of dear Aunt Talitha if she were to take all three of you on a picnic while Mama entertains visitors this afternoon.' "

"Thank you," continued Tally, her voice tinged with acid, "but I believe that I would rather make my own way as a 'scribbler' than serve as an unpaid nanny in Henry's household."

Miss Adlestrop sighed once more, her plump chins atremble and easy tears appeared in her pale blue eyes.

"To think that your dear papa should have left you in such straits. Fifty pounds a year is certainly not what he could have intended for you. He can't have meant to leave things in such a bumble broth."

"No," agreed Tally slowly. "I've gone over it all a hundred times in my mind since Papa—since Papa died, and I can only conclude that he intended to make out a new will, but simply never got around to it. You know how he was—'Never put off until tomorrow what you can push off till next week.' "

Finding herself sinking deeper into a quite unacceptable mire of gloom, she shook herself.

"Well, at any rate, Henry has behaved very handsomely in regard to this trip to Town." She smoothed the skirt of her kerseymere carriage dress. "For such a nip-farthing, it must have gone much against his grain to dress me in style."

Miss Adlestrop glanced dubiously at the gown, an ill-fitting creation in a muddy shade of olive. She reflected

for the hundredth time on the parsimony of the present
earl, and on the wretched taste of the earl's wife, to
whom he had turned over the procuring of Tally's wardrobe. Not that Lady Tally's taste in fashion was much
better. The girl simply had no concept of how to dress
becomingly; nor did she care that her natural appeal was
completely obliterated by the dreadful clothes she wore.
The governess said nothing of all this, however, merely
pointing out that they had reached the outskirts of the
city.

Tally whirled to peer through the coach window and
was instantly assaulted by the sights, sounds, and smells
of the metropolis. "Oh! Oh, yes—we *are* here—at last!"

She had forgotten the incredible vitality of the place,
but as she watched the crowds of passersby and street
hawkers, she felt as though she had never been away
from the raucous, brawling, sprawling cacophonous hive
that was London.

The old carriage, negotiating its way gingerly through
winding streets and crooked lanes, finally drew into the
narrow confines of Paternoster Row, and lumbered to
a stop before Number Three, a shabby building which
proclaimed itself the headquarters of George Mapes and
Son, Book Publishers. The hazy bulk of St. Paul's
loomed in the background.

Without waiting for the assistance of the footman who
was unhurriedly climbing down from his perch, Tally
flung open the carriage door. Clasped to her bosom, beneath which her heart had suddenly begun to lurch in an
alarming manner, was a fat packet of parchment paper.

"Oh, Addie, wish me luck!" she breathed. "I shan't
be long, but if I don't return shortly, tell Greavey it's all
right to walk the horses. How do I look? Oh, I do wish
we had time to stop at Cat's house so that I could freshen
up. Do you think . . . ?"

Miss Adlestrop smiled. "My lady, if you don't stop
chattering like a ninnyhammer, you will be late for your
appointment."

Tally gulped, and in a burst of nervous fury, catapulted
herself into the space between the vehicle and the doorway to Mapes and Son, Book Publishers. Unfortunately,
that particular space was already occupied by a tall, extremely solid, and definitely masculine body.

The most striking feature of the collision that ensued was the paper flurry it produce. Tally clutched wildly at the gentleman with whom she now found herself entangled in an awkward embrace. Sheets of drawing paper flew into the air and then fell in a swirling cloud. Joining them was a small blizzard of manuscript leaves, which had been wrenched from the gentleman as he gathered Tally into his arms to prevent her from falling.

In the instant during which Tally's face was pressed into a fragrant shirt front, she became aware of its owner's almost overpowering masculinity. The next moment, she found herself gazing into a pair of startled, gray eyes.

"You're not hurt, are you, Miss?"

Tally demonstrated that she was unharmed by pushing firmly against his chest.

He abruptly shifted his attention to the eddies of paper fluttering about them, and scrambled to retrieve his property, ignoring the danger to his superbly tailored pantaloons. Tally, abandoning any attempt at decorum, dropped to her hands and knees beside him, frantically grasping at the fluttering parchment sheets.

"You might warn a fellow before plummeting out of a carriage onto the public thoroughfare," he continued in some irritation. "Here, that's mine." He turned to snatch a fragment from Tally's hand.

The apology she had been about to utter died on her lips, and stiffening, she favored him with a haughty stare.

"Perhaps," she snapped, "if you had been watching where you stepped, you would not have—oh, that's mine!" She plucked a piece of parchment from his fingers.

By now most of the papers had been retrieved by helpful passersby, and by the footman, who had finally come to a sense of his duty. These were thrust at Tally and the gentleman, and it was left to them to continue the sorting-out process. Tally glanced at the sheet uppermost in her pile and noticed that it was covered by a dark, bold scrawl. The first sentence caught her eye.

"Cliffie, what do you say to a toddle in the Park? Then, perhaps we should slide round to the Daffy Club."

The paper was snatched from her.

"I believe that is mine," the man remarked coldly as he added it to his own handful. "And these"—he thrust several drawing-covered sheets at her—"must be yours."

Without asking permission, he grabbed the rest of Tally's collection from her and sifted through them rapidly, retaining some and handing the rest back to her. As he was about to relinquish the last of the parchment sheets, he paused and stood still for a moment, examining the drawing he held in his hand.

He gave a shout of laughter. "By Jove, if that isn't the Duchess of Wigand to the life!"

Abruptly he grew still, and again without asking permission, drew several more of the parchment sheets from Tally's hand and examined them closely.

Tally found her voice.

"Now, look here . . ." she sputtered, but it was as if the young man had not heard her. He continued to peruse the drawings, and it was several moments before he raised his head.

"These are very good," he said. "Who did them?"

"I cannot see that they are any concern of yours, sir, but as it happens, I am the artist."

"But . . ." He peered at her in some puzzlement. "You are a female."

Tally drew a deep breath and assumed an expression of vapid sweetness that would have boded ill to those who knew her well.

"Your quick perception must be a constant delight to your friends, sir," she returned smoothly. "You have penetrated my disguise. I am a female. And," she continued, "those are my drawings. Will you please return them to me at once? I have an appointment with Mr. Mapes." She nodded toward the ancient facade of Number Three. "I fear I have no more time to waste in chatting with idlers."

A flush spread over the man's outrageously handsome features. In some haste, he returned her drawings and lifted his hat. He ran strong fingers through his thick, neatly trimmed thatch of dark hair, and bowed over the small, wrathful form before him.

"I am sorry—that was stupid of me. It's just that one

is not accustomed to finding a true artist gowned in kerseymere and ribbons."

Tally, always susceptible to praise of her talent, found her antagonism melting under his words. The charming grin that accompanied them completed the thaw.

"I am Chelmsford," he continued with a devastating grin, "the Viscount Chelmsford, that is. As it happens, I, too, have an appointment with George Mapes. Shall we go in?"

With a flourish, he opened the door to Number Three and ushered Tally inside. Tally, unaccountably tongue-tied, hurried into the building.

The offices of Mapes and Son occupied the ground floor of the building, and the viscount was evidently well known there. A bespectacled clerk, occupied at a desk in the anteroom, sprang to his feet at their entrance. Ignoring Tally, he advanced toward Chelmsford and bent so low that his nose nearly became caught in his furious hand-washing.

"My lord!" he exclaimed. "Mr. Mapes is waiting for you. May I take your hat, my lord? And your gloves? Would you care for a cup of coffee—or a nip of something stronger, perhaps?"

With an expression of distaste, the viscount eased himself out of the clerk's obsequious grasp.

"Nothing for me, thank you, Porlock. But perhaps some tea for Miss . . . er, Miss . . ." He turned questioningly to Tally.

"My name is Talitha Burnside, my lord. And, thank you, I do not wish for any tea."

The clerk deigned to glance at Tally.

"Miss Burnside? Yes, I believe you, too, have an appointment with Mr. Mapes. If you will wait here, Mr. Mapes will see you—after his business with his lordship is concluded, of course," he said with condescension.

Tally stiffened. Though she had chosen in her correspondence with Mr. Mapes to represent herself as plain Miss Burnside, she was unused to being spoken to in such a manner by persons of Mr. Porlock's order.

She turned to the clerk, drew herself up to her full five foot two inches, and in a voice of calm authority said, "But, my appointment was for four o'clock, was it not?

And it is now just a few minutes past. I'm afraid his lordship will have to wait his turn."

Mr. Porlock's mouth dropped open. Before he could deliver a reply, the viscount interjected, and Tally could have sworn she heard amusement in his voice.

"You are absolutely correct, Miss Burnside. It is I who am at fault, for I am quite half an hour late for my own appointment. By rights I should forfeit my precedence. However, I wonder if I might prevail on your good nature. You see, I am expected elsewhere soon at another appointment—an important one, I'm afraid. May I see George ahead of you? I shall only be a few moments. Please?"

Again, his smile bathed Tally in its blinding warmth. She cast her eyes down, and in doing so, caught sight of the untidy bundle of parchment she still clasped in her arms.

"That will be agreeable, my lord. I believe it will take several minutes for me to rearrange my drawings more presentably." She nodded her head regally, wishing she did not feel so stiff and stilted and foolish.

With another smile the viscount walked from the ante-room into the passage beyond. Rigid with disapproval, Mr. Porlock waved Tally to a seat and returned to his own desk, where he busied himself with some papers, refusing to look at her again.

Tally sank onto the hard wooden chair and let her papers fall into her lap. She began smoothing them out, but after a few moments her fingers stilled. She lifted her head, and her eyes gazed unseeing at the back of Mr. Porlock's head.

She thought back to her descent from the carriage a few minutes earlier and relived the subsequent collision and the instant she had found herself clasped in the arms of the Viscount Chelmsford. She could still feel their strength and warmth.

She had recognized him at once, of course. It was obvious that he did not remember her, but she had not expected that he would. Why should the *ton*'s most notable ornament remember a single dance that had taken place five years earlier? A dance in which he had partnered one of the *ton*'s most unremarkable young misses.

It had been a dance Tally would never forget.

Chapter Two

Even after all these years, Tally could not look back on the night of her come-out ball without experiencing a tightening of her throat and a sick feeling in the pit of her stomach.

She pictured herself at seventeen, small and thin, all big, scared eyes and awkward angles. She had no doubt she resembled a fledgling stork rather than a young lady making her entrance into the Polite World.

She had been sponsored by her mother's sister, Sophronia, Lady Spilting, an elderly widow of reclusive habits, who lived in a cavernous old town house in Cavendish Square. She had selected Tally's wardrobe with an eye more to durability than fashion, and the pale pastels favored by the *ton* for debutantes did nothing to enhance Tally's delicate features and honey gold complexion.

Not that Tally cared. She had resigned herself at an early age to the fact that she would never be a beauty. Even her father had once told her, "Never mind, my dearest, you are lovely inside—and that beauty will endure long after Jeannie Fox's golden curls have faded, or Sarah Smythe-Beddoes's figure has given way under all those comfits."

Tally didn't believe any of it for a minute, but when it became apparent that her fingers contained a special magic, she was able to persuade herself that her talent outweighed her plainness. She became immersed in her drawing. Now, a social gathering was merely an opportunity to study faces and forms. On this particular evening, therefore, she did not feel slighted that her only partners were young men who had been coerced into the position by propriety-conscious mamas. At least, so she told herself.

Still, she loved to dance, and when, inevitably, she

found herself partnerless at her aunt's side, she gazed longingly at the couples whirling about like brilliant blossoms tossed in a stream. Suddenly Lady Spilting had hissed in her ear.

"Well! You can count your evening a success, my dear. Chelmsford has honored us with his presence."

Tally turned to look and then caught her breath at the magnificence of the tall stranger who had just entered the ballroom. His mahogany-colored hair was cut in a careless Brutus style, and his eyes, the color of summer mist, were a pale blaze against his bronzed skin. The quiet elegance of his evening attire made every other man there seem just a little shabby, and his lazy smile seemed to warm the entire room. When he dutifully presented himself to Lady Talitha for one of the country dances, she was overcome with shyness. To his polished courtesies she responded with mechanical civilities, uttered in a strangled monotone.

When the music died away, the viscount brushed her fingertips with his lips and turned to seek entertainment elsewhere. His course led him unerringly to a beautiful, vibrant creature who had been the center of attention all evening. She was tall and slender, and from behind her fan, eyes of twilight blue flashed and sparkled at her court. Golden curls tumbled over a perfect forehead of smoothest ivory and drifted airily about classically curved cheeks. Her mouth, red and full-lipped, trembled in a coquettish smile as the viscount swept her into a waltz.

Then, scarcely an hour after he arrived, he was gone. Aunt Sophronia frowned in exasperation.

"Not that one would expect him to linger," she grunted. "The man is notorious for his lightning appearances. I suppose we must count ourselves lucky that he showed up at all. His mother must have exerted her influence. Lady Chelmsford and your mother were bosom bows at school, you know."

"And the lady he partnered for the waltz?" Tally asked in a carefully casual tone.

"Umph. Clea Montmorency. 'The Unattainable,' they call her. She's the youngest daughter of some baronet that nobody ever heard of, but Clea has made quite the splash. Has half the blades in London mad for her. According to the *on-dits*, she's hanging out for a title and money—lots of it. Looks like she may have found her target there in young Chelmsford. Heaven knows, he has both in abundance."

Tally experienced an unexpected pang at these words, but she chided herself immediately. Surely, she was not a susceptible widgeon, driven to rapture by a godlike countenance. And even if she were, what possible chance could she, a dull country wren, have against the exotic beauty of Clea Montmorency?

Suddenly weary of the scented ballroom and the buzz of stilted conversation about her, she slipped off to seek a moment's solitude in an alcove near the cloakroom. Just before she reached the little nook, she met the viscount, who had donned his evening cloak and was making his way toward the staircase. As Tally moved aside, he smiled at her, then paused.

"Your ball appears to be a success, Lady Talitha. I look forward to encountering you again—perhaps at Almack's?"

Her eyes met his, and she returned his smile shyly. Just then a shrill, masculine voice burst from the interior of the alcove, piercing the subdued hum of voices and sedate string music that surrounded them.

"Confound it, Mama, I'm not going to dance with the Burnside chit! You always force me to stand up with the drabbest nobody in the place, and I'm sick of it. And she's only moderately endowed. Get Roddy to do it! God knows he'd be happy to propel the Witch of Endor around the floor if she had but tuppence to her name!"

Tally stood paralyzed in the echo of those wounding words. The viscount's eyes still held hers, and for an instant, she stared at him in shamed horror. A single embarrassed titter from the surrounding group of listeners caught her with the force of a blow, and with the instinct of a wounded forest creature, she whirled to flee. To her dismay, the viscount grasped her wrist, forcing her to immobility.

"Please," she whispered in a choked sob. "Please—let me go!"

"Don't be a fool." The words were spoken in a tone of cold disinterest. "Do you wish to be perceived as a spiritless ninny—as well as a drab nobody?"

Tally whitened, and the viscount continued brusquely.

"I fail to see why you should crawl into a cave and whimper just because some idiot has chosen to vent his extremely ill-bred spleen in such a public manner. Come."

The viscount, calm and smiling, swept his cloak open and tossed it to a nearby lackey.

"But I cannot leave without one more dance with you, Lady Talitha." He did not raise his voice but somehow made his words heard clearly to those surrounding them. "May I claim your hand for the waltz?"

He was apparently oblivious to the fact that as a young girl just making her come-out, she could not have received the requisite permission from the patronesses of Almack's to participate in that controversial dance. Without waiting for an answer, he brought Tally's hand to his lips and, still holding her icy fingers clamped in his own, strode into the ballroom. He swung her into the rhythm of the dance, and, observing the tears that threatened to overflow, he bent to remark caustically, "Apparently, I was right. You are a spiritless ninny. Fortunately for you, I have determined that you are not to give way to an attack of the vapors, or whatever else you may have planned to relieve your bruised sensibilities."

Tally gasped as though she had just been drenched in ice water. How *dare* he speak so to her! She tried to break free of his grasp, but his slender fingers imprisoned hers with a grip of steel.

During the course of the dance, he maintained a flow of light conversation, sometimes throwing his head back in laughter, as though Tally had overcome him with her wit. In truth, she had almost nothing to say. Inwardly, she raged at the viscount's incredibly insulting behavior, but could not form the words to give him the set-down he so richly deserved.

The eyes of the gathered ball guests were on her, and all she wanted was to find a dark corner in which to lick her wounds. What right had he to drag her from the refuge she sought—and in such an insufferable manner? He had as much as told her she was indeed a drab nobody! She felt suspended in a nightmare, all her pain centered on the man who held her so lightly. To her cringing senses, he represented the entire Polite World, with all its arrogance and casual cruelty.

Suddenly she was fired with a determination that neither he nor any of the bejeweled butterflies surrounding her should discern her anguish. She glared straight into Chelmsford's cool gray eyes, and with her head held high and an expression of inutterable boredom on her face, she floated over the floor in the viscount's arms.

When the music stopped, Chelmsford bent to whisper in her ear, and though his words expressed the most commonplace sentiments—"Thank you for a most enjoyable dance, Lady Talitha."—his demeanor spoke of future assignations in secluded bowers. He was making a joke of her humiliation! Of all the insensitive boors! As though he guessed her thoughts, he laughed down into her eyes. Tally would have given all she possessed to plant a jarring slap right across those perfect teeth.

He pressed a warm, lingering kiss on her hand, then bowed himself away, conveying the impression that it was all he could do to tear himself from her presence.

Still seething, Tally turned once again to seek haven, but to her surprise, her hand was claimed by an aspiring dandy who had earlier passed her by without a second glance. By the end of the evening, a puzzled but gratified Aunt Sophronia had seen her niece become the most sought-after damsel in the room. Clearly the Viscount Chelmsford's gallantry, even for a few moments, was enough to guarantee a flattering degree of attention from every other male in the room who aspired to fashion.

It did not last, of course. The next day several gentlemen called in Cavendish Square, but when it became apparent that Lord Chelmsford was not to be among them, interest in the Earl of Bamfield's unprepossessing little daughter waned, and by the end of the week, the flow had dried up completely. Soon even Aunt Sophronia had forgotten Tally's spurt of popularity.

But Tally did not forget. Over the years she had come to realize that the viscount's blunt tactics had prevented her from making a further fool of herself by hurtling out of the room in tears. She was far from understanding his motive in interfering in her predicament. An arrogant whim, perhaps—a desire to prove that he had it in his power to transform her in an instant from a scorned outcast to the belle of the ball. He had been insufferably rude, and—and he had laughed at her! She was sure she hated him.

But the image of the viscount's cloudy eyes laughing into hers remained permanently etched in her mind. She would always know the feel of strong fingers cupping her hand in his. The memory of his powerful stride—the very cologne and leather scent of him still haunted her dreams.

The sound of a door opening and a rumble of jovial voices from beyond the antechamber jerked Tally from her reverie. She looked down to find that the parchment sheets were still scattered in disorder over her lap.

"Ah, Miss Burnside."

It was the voice of the viscount, and Tally, relieved as she was that no memory of her humiliation lingered with him, experienced a pang of disappointment that he did not remember her at all.

"You see," he continued, "I have honored my promise. I kept George occupied for less than ten minutes. Now, he assures me, he is completely at your disposal."

Behind the viscount, a plump young man bobbed his head in agreement. In a few moments Lord Chelmsford, with a cheerful nod, had departed, and Tally was ushered into the publisher's office.

Outside the shabby old building the viscount closed the door behind him. He settled his curly-crowned beaver on his head, and his lips curved in an odd smile. What a singular coincidence, to be sure. He had recognized the girl at once, of course. He doubted he had once thought of her since that night some four years ago, when he had, with intentional brusqueness, forced her to face down her tormentors. Time had done little to improve the aspect of the colorless damsel whom he had partnered in the oddest dance of his career, but those great brown eyes had stayed with him. He smiled again as he remembered the pride in which she had garbed herself, like the raiment of a queen.

Now she presented herself as plain Miss Talitha Burnside. He experienced a mild curiosity at this, but his mind leaped to the fact that under "Miss Burnside's" plain exterior lurked a blazing talent, a talent for which he had, at the present, a most pressing need.

Apparently she had not recognized him. He found himself unexpectedly piqued at this. But then, why should she? She had no doubt exorcised the whole, humiliating incident from her memory. He certainly had no intention of resurrecting a painful moment by reminding her.

But what a stroke of luck that he had met her again, and right on Mapes's doorstep! He smiled, picturing the scene that must be taking place behind the doors of Number Three, and he whistled as he made his way to his next appointment.

In the publishers' office Tally settled herself in a large chair opposite the plump young man.

"But," she began, looking doubtful. "I was not expecting . . ."

"Yes, Miss Burnside? Your appointment was with George Mapes, and I am certainly he."

Mr. Mapes laughed, his spectacles glinting in the late afternoon sun pouring through the office window.

"You were expecting to meet my father, Mapes, Senior. He was called away unexpectedly, so you will have to make do with me, I'm afraid."

"Oh, it's nothing like that. It's just that—well . . ." Tally trailed off uncertainly.

"I understand, Miss Burnside. You had corresponded with my father, and he is the gentleman with whom you expected to deal. Please be assured that he has given me your letter, and I am fully cognizant of your reason for being here."

He peered again at his guest, and Tally thought his gaze held some degree of reluctance. She tensed herself for the attack.

"Very well, then," she began briskly. "You are aware that I am applying to you as a caricaturist. I have here a representative sample of my work, as well as a letter of introduction from Thomas Beecroft."

"Mm, yes. You mentioned Beecroft in your letter to my father. His name, as you might imagine, carries a great deal of weight. Until he retired ten years ago, he was one of England's premier caricaturists." He gazed uncertainly at Tally for a moment. "You actually studied with him?"

"Oh, yes," replied Tally firmly. "As you may know, he retired to Cambridgeshire. His present home is not five miles from my own. I met him soon after he moved in—I was only a child then."

Tally paused. Should she tell him just how she, a grubby twelve-year-old had met the Great Man? She chuckled unself-consciously and was surprised at the encouraging grin returned by Mr. Mapes. She could not know that her eyes, when she laughed, narrowed to sparkling slits that seemed to invite an answering smile.

"As it happened," she began, the corners of her generous mouth lifting in an engaging curve, "Uncle Bee—that is, Mr. Beecroft, caught me stealing apples from his orchard. He rang a tremendous peal over me, and in retaliation, as soon as he had stumped off, I sat right down and drew a picture of him. I have always had a love of drawing and take my sketch pad with me everywhere. I'm afraid I was rather in the habit of scribbling horrid drawings of people I particularly disliked. I always destroyed them right away, but in Uncle Bee's case, the wind caught my paper just as I finished, and blew it right into his front garden.

"When he found it, he was not angry, as I expected he would be. Instead, he came to my father and offered to instruct me. Ever since I have spent every moment I could spare learning about line and form and balance, and all the other components of art. And these"—she indicated the drawings—"are the result."

She laid the untidy bundle on the desk, and Mr. Mapes reached for it, his expression resigned.

As he leafed through the sheets, however, his face lightened. When he had looked at them all, he began again, subjecting each to a minute scrutiny. At last, he looked up with a smile.

"Well, now." He sat back in his chair and stared at her thoughtfully. "Miss Burnside, your skill is, quite frankly, astonishing, especially for a female. I think we can use your talent."

Tally released the breath that she had been holding for what seemed like the entire time she had been in Mr. Mapes's office.

"Ordinarily," he continued, "Mapes and Son does not handle caricature work. We produce in the main, serious tomes on science, religion, the arts, and current events. It has only been within the last year that I have been able to convince my father that the public is crying out for something more frivolous. The phenomenal success of the Ackermann firm with Rowlandson's work finally convinced him to take the plunge.

"Thus, it happens that we are preparing for publication, in serial form, a book called *Town Bronze*. It is the story of the adventures—or rather, the misadventures—of a pair of men about town called Clifford and Clive."

Tally frowned. There was something familiar in all this.

"These two scapegraces," continued Mr. Mapes, "cover the length and breadth of London, as well as its heights and depths. Clifford is a peer, newly arrived in Town, who meets Clive, a kindred spirit, ripe for any spree. Their activities take them from the most exclusive gaming clubs in St. James's Street, to the sluiceries of the East End—from the Duchess of Devonshire's ball to Cribb's Parlour. Does this sound like something you could handle?"

Tally nodded firmly, wondering what a sluicery might be, and who or what was Cribb—and what was so special about his parlour?

"Of course, Mr. Mapes. I am reasonably familiar with the London scene."

"Mm," responded Mr. Mapes enigmatically. Then he hitched himself forward in his chair and his voice became intense. "But the most important aspect of *Town Bronze*, at least to our firm, are the characters portrayed in it. Our readers will meet Lady Beddable, Lord Deeppockets, Sir Toby Potwell, Lily Lightskirt, and Miss Primrose Promise, among others. All of these will be easily identifiable as persons of note in our little metropolis. Particularly, if the 'portraits' are suitably drawn in the book's illustrations. Do I make myself clear?"

"Y-yes, I think so. I suppose the persons involved are those who have already made themselves ridiculous in the eyes of the world."

"Quite." Mr. Mapes smiled, delighted at Miss Burnside's quick grasp of the essentials. "People want to read about the nobs. They want to see the foibles and fribbles of those who aspire to be the shapers of our world. Your sketch of the Duchess of Wigand, for example, is perfect! You've captured her arrogant self-satisfaction in a few strokes without falling into the grotesqueries of poor old Gillray (he's gone quite barmy, you know) and young

Cruikshank. This is the kind of thing we want for *Town Bronze*."

Tally felt a stirring of eagerness. She could do this! She knew her fingers contained the talent to bring to life all the silliness, the artificiality, yes, even the cruelty of the denizens of London, from the lowest chimney sweep right up to the Prince Regent, if necessary.

Mr. Mapes was sunk in another thoughtful pause, his fingers steepled in front of him. Tally watched him expectantly, and at last he spoke again.

"We cannot pay you a great deal, Miss Burnside. It was my father's stipulation that if we were to venture into 'trumpery satire,' as he put it, we would expend very little money, at least until it becomes a proven success. The author of the book has agreed to work for next to nothing. He is . . ." Mr. Mapes appeared to be groping for words, "a, um, peer. A wealthy man who writes for enjoyment. It is his stipulation that his name not be revealed as the author of *Town Bronze*."

Tally's eyes widened. The lines scrawled on the viscount's vellum page leaped to her mind. "I say, Cliffie, what do you say to a toddle in the Park?" Chelmsford must be the author of *Town Bronze*! That's why he had insisted on seeing Mr. Mapes ahead of her. He had recognized in her just the sort of mouse who could be bullied into selling her talent for a pittance.

Tally sighed inwardly. She would dearly have liked to show him that he was very much in error, but she was in no position to dictate terms. She desperately needed to get her foot in the door of the publishing world, and, yes, she would work for a pittance. At first, anyway.

She straightened in her chair and faced Mr. Mapes squarely.

"Sir, I will be frank with you. First of all, I must assume that the author of *Town Bronze* is the Viscount Chelmsford."

The young publisher's response was an audible gasp.

"But how—that is to say—what a ludicrous idea, Miss Burnside."

"I think not, Mr. Mapes. But," she continued in a kind tone, "you need not fear a lack of discretion on my part. You see"—and here her eyes fell to her lap, where she had begun to twist a small ring she wore—"I, too, wish to remain anonymous. I have my reasons," she finished, as she observed Mr. Mapes's expression change to one of guarded curiosity.

"Of course, Miss Burnside," he answered smoothly. "That is quite commonplace among female scriveners. As you may know, the author of *Sense and Sensibility* is featured on her book covers simply as, 'a lady.' There is little or no precedence for a female caricaturist, but I should imagine the same arrangement would suffice."

"No." Tally's response was abrupt. "I have decided to produce my work under a pseudonym. My drawings will be signed simply 'Mouse.' " She continued quickly. "It was a pet name my father used for me when I was very small."

Accustomed to the foibles of the literary world, Mr. Mapes merely smiled briefly.

"Very well then, Miss Burnside. Lord Chelmsford, by the by, has chosen to be known as 'Dash.' "

"Yes. Well," Tally rushed on, determined now to conceal nothing from the man who was about to become her employer, "I am not really Miss Burnside."

This produced another gasp from Mr. Mapes.

"I mean, well, of course, Burnside is my family name, but I am called Lady Talitha Burnside, my father being the Earl of Bamfield."

George Mapes's countenance now took on the expression of one who has been granted a heavenly vision. His plan for what he contemplated would be the runaway success of *Town Bronze* counted heavily on the discreet rumor he planned to circulate that its author was an unidentified peer. And here, dropped into his lap, lay additional grist for his mill. The paltry sum he had been about to offer in remuneration was quickly revised upward.

To his pleasure, Miss Burnside, or rather Lady Talitha, agreed to the amount, with the stipulation that she be accorded a small percentage of the book's sales. Mr. Mapes smilingly agreed, and thus the interview closed.

"I must say," said Mr. Mapes, "that your being aware of the author's identity will smooth the way in your collaboration with Lord Chelmsford, for of course, it will be advantageous for you to meet with him from time to time."

Tally felt a flutter of dismay.

"Oh, no! I do not plan to be out and about, and—I'm sure his lordship and I can conduct whatever business is necessary through your office."

Mr. Mapes's brows rose.

"Dear lady, you cannot have considered. Since the book is to come out in serial form, it will be necessary for you to know, even before his lordship has finished his first draft, the persons and places described in each chapter, so that by the time he has readied an installment for publication, your illustrations will also be completed.

"As for going out and about, again you must realize that if you are to bring Lord Chelmsford's London to life, you must be *au courant*. You must be familiar with the interior of the Italian Opera, the pathways at Vauxhall, Hyde Park at promenade. Your ladies must be dressed bang up to the echo. I notice here that the Duchess of Wigand's gown is at least three years out of style. The public notices things like that, Lady Talitha."

The sick feeling had returned to the pit of Tally's stomach. She knew that Mr. Mapes spoke the truth, but how could she bear to open herself to the bored ridicule she had experienced during her first visit to London? More important, how could she bear the constant company of Lord Chelmsford? In the years following her departure from the realm of the *haut ton*, she had outgrown the childish feelings of hurt and humiliation of those brief, painful months. In Lord Chelmsford's presence, she would be constantly reminded of them.

She stood in thought for several moments before she squared her slight shoulders and faced Mr. Mapes.

"Yes, you are quite right. Please tell the viscount that I shall be pleased to meet with him at his convenience for the purpose of conferring on our project."

Tally left Mr. Mapes's office a few moments later, with his expressions of good will and satisfaction ringing in her ears.

She was exhilarated at the success of her interview with the little publisher, but before her floated the image of a pair of cool, gray eyes. The thought of a collaboration between herself and the exalted Lord Chelmsford filled her with deep misgiving, mingled with a stirring of unacknowledged anticipation.

Chapter Three

By the time Tally had deposited Miss Adlestrop at her sister's home, the hour was far advanced, and when the ancient carriage shuddered to a stop before a fashionable town house in Half Moon Street, dusk had begun to descend.

Flambeaux on either side of the entrance cast a warm glow into the advancing twilight as the coach, creaking in leathery protest, pressed against one side of the narrow street. The door of the town house flew open, and a tall, slender figure stood poised for moment, silhouetted against the light streaming from within, before hurling herself upon Tally as she emerged from the vehicle.

"Tally! We had given you up for lost! We've been envisioning highwaymen on the heath, and vile kidnappers in the hills!"

The young woman enveloped Tally in a warm hug and scattered directions at various functionaries, causing them to scurry like obedient mice to assist in the disembarkation.

Tally laughed unaffectedly.

"Well, I hardly think kidnappers, however vile, would be likely to bother with Henry's old coach. Oh, Cat," she breathed, "it is *so* good to see you!"

Drawing her friend into the warmth of the house, Cat led the way to a small, exquisitely furnished salon.

"Now!" she exclaimed. "You must tell me what it is that has brought you to London. You were very mysterious in your correspondence. Yes, I know what you said, but I do not believe in your 'sudden craving for a space of town life.'"

Tally shrugged herself out of her pelisse and turned to Cat, her eyes wide and disingenuous.

"But, dearest, I simply must change my ensemble."

She gestured to the kerseymere carriage dress, smoothing its wrinkled olive skirts. "I cannot sit down to dinner in all my dirt."

"Mm, yes, the sooner you get out of that outfit the better," replied Cat cryptically. "We've having your favorite, buttered crab, but remember, not one bite shall you get until you explain all."

In her room Tally made a hasty toilette and donned a gown more suitable for evening wear, this time a robe of puce satin, with rows of ruffles churning furiously about neckline and hem. When she returned to the small salon, she found that Cat had been joined by her husband, Richard Thurston. Observing them together, Tally decided that Richard was precisely the sort of mate one would choose for one's best friend. He was of medium height and compactly built. A shock of brown hair fell in a curve over a pair of smiling brown eyes, and his mouth was spread, as it almost always was, in a friendly grin.

Richard was the youngest son of the Earl of Trumpington, but had fared much better than most young men in his position. He had inherited a comfortable living from a wealthy uncle and was thus able to support his bride in a more than tolerable life-style. He had also discovered in himself a talent for what he called 'bringing people together,' and when he entered the Foreign Office, under the auspices of yet another well-placed relative, his rise had been swift. He was at present a senior aide for Lord Whittaker and privy to the sensitive machinations of the department.

As Tally entered the room, Richard advanced and wrapped her in a vigorous hug. He planted a noisy kiss on her cheek.

"Tally! By all that's wonderful! You've finally decided to make a return trip to the metropolis. I hope you'll be with us for a long while?"

"Yes, she will." Cat answered for her friend. "Now that I finally have her in my clutches, she shan't see her precious Summerhill for some time to come."

"But," continued Richard, "Cat tells me you're being very mysterious as to the reason for your visit. Come now, you must divulge to your two best friends whatever plot it is you're hatching."

Tally, comfortably ensconced in an armchair of cherry-striped silk, waved an airy hand.

"Oh, it's nothing, really. Simply that I come to you as London's newest, soon-to-be-the-rage caricaturist!"

To a most satisfactory accompaniment of gasps and widened eyes, Tally related the events of the afternoon, carefully omitting any reference to my Lord Chelmsford. At the end of her discourse, she swore her host and hostess to secrecy, to which they agreed in hushed voices.

"Oh, Tally," breathed Cat. "I always knew you had the talent, but to walk into a publisher's office and—and simply ask for work!"

"That's the part I don't understand," interjected Richard. "I mean, yes you draw very well, but, well—you're a female."

Cat moved to lay her hand on her husband's sleeve.

"My dear"—she laughed—"if I were you, I should retract those words immediately before you earn the finest trimming of your life."

"Not at all," replied Tally stiffly, her straight brows pulled together in an awful frown. "This is the second time today I have heard them. I am inured."

"But—but, I only meant . . ."

"That intellectual or artistic creativity cannot be found in any person wearing skirts," Tally finished through gritted teeth. Then, noting the dismay in Richard's face, she relented.

"There now. I have just presented you with yet another feminine stereotype, the sharp-tongued shrew. But," she continued thoughtfully, "there is a precedent, you know. Late in the last century, a lady—whose name escapes me—became quite famous for her caricatures. Of course, she was not paid for her work."

"Well," interposed Cat with a giggle, "if anyone can crash such a masculine bastion, it's you, Tally. After all, you've done it before."

Tally shot her a questioning glance. Cat, in turn, slid her gaze mischievously toward Richard.

"Did you know that when Tally was just a slip of a girl, it was her habit to don her cousin Andrew's shirt and breeches?"

Ignoring Tally's gasp of indignation, she continued. "At daybreak, she would shinny down the tree outside

her window, creep to the stables and ride for an hour—
astride, if you please—and hurry back to her room before
her family was any the wiser. I only found out about it
when we were at Miss Winterford's School. One morning
I spied her sneaking off in her boys' clothes toward the
school stables and followed her. The next thing I knew,
she was galloping off over the hills into the mist. I was
never so shocked in my life!" she finished primly, the
impish sparkle in her eyes belying her words. "And then
there was the time . . ."

"Cat Thurston," hissed Tally, "if you say one more
word, I shall be forced to reveal the infamous Affair of
Miss Pinfold's Parrot!"

"Tally! You wouldn't!"

At this point Richard intervented, his eyes alight.

"But I must hear this! I fear my wife has been conceal-
ing details of a sordid past."

"Nothing of the sort." His unrepentant helpmeet
laughed. "Tally refers to a slight, er, contretemps that
occurred one afternoon during our annual Visitor's
Day."

She pointedly ignored the muffled snort that escaped
from her friend.

"You see," continued Cat, "Miss Pinfold was Miss
Winterford's assistant, and she owned a parrot, brought
to her by her brother, who was a sea captain. His name
was Ezekiel—the parrot, not the sea captain—and he had
in his youth, acquired an extremely, er, salty vocabulary.
Miss Pinfold, the very picture of rectitude, had devoted
many hours to eradicating this unfortunate flaw in an
otherwise blameless character by teaching him instructive
verses from the Bible.

"Ezekiel's cage stood in the school parlor, but when
visitors were entertained, his cage was kept covered—to
avoid any lapses on his part. I discovered that while
Ezekiel had dutifully learned his verses, he had by no
means forgotten his wicked life on the bounding main."

"Much as it distresses me to tell you this, Richard,"
interrupted Tally, "Cat encouraged the poor bird to slide
back into his old, sinful ways. On Visitor's Day, when
all the students' nearest and dearest were gathered in the
parlor for tea, Cat crept over to Ezekiel's cage and
whisked off the paisley shawl that covered it. She whis-

pered a few words to him—just enough to set him off, whereupon he regaled the assemblage with several very bawdy sea chanteys and concluded his program with an extremely indecent suggestion to the Duke of Barstoph, Susie Wither's grandfather.''

"So, you see"—Cat laughed—"it was nothing at all, really.''

"Nothing!" cried Tally with some indignation. "I would hardly call it nothing that Miss Winterford blamed *me* for the whole ugly episode, for of course 'sweet Catherine Wenderby would *never* be involved any such impropriety.' The upshot was that I spent the next two weeks copying instructive verses from the Bible!"

The burst of merriment that ensued was interrupted by the entrance of Bates, the butler, who informed them in disapproving tones that dinner was served.

Tally sighed with satisfaction at the sight that greeted her in the dining room. The table gleamed with snow white napery and shining silver, and it was burdened with a staggering array of dishes, among them, she was pleased to note, a large platter of the promised buttered crab. She applied herself enthusiastically to each dish in its turn, until finally, as the last covers were being removed, she sighed again.

"Cat, this is wonderful," she mumbled through a mouthful of Gateau Mellifleur. "I haven't had a meal like this in donkey's years. The menu at Henry's board, you know, runs more to stewed mutton and potted hare.''

"Ah," responded Richard, "then perhaps we can fatten you up while you're here. Not," he added hastily, "that you're too, er . . .''

He broke off, blushing at his rare social lapse.

"Thin," finished Tally with a chuckle. "Oh, Richard, I don't mind. It's perfectly true—I'm thin and I have no countenance, and I don't give two whoops for it. Papa always told me that it doesn't matter that I'm plain—that it's what's inside that counts—and he said I have perfectly lovely insides, whatever that means. At any rate, I've always felt . . ." She cast a twinkling glance at her friend, "that being beautiful is a dreadful nuisance. Just look at poor Cat. During her Season, she was positively awash in flowers and bad verse, and she couldn't step outside the house without squads of swains springing out of the sidewalk, offering to carry her parcels, or take her driving, or to Gunter's for an ice. I believe that's why she chose you, Richard, simply because you never wrote odes to her left ear, or any such drivel."

Richard turned to Cat, his expression hurt.

"And here I thought it was my masculine beauty that won you, my precious. And my wit. And, of course, there was my compelling charm."

"It was all of those, my darling."

Cat's words were uttered in an airy tone, and her fingers brushed his cheek with the lightest of touches, but the glance that flashed between them conveyed such intimacy that Tally turned her head away from its message.

It was not, she assured herself, that she begrudged Cat and Richard the happiness that fairly shimmered about them. Indeed, she was truly pleased for her friend. But somewhere deep in her heart stirred the thought that it must be wonderful to have somone for one's very own. Someone with whom to share all of life's pleasures and griefs—someone to complete one's self like two halves of the same whole.

Without volition, her thoughts flew to the Viscount Chelmsford, and once more she felt the strength of his arms about her as he had pressed her to him after their collision. She reddened, experiencing again the thud of his heart against her own, and the scratch of his starched shirt linen against her cheek. And the wonderful soap and leather scent of him.

Coming to herself, she realized that Cat had risen to lead the way from the dining room, leaving Richard in lordly solitude with the brandy decanter. Before they had proceeded very far along the corridor, however, they heard his stride in pursuit.

"I fail to see why I should be burdened with my own company while you two gossip over your embroidery." He smiled and offered an arm to each lady as he escorted them to the music room.

The rest of the evening passed in companionable conversation interspersed with songs played by Cat on the pianoforte, to which Tally and Richard added their voices in reasonable harmony. Later, after the tea tray had made its appearance, Tally yawned and declared herself ready for her bed.

"Well, of course," exclaimed Cat in sympathy. "You must be worn to ribbons, with your journey and your interview with Mr. Mapes and all. You'll need a good night's sleep, for tomorrow we shall be out till all hours.

"Sally Jersey is holding her soirée. She has prevailed upon Madame Catalani to sing, and all the world will be there. You will come with us, of course." Noting Tally's hesitation, she continued swiftly. "Remember what Mr. Mapes told you about getting out and about. Lady Jersey's social event will be your perfect opportunity to make mental notes, or whatever it is London's newest and most talented and soon-to-be most famous caricaturist does for inspiration."

"Y-yes," began Tally, "but . . ."

"I forgot to tell you, love," interposed Richard, tapping Cat's wrist for her attention. "I ran into Chelmsford this afternoon, and he sent his regards. I asked him to dine with us next week."

Tally's heart gave a sudden lurch, but she managed a casual tone as she asked, "Chelmsford?"

"Yes," replied Richard. The Viscount Chelmsford. Do you know him?"

"We—we've met. That is, he came—he came to my come-out ball." Tally felt that her heart had come loose from its mooring to lodge in her throat. "I—I really don't know him."

"Been acquainted with him for years, of course, but we became friends last year when I assisted him with a small commission he undertook for the Foreign Office."

"I suppose," said Cat in a brittle tone, "he will be attending the soirée with Clea?"

"Clea?" murmured Tally thickly, beginning to feel like Ezekiel, the parrot, on a particularly dull day.

"Chelmsford became betrothed to Clea Forrest, the Countess of Bellewood, that is, earlier this spring," replied Richard in a flat voice.

At these words Tally experienced an odd chill that seemed to settle in the pit of her stomach.

"They are to be married in June," added Cat in an equally expressionless tone, "in St. George's in Hanover Square, of course."

"Why 'of course'?"

Tally asked the question only because Cat seemed to expect it. She had, she told herself, no interest in whom the Viscount Chelmsford planned to marry, or where he planned to do it.

"Because St. George's in Hanover Square is the most fashionable church in London, and Lady Belle would rather be nibbled to death by ducks than be wed in any other."

Tally knew she should simply let the subject drop, but she found herself incapable of doing so.

"I believe I met her once—when she was Clea Montmorency. She is very beautiful, is she not?"

She pictured the golden vision of loveliness who had held the center of attention, including that of the Viscount Chelmsford, at that disastrous come-out ball.

"I suppose some would call her so," sniffed Cat.

"Come now, love," her husband interposed with a chuckle. "You know very well she is a diamond of the first water. She has held every eligible male under her pretty thumb since her come-out."

"And the diamond certainly went to the highest bidder." Cat's soft voice was edged with uncharacteristic malice. "Do you remember? She and Chelmsford had been in each other's pockets for months, when she suddenly became betrothed to old Bellewood."

"But what happened?" Tally stopped short, wishing she had bitten her tongue before betraying any interest in the viscount and his romantic entanglements. "I mean, between Miss Montmorency and the viscount," she finished lamely.

"No one is sure," replied Cat. "The story put about by Lady Belle, as she became known, is that her father had some sort of dispute with his father. They grew up as neighbors, you know, in Buckinghamshire. Another theory, one which is my personal favorite, is that captivating Clea thought it would be more pleasant to be married to an earl than to a viscount, particularly one who was even wealthier than Chelmsford. But, even after she was married to poor Bellewood, she acted as though she and her Jonathan were the most star-crossed pair of lovers to exchange hearts since Romeo and Juliet. She cast anguished glances at him from across the room and went pale when his name was mentioned—all that sort of dramatic nonsense. Chelmsford acted in a similar fashion; he was so devastated that for a while we all thought he might put a period to his existence!"

"That didn't last long, as I recall," put in Richard dryly. "He was seen with a different ladybird on his arm every week, and how he managed to wiggle around all the lures that were cast out to him without being eaten alive, I don't know."

"Yes," retorted Cat, "but when Clea's husband obligingly passed on to his reward last year, there was Chelmsford, back at the old stand, all but singing outside her window. And didn't she just eat it up!"

Richard turned to Tally.

"My wife does not care over much for Lady Bellewood," he pronounced in an informative tone.

"Mm-mm, yes," replied Tally gravely. "I somehow sensed that."

Cat, unable to withstand their teasing, allowed a smile to curve her lips.

"Nonsense. Beyond the fact that she's selfish, arrogant, and hard as nails, I daresay she's perfectly amiable when one comes to know her."

With mock dignity, she swirled a bow to her husband, somewhat marring its effect by sticking her tongue out at him. She turned to Tally and offered her arm.

"I shall escort you to your room, dearest, as I can see your eyes are fairly drooping."

With this, the two ladies made their exits, each with much on her mind.

Chapter Four

Tally's preparations for the ball were minimal. She had only one gown that could be considered adequate for such an occasion, an India muslin robe of a rather startling shade of yellow. Thanks to the ministration of Cat's maid, Tally's hair had been tamed to a semblance of propriety, but even Lisette's talents were no match for the thick chestnut rope that hung nearly to Tally's hips. Fastening the strand of pearls bequeathed to her by her mother, Tally scuttled into the small salon just as an exquisitely gowned Cat was being assisted into her cloak by Richard.

"Good Heavens!" were Cat's only words on observing her friend's entrance.

"I'm sorry to be so late," apologized Tally, "but Lisette seemed to experience some difficulty with my hair."

"I should imagine so," murmured Cat. "It's no matter, however. Heaven forfend that we should arrive on time. We should be laughed at as provincials."

Indeed, by the time Mr. and Mrs. Thurston arrived at the town home of Lord and Lady Jersey with their guest, the Lady Talitha Burnside, the gathering had already been voted a sad crush. No hostess could, of course, hope for a higher encomium. Tally thought she had never seen so many human beings packed together. She shyly acknowledged the introduction to her hostess and followed Cat to the bulwark of matrons who lined the far wall of the huge ballroom. She exchanged proprieties with these formidable ladies, and soon found herself engaged in a *bourée*, enjoying herself as she rarely had in her previous foray into the world of the *haut ton*. Her card was not entirely full, but it held a respectable list. This was due, Tally was aware, to Cat's good offices, but she did not allow this fact to dim the glow of the first night of what she considered her New Life.

All the while, behind the glow and beyond the chatter, Tally's mind was furiously active, taking notes for her sketches. Into her mental portfolio went Lady Webster, whose small eyes glared petulantly out at the world from beneath a garish headdress. The Earl of Mindenhall followed, with his quivering moustaches, of which he was inordinately proud. Also included was Ceddy Bagshot's quizzing glass with which he delicately punctuated his rather vapid conversation; and in went what appeared to be the entire contents of Miss Fanny Wibbleston's jewel box, draped around her plump arms, neck, and fingers.

Tally had just added to her files Lord Clathersham's imposing paunch, over which stretched an ornate waistcoat, dripping with fobs, when her eyes were drawn to the doorway. A newcomer had entered the room, and Tally's heart gave a panicky lurch as she recognized the Viscount Chelmsford's tall figure. As on that night four years ago, beside his quiet elegance, every other man in the room seemed to fade into insignificance.

The viscount was not alone. On his arm was a veritable Vision, dressed in an azure stain underdress, over which floated a tunic of sheerest silver net. Tally recognized her at once as Clea, Countess of Bellewood, at her most bewitching.

Her slender fingertips rested on the viscount's sleeve, and her head was uptilted toward him, emphasizing the graceful curve of her throat. A dainty diamond tiara glistened in the spun gold nest of curls piled high on her head, and on her deliciously curved breast blazed a spectacular necklace of diamonds and sapphires. Jonathan bent over his fiancée with an expression of pleased appreciation that bordered on the fatuous.

The progress made by the pair into the center of the ballroom was almost royal. Friends were greeted, and compliments acknowledged by the *ton*'s reigning beauty. Conversation seemed to still as the viscount and his Clea greeted Lady Jersey and were bathed in that flighty lady's most gracious smile.

Tally turned her back and began to speak brightly to the person nearest her, a timid young girl in her first Season. The conversation elicited from this maiden, whose attention was still riveted on the splendid scene taking place beyond Tally's left shoulder, could not have been described as scintillating—or even coherent, for that matter.

The orchestra launched into a spirited country dance, and those who had gathered around the celebrated newcomers separated to form sets. Tally swung around again just in time to watch Jonathan take Clea's slender hand into his own as the pair swung into the lively dance.

Once again Tally turned away from the enchanting picture, only to find that the shy recipient of her monologue had been whisked away by the Earl of Mindenhall.

"Well!" breathed a voice in her ear. "Did you observe the Grand Entrance?"

Tally's lips curved in a faint smile. At least there was one other in the room who was not enthralled by Lady Belle's fairy princess aspect.

"Oh, Cat. You cannot say she is not the loveliest creature in the room."

"No," replied Cat ruefully, "though it would give me a great deal of pleasure to be able to do so. Come along, Tally, there is someone I particularly want you to meet."

The someone proved to be yet another perspiring dandy, who, under Cat's minatory stare, requested Lady Talitha's hand for one of her open dances. Then, with an air of one carrying duty to its limits, set off to procure lemonade for the ladies.

"Cat," whispered Tally in anguished accents, "this really is not necessary."

Cat merely turned upon her a stare of questioning innocence.

"I mean," continued Tally, "these—candidates you have been presenting all night. I'm sure they're all very nice young men, but at the moment I do not require a nice young man. I am perfectly happy as I am."

"Nonsense," returned Cat serenely. "I am merely ensuring that you have a good time tonight. And don't tell me you'd rather be sitting on a chair discussing the best remedy for chilblains with all the dowagers."

"No, but I know you, Cat Thurston. You have matrimony on that scheming mind of yours, and I am *not* on the lookout for a husband, thank you very much."

"Nonsense," repeated Cat. She smiled, gesturing toward the entrance to the card room.

"Look, there is Richard. I thought he would never be finished in there."

As her husband made his way toward her, he passed Lord Chelmsford and Clea, who, having finished their dance, were recruiting their strength with a champagne cup. Clea bestowed a blinding smile on Richard and reached up on tiptoe to bestow a kiss on his cheek.

"I didn't know Lady Bellewood and Richard were so well acquainted," she remarked in some surprise.

"Oh, yes," replied Cat with elaborate unconcern. "They have become quite good friends since she and Chelmsford became betrothed." She gave a high little laugh. "It's odd, really. Before the betrothal, Richard had little good to say of her. I expect he has come to terms with her for the sake of his friendship with Chelmsford."

"Oh," Tally remarked dubiously, noting the enthusiasm with which Richard returned Clea's kiss. She was prevented from any further observations by the approach of the little party, which appeared to be in the highest of spirits.

Clea reached out a gloved hand to Cat.

"My dear," she bubbled, her blue eyes sparkling with an almost febrile vivacity, "I was just saying to your wonderful husband that I vow he is the handsomest man in the room—except for my Jonathan, of course."

She turned a melting gaze to the viscount, who drew his fingers along the curve of her cheek in an affectionate gesture. He turned to the rest of the group.

"My fiancée must be excused for a certain degree of partiality."

He bowed gracefully over the hands of the other ladies present and turned to Tally.

"Lady Talitha, what a pleasant surprise to see you again. Thurston tells me you are a guest in his home."

Startled, Tally's eyes flew to his. By using her title, was he telling her that he remembered That Awful Night, after all? She was sure she detected a twinkle lurking deep in his smoky eyes. All at once she was seventeen again, and painfully aware of her inadequacies. Why, she agonized, was her wit and sparkle confined entirely to the talent in her fingers? Why was she so plain? Could not the Creator, who had been so generous with Lady Belle, have spared just a little beauty and charm for her?

"Yes," she croaked in response to the viscount's words. "I—I just arrived yesterday."

"And will you be staying long?"

After one more scared glance at Chelmsford's face, Tally detected a definite spark of mischief in his smile. *And, why did that smile have the power to make her senses hum?*

As though from the depths of a nightmare, she answered, "Yes—that is, I'm not sure. It depends. . . ."

The last thing in the world Tally expected to feel for Clea Bellewood was gratitude, but when that lady interrupted her, Tally went limp from relief.

"But I want to show off my new present," purred Clea, with an impatient pout. She lifted one shapely wrist looped by a sparkling bracelet of sapphires and diamonds. It matched the necklace that lay shining above her enticing décolletage.

"Jonathan gave it to me just today to wear this evening. Isn't it lovely?" She waved her wrist delicately so that the jewels fairly blazed in the candlelight.

"It's breathtaking, Clea," returned Cat, her eyes wide.

"Yes." Clea's voice was creamy with satisfaction. "The necklace, you know, was Jonathan's betrothal gift to me, and it simply cried out for the finishing touch."

After one more fond look, Clea allowed her arm to drop gracefully to her side, then turned her attention to Tally. In one, raking glance, Tally felt herself brutally exposed for the dowdy provincial that she was.

"Lady—Talitha, is it?" Clea queried in a tone of total disinterest. "What an extremely quaint name, to be sure."

"My father was a biblical scholar," replied Tally, her voice barely audible. "It means, 'little girl.' "

Clea's expression clearly expressed her agreement with the biblical scholar's choice of name for his unremarkable daughter. Then her attention turned to a subject more to her liking.

"Richard," she said pouting, "you have not yet told me how you like my gown. I had it made after you told me you thought that blue was my best color."

For a moment Richard's response was a blank look. He quickly recovered however, and bent his lopsided grin on her.

"And I was right. That confection makes your eyes look as though angels had fashioned them from bits of summer sky."

Clea's silvery laugh trilled in pleased appreciation. Cat and Tally merely gaped at Richard, and Jonathan raised his quizzing glass to favor him with an astonished stare.

"If that isn't the outside of enough," he snorted, in mock indignation. "Do they teach you that stuff at Whitehall? I'll thank you to stop talking fustian to my fiancée, my good man. You have a beautiful wife of your own to pitch fulsome compliments to."

Richard turned to Cat, and his eyes warmed.

"As well I know." He smiled. "But I know she doesn't require any fulsome compliments from me to assure her of that fact."

Cat rapped his knuckles playfully with her fan.

"I hate to topple your image of me, my good man, but I am just as susceptible to a well-turned phrase as the next woman."

"Well, then," replied Richard with an exaggerated leer. "Come with me, my pet, for a turn on the terrace, and I shall whisper delightful words into your shell pink ear."

With that he whisked his wife off toward the French doors that lined one wall of the ballroom. Just then Clea was approached by a very young officer of cavalry, who shyly bespoke her hand for the set of country dances now being formed. With another tinkling laugh, she whirled away on his arm.

To her dismay Tally found herself alone with the viscount. His eyes smiled down into hers, but his voice was grave as he spoke.

"We seem to find ourselves deserted by our nearest and dearest, Lady Talitha, and must cling to each other for support. Shall we join the dancers?"

Tally dropped her eyes. Her heart was banging like a child's drum beneath the yellow muslin pleated in awkward layers over her bosom. Her tongue seemed to have swollen to twice its size and was now stuck to the roof of her mouth.

Chelmsford's dark brows lifted quizzically.

"I have not asked you to take part in an execution, you know. Do you find a dance with me so distasteful?"

"No!" replied Tally in a strangled gasp. "No, of course not! It's just that—just that I—I do not enjoy dancing," she finished lamely.

Jonathan experienced a moment of amused surprise. He was unaccustomed to having his invitations to the dance received with anything less than delighted acceptance, and, as wide brown eyes stared into his with what could only be described as consternation, he felt a stir of interest.

"Excellent," he replied. "I, myself, have little taste for country dances. Besides, I believe the Italian soprano will be inflicted on us soon. I shall procure some punch for you, and then we can retire to one of the smaller salons for a comfortable coze."

From the expression on the Lady Talitha's mobile features, it was obvious to the meanest intelligence that she found this prospect similarly unpleasant. Undaunted, Jonathan took her small hand in his own, suppressing an urge that was as unexpected as it was unbidden to warm those cold fingers with his lips. He drew her toward the refreshment table, and shortly thereafter, punch cups in hand, he settled her on a small confidante in a secluded nook.

"Now, then, Lady Tally—or should I say, Miss Burnside—I think we have matters of import to discuss."

Once again her eyes flew to his face, and once more Jonathan felt himself oddly affected by the unusual combination of strength and vulnerability displayed in her brown velvet gaze.

"I was," he continued, "in communication with George Mapes this afternoon, and he tells me that you and I are to be collaborators. I must say, I look forward to our partnership."

He glanced down to where Tally nervously twisted the small ring she wore. It was hard to imagine those fluttering fingers gripping a pencil with surety and purpose.

Tally followed his gaze and blushed, separating her hands with a jerk, only to resume the activity almost immediately.

"It is a most unusual ring, Lady Talitha."

He smiled, and with an effort, she once more curled her fingers into her lap.

"I can see why you are fond of it."

Tally stared mutely at the oddly shaped pearl which formed the ring's centerpiece. Around it swirled a delicate pattern of seed pearls, the whole nestled in an old-fashioned setting of wrought gold.

"It was my mother's," she murmured. "One of the few pieces of jewelry she left me. I wear it always."

So saying, she folded her hands firmly on her knees and faced the viscount.

"I—I hope you don't mind that I divined the book's authorship, my lord. You see, I caught a glimpse of one of . . ."

"No—that is—I would have wished that no one be aware of my literary efforts, but, since you have the same desire, I feel I can trust your discretion—as you will have to trust mine. Besides, it will make matters a great deal easier. As George pointed out, it will be better if we meet on a fairly regular basis, if we're to pull this thing off."

"Mm-mm, yes," Tally replied, her breathing returning to normal now that the conversation had taken a more businesslike turn. "I fear there will be some difficulty, my lord. You see . . ."

"Do you think," Chelmsford teased lightly, "that we could dispense with 'my lord'? Since we are to be partners, and, I hope friends, perhaps we could flaunt propriety and leap directly to the use of our first names."

A gasp of laughter escaped Tally.

"Very well, Jonathan. Partners and friends. Now," she continued more soberly, "about these meetings. I don't see how we are to see each other on a regular basis without exciting comment. Perhaps you could send our material via messenger."

"Mm." Jonathan frowned. "I don't think that would work well at all. Look here, we can't go into this right now. Would you meet me tomorrow? Early? How about a ride in the Park?"

Tally brightened.

"Oh, I'd like that! I used to ride every morning at Summerhill, and I brought my little mare, Blossom, with me to Town. Would seven be too . . . ?"

"There you are!" A high feminine voice interrupted. The speaker was revealed as Lady Belle as she peeped into the room. She looked none too pleased to find her fiancé in a tête-à-tête with a strange female, but when, on closer inspection, the female was shown to be the newly arrived country mouse, a sparkling smile curved her lips.

"How very naughty of you, Jonathan, to hide away. I have been searching for you this hour!"

Jonathan rose and drew Clea into the room.

"But we have been here only a few minutes, love. Tally is not used to our giddy party ways and required sustenance and a place to catch her breath.

Clea's perfect brows lifted for an instant at the sound of the mouse's first name on the lips of her betrothed. She cast Tally a sidelong glance.

"And have you been enjoying a giddy time, Lady Talitha?" she murmured, her tone conveying only too clearly the absurdity of such an idea.

Tally raised her chin.

"I have enjoyed the dancing, my lady."

Clea's smile was brittle as she turned to Jonathan. "Only see, dearest," she cried as she opened her reticule. "I have been lucky at cards tonight!"

Jonathan's smile was a trifle thin as he replied. "Perhaps that will offset the guineas you lost last night."

"Oh, don't scold, darling. You do not wish to spoil my pleasure, do you? I do enjoy my little flings at the table."

As Tally watched uncomfortably, Clea drew close to Jonathan and rubbed her cheek against his shoulder. She clasped his hand in her gloved fingers and twisted slightly, so that it seemed entirely by accident that her breasts moved tantalizingly against his arm, and his hand was drawn along the curve of her hip.

Jonathan stilled for a moment, and the response that flickered in his eyes made Tally turn her head.

As though having accomplished her purpose, Clea drew back, and, grasping Jonathan's sleeve, began urging him toward the doorway. Jonathan hesitated.

"It will be time for the first supper soon, Tally. With whom will you go down?"

"I have been promised to Sir Geoffrey Prestwood,"

she replied modestly, observing with pleasure the startled expression that crossed Clea's face. Sir Geoffrey, a man possessed of considerable wealth and charm, was a highly eligible bachelor. That Tally owed his attention to Cat's machinations, she had no intention of divulging to either the viscount or his fiancée.

Tally did not speak with Jonathan during the remainder of the evening, though she was intensely aware of his presence. Her eyes were drawn again and again to that thatch of dark hair rising above a pair of broad, muscled shoulders.

Chapter Five

It was late when Richard ushered his ladies into the house on Half Moon Street. Tally, thinking of her early morning appointment with Jonathan, bid Cat a hasty good night and repaired to her bedchamber. Much to her surprise, she had just snuggled under her comforter, when a light tap sounded on the door, and Cat thrust her head into view.

Observing that Tally was still awake, she paused for a moment, and, chuckling mischievously, she scuttled into the room and launched herself in a flying leap onto Tally's bed. Tally, after an astonished moment, snatched up a pillow and began to pummel her friend. Cat availed herself of a second pillow and retaliated with a fierce barrage of feathery thumps. Soon the two young women dissolved in a fit of giggles.

"If Miss Pinfold could only see us now," gasped Cat at last.

" 'Young ladies, I declare!' " cried Tally, contorting her face into an expression of frigid disapproval. " 'You must stop this instant, or I shall be forced to . . .' "

" '. . . deal with you *most* severely!' " they finished in unison.

The two collapsed against each other in a final burst of laughter.

"Oh, Cat," wailed Tally, "you absurd creature. Whatever made you think of those days? You're a respectable matron now!"

"I don't know. I guess it was the sight of your two big, brown eyes, peeping over the comforter, looking for all the world like the mischievous chit I remember from so many years ago."

With a last swipe at her tormentor, Tally replaced the

pillows and leaned back with a sigh, while Cat disposed herself comfortably on the counterpane.

"It was a long time ago, wasn't it?" sighed Tally. "And look at us now. You, happily married, and I . . ."

"And you on the brink of a new life," finished Cat. "Which brings me neatly to my next subject, Lady Talitha Burnside. You are starting out anew," she continued in response to Tally's questioning expression. "You said yourself that you will be going out and about. Now, Tally, I hope you won't take offense at this, but you need a new wardrobe for your new life."

"But, I *have* a new wardrobe. The gown I wore to the ball—the carriage dress I arrived in yesterday—Cat, what on earth are you talking about?"

"Who selected that new wardrobe?" demanded Cat.

"Why, Henry's wife, Gertrude."

"I thought so. And who was your modiste?"

Tally uttered a muffled snort.

"Modiste! Surely you don't think Henry would go to the expense of hiring a modiste. He won't do that even for Gertrude. No, the job of putting together my ensembles went to the village seamstress."

Cat closed her eyes.

"Tally, have we or have we not been like sisters for the past sixteen years?"

"Well, yes, of course we have, you goose, but . . ."

"Then, as a sister, let me tell you, my dear, those clothes are absolutely dreadful!"

"Um, I guess they are, rather," agreed Tally mildly. "But what difference does it make? I mean, they are in a reasonably fashionable mode, and they cover the areas of my person that are supposed to be covered. What more can I ask?"

Cat stared at her as though she had just given it as her opinion that tomorrow the sun would turn blue.

"Tally, even if those gowns fit properly, which they do not, they are screamingly unbecoming."

"Well, I can see why that would be a consideration for you. You're beautiful, and a beauty should be complemented by what she wears, but I . . . Well, I guess that's one more advantage of being plain. I could dress in a dish clout and it wouldn't be particularly noticeable. Oh, I don't mind, Cat," she added quickly, as she observed her friend's stricken expression. "Papa taught me when I was quite small that it didn't matter that I am not pretty, since exterior beauty cannot compare with beauty of the spirit."

At this Cat caught an astonished Tally by the shoulder and shook her.

"I can just hear him saying that," she growled. "I remember once listening to him call you plain as a pump handle."

"Yes," replied Tally defensively. "Papa, you know, valued Truth Above All."

Cat cast her hands skyward.

"Heaven knows your father was a fine man, with a brilliant mind, and no doubt his words were spoken out of love, but I think at this moment, if he were here in this room, I'd—I'd—well, I'd give him a piece of my mind—and all those feather-witted nannies and governesses to whom he left your upbringing, as well. As for you!" This, accompanied by another shake. "I could just strangle you. You may not have been a pretty child, but have you looked in a mirror even once during the last four years? Yes, you are plain, but now it's because you make yourself so."

She tumbled off the bed, and with Tally still in her grasp, she brought the bedside candle to the dressing table and thrust Tally into the seat.

"Now, look at yourself. To begin with—you're not even thin anymore. You've filled out. Now—well, now, you're slender. Do you understand? And see? You have lovely, velvety brown eyes, and long, curly lashes."

Tally gazed at her reflection for a long moment. Yes, it was true. She had been vaguely aware that the clothes she had worn in London before were now a bit small, especially around the chest. That was one reason Gertrude had consented to talk Henry into the new wardrobe. And her eyes. Yes, in a dim light they could surely be called pretty.

"But my nose," she said plaintively. "It turns up at the end, and you have to admit, my mouth is just huge."

"I would rather call it generous. And those are those, you know, who consider a turned-up—that is, a slightly uptilted nose quite piquant. The thing is," she continued before Tally could utter any more caveats, "the thing is, if you are going to be seen in the Polite World, you are going to have to get another wardrobe. That's all there is to it," she finished with immutable finality.

Tally simply gaped at her.

"I think you must be mad! It took every penny I could squeeze from Henry to provide me with the clothes I have now. Right this minute I couldn't so much as purchase a reticule. Perhaps, after Mr. Mapes begins paying me for my drawings . . ."

"No, no, no. That's unacceptable. Now, I have talked this over with Richard, and he has agreed that we will stand the ready for anything you require."

Tally drew herself up in some indignation.

"Now, I really do believe you're gone round the bend! Do you suppose for one minute I would let you and Richard pay to dress me in finery that I neither want nor need?"

Cat laid a placating hand on her arm.

"Tally, please don't fly into the boughs. You'd think we were suggesting you join the muslin company! We only want what's right for you—you must know that."

"Oh, of course I do, dearest Cat. But cannot you see that I couldn't let you . . ."

"Would you consider a loan, then?"

Tally remained silent.

"Look at it this way," continued Cat. "For a while, at least, you will be appearing at social events under our sponsorship. Your appearance will reflect on us."

At this Tally sat up very straight.

"Cat, is that what this is all about? Are you ashamed of me?" Tears shone bright in her eyes.

"Oh, don't be such a widgeon. Of course not. It was the only thing I could think of that might sway you."

"But you're right," murmured Tally after a few minutes' thought. "People will wonder that the exquisite Mrs. Richard Thurston would be entertaining a perfect dowd."

Suddenly she pictured herself, beautifully gowned and coiffed, soaring about the dance floor in the arms of Jonathan, the Viscount Chelmsford. Not that new feathers would make her anything but the brown wren she was, but—well, why shouldn't the wren at least make the most of what she had?

She turned to face Cat.

"I think I should probably do something about my hair, too, don't you think?"

Cat broke into a delighted burst of laughter. "Definitely we'll do something about your hair! For too long have you gone about looking more like some small creature of the forest peering through a hedge than the attractive young woman you are. We'll start out the first thing in the morning, and . . ."

"Oh, no," Tally broke in nervously. "Not first thing, that is. I have an—an engagement, you see. To go riding," she added, in response to Cat's look of inquiry.

"But that's wonderful," exclaimed Cat. "With whom? Is it Ceddy? He's always very quick off the mark. Or, no—it must be Lord Shingleton. He seemed quite smitten with you, I thought. Oh, tell me!"

"No! No—it—it's nothing like that. I just—that is, I was telling Lord Chelmsford how much I enjoy a good gallop early in morning, and he suggested I join him. It's nothing—really."

Cat's face fell ludicrously.

"No, I shouldn't think it would be. He obviously took a liking to you, and it's just like him to befriend a stranger in our bewildering metropolis—he has the kindest of hearts, you know. Well," she sighed, "it's early days yet, and I'm sure that in no time at all we'll have gentlemen lining up at the door to take you riding in the Park."

Tally returned Cat's good-night hug with a wan smile and, after her friend whisked herself out of the room, she lay staring into the darkness.

"He has the kindest of hearts, you know."

Cat's words rang in her ears. How could someone as cold and supercilious as the Viscount Chelmsford have won a reputation for kindness?

Her innate sense of fairness surfaced at that point, and she was forced to admit that the Viscount Chelmsford with whom she had conversed tonight bore little resemblance to the monster of arrogance with whom she had held so many mental confrontations during the past few years. She could hardly believe that the fingers which had brushed hers so softly over the punch cups a few hours ago had once gripped her unmercifully, preventing her intemperate flight. She could not imagine that the voice which had once scarred her very soul with its harshness could speak with such warmth and charm.

Resolutely, she thumped her pillow. She was willing to admit that Jonathan possessed charm in abundance. Kindness of heart she was not yet willing to concede. Still, the image of those gray eyes smiling into hers stayed with her and drifted annoyingly in and out of the landscape of her dreams.

Chapter Six

Jem, the Thurston's second undergroom, rubbed the last of an all-too-short night's sleep from his eyes and assisted Lady Talitha into her perch on what Jem privately considered a mare entirely too tricksey for such a little dab of a woman. He hoped he would not be called upon to perform any rescues this morning, his head being what it was after too much Blue Ruin at the Running Footman the evening before.

Jem sighed and heaved himself onto the back of his own steed. Warily, he followed his master's guest at a respectful distance. He relaxed after a few paces, noting the mare's stately gait and my lady's dignified demeanor. This state of affairs lasted until they reached the Park. Then, upon turning onto a long stretch of tanbark, my lady bent to whisper in her Blossom's ear. With a flick of her tail, the mare hurtled down the path, mane feathered in the wind, and harness ajingle with a joyous abandon reflected in the rosy cheeks and sparkling eyes of her mistress.

With a start of horror, Jem urged his mount forward, fearing at any moment to see her ladyship spilled lifeless upon the tanbark. Much to his surprise, the little dab of a woman seemed to experience little difficulty in managing her steed. Still, he was vastly relieved when at that moment an elegant male form appeared at the far end of the bridle path. Lady Talitha, evidently brought to a sense of her transgression, drew up sharply.

Tally's first thought on seeing Jonathan was that he looked magnificent in his admirably tailored riding coat of blue superfine. Doeskin breeches molded themselves to his powerful thighs like smooth bark to a tree. Tally blushed at her wayward reflections. And what must she look like, with her windblown hair, and her neckcloth askew? As though she'd been pulled through a bush backward, no doubt. Not that she cared what sort of impression she made on him, but she was aware that her habit, the only item in her wardrobe that she had not replaced, was six years old. It was faded and threadbare in spots; it fit a trifle too snugly around waist and hips, and it curved much too tightly about her chest.

"Good morning, my lord," she cried, rather breathlessly, as she drew abreast of Jonathan's mettlesome stallion. "What a magnificent animal! He quite takes the shine out of poor little Blossom."

"Good morning to you, Lady Talitha," answered Jonathan, "although I thought we were to dispense with tiresome formalities. And my magnificent animal thanks you. His name is Horatio, after the Hero of Trafalgar, but I'm afraid it is a misnomer, for he is the most complete humbug. He shies at squirrels and will grovel shamelessly for a lump of sugar."

As he spoke, Jonathan surveyed Tally briefly. He had not realized that she possessed such a lithe, trim figure. Nor would he have believed that flushed cheeks and a sparkle in those enormous brown eyes could make such a difference in her appearance. What was there about her, he wondered, that made him want to discover the unexplored facets of this seemingly unprepossessing little female. He smiled as Tally stroked Horatio's nose.

"There," she crooned to the magnificent animal, who apparently did not draw the line at groveling for some praise and a good scratch, either. "Did you ever hear such calumny? You're obviously a pearl among horses, and it's a great pity your master does not appreciate your true worth."

Jonathan joined in Tally's laughter, and they turned to center in silence for a few moments before Tally lifted her head in a sidelong glance.

"How—how does it happen, my—Jonathan, that you chose such an unusual, um, hobby?" She rushed on in response to a questioning lift of his dark brows. "I mean, a man of your rank certainly needs no profession, so I must conclude that writing is an amusing pastime for you."

"Yes, I suppose you might consider it so, but I work at my—hobby with the dedication of the most serious author, I assure you. And you, Tally—what is your purpose in taking up an artist's pencil? George Mapes tells me you are intent on making a career of your work."

Tally read in his tone a note of derision, and she stiffened. Did he view her as one of those aristocratic women who busied themselves in meaningless pursuits, simply to ease the endless boredome of their pampered lives?

"Let me assure *you*, sir, that unlike yourself, my work is not a hobby, but my career. I intend to support myself with my earnings as a caricaturist."

Jonathan could not have been more startled if the young woman had suddenly announced her intention of flying to the moon in a balloon.

"But you are . . ." he began.

"Yes, I know," finished Tally wearily. "A gently bred female, which, of course, makes it completely unsuitable for me to consider making my own way in the world. I must not put my talent to profitable use, but must repose by the window with my embroidery, waiting for some male whose desire to marry into a titled family outweighs my lack of dowry." She did not add the words "and my plainness of face" for fear of the agreement she might find in the viscount's eyes.

Jonathan was taken aback by the unmistakable note of bitterness in Tally's voice. He admitted to himself that he had never considered the plight of the battalions of young women who appeared in London every year for their Season. What must it be like for those who were endowed with neither wealth nor beauty? For, undoubtedly, the maiden who did not "catch" was doomed to a dreary existence as a spinster, living on the sufferance of her relatives.

He kept his voice matter-of-fact as he answered.

"Mmm, yes, I can see your point. Such a situation would be intolerable to one of your extraordinary ability, married or not. I have found my own situation to be somewhat of a burden at times. Do you know"—he turned to her with that treacherously warm smile—"there are days when I think how pleasant it would be to be plain Jonathan Jones, writer—to sign my own name to my work, and accept the acclaim of the masses for my brilliance?"

"Have you written other works for publication besides *Town Bronze*?"

"Oh, yes. Under various *noms de plume* I've written political satire, sporting news, and the occasional thoughtful piece on current events. *Town Bronze*, however, is the first novel I have attempted. Actually it's not so much a novel as a collection of observations on the London Scene. Mapes seems to think it might see some success."

"Ah." Tally laughed delightedly. "I don't know how I shall contain myself when the doings of Clifford and Clive are on the lips of every important personage in town. I'll want to stand up and shout, 'I know who wrote it—I know who Dash really is!' "

"Mmp. If it creates the reaction that Mapes hopes for, you may well cower in a closet when it comes out, hoping no one will connect you with a piece of rank libel. Particularly, I might add, if the illustrations of said piece contribute to its libelous nature."

"Which I certainly hope they will," added Tally with a demure smile.

Jonathan threw back his head in a shout of laughter, giving Tally ample opportunity to reflect that it was no wonder this man was the catch of the marriage mart. It simply wasn't fair for one man to possess wealth, and charm, and a face that belonged on a Greek vase, to boot. What a good thing it was that she had seen this deity's true aspect—his abominable rudeness and his icy disdain—his utter disregard for the feelings of others. If only she didn't have to keep reminding herself of that other aspect. She was much too prone to enjoy the viscount's charm.

In the next instant Tally's mind flicked back to Lady Jersey's soirée the evening before, and the moment when Jonathan and Clea had swept from that little alcove. Jonathan had been unwilling to leave her until he had ascertained that she had a dinner partner. Was this the act of a man who was in the habit of running roughshod over the feelings of others?

Giving herself a little shake, Tally abandoned this line of thought and concentrated on what Jonathan was saying.

". . . which brings me to the point of this morning's

jaunt. How are we to conduct our, er, collaboration without it seeming to others that we are sitting in each other's
pockets?"

"I've been giving that some thought," replied Tally
slowly. As you know, I'm staying with the Thurstons."

Jonathan nodded.

"You see, Cat and I have been friends for years and
years. I know her to be the soul of discretion—when
it's necessary. And Richard works with important State
information. He certainly knows how to keep a secret."

"Are you suggesting . . . ?"

"Yes. I've already told them that I have been hired to
illustrate a soon-to-be published satire—by an anonymous author—and they have both promised not to utter
a word."

"Yes, but . . ."

"Now, you and Richard are friends. If you are willing
to trust him—and Cat—we could work together in their
home. You could, perhaps, find some pretext to further
your acquaintance, um, such as working on some public
charity together. No one would question your visits, and,
of course, we shall probably not need to meet that often,
anyway."

She raised her eyes to Jonathan's, and found his expression dubious.

"I don't know," he mused softly. "I have been so careful. I rarely appear at the publisher's, and except for
Mapes himself, the staff believes that I am simply a bib-
liophile who has retained the firm to seek out rare old
books for me.

"I've had my desk moved into my room, and the
chamber maids are under threat of a punishment too terrible to mention if they so much as whisk a dust clout
near it. Even my valet is unaware of my double existence, though I'm sure he's wondered at the puddles of
candle wax he finds in the morning."

"Yes," responded Tally, "but I certainly cannot come
to your home, and that leaves us the option of meeting
elsewhere; Mapes's perhaps—but then I would have
coachmen and grooms to contend with, plus that odious
Porlock, whom I do not think I trust at all. We certainly
can't continue meeting in the Park at the crack of dawn,
and . . ."

Tally was interrupted as a thud of hoofbeats announced approaching horses, and in a moment a pair of riders swung into view. One of them, to Tally's surpirse, was Lady Bellewood, wearing a fetching habit of midnight blue, with a hat of the same shade perched rakishly on one side of her head.

Catching sight of Jonathan, Clea drew to an abrupt halt, and for an instant, moved as though to turn back the way she had come. Her companion, a tall, slender gentleman, dressed in elegant, if somewhat showy riding attire, placed his hand on her bridle, and bent to whisper in her ear. Straightening, Clea waived gaily to Jonathan and approached at a smart trot.

"Jonathan," she cried in pleased accents, "what a nice surprise!"

"Good morning, my love." Jonathan lightly clasped the gloved hand extended to him by Clea. He nodded briefly to her companion. "But what are you doing out in the world at such an early hour?"

"Oh, it's the silliest thing." She giggled nervously. "Miles said that after such a late evening of dancing I would not be seen until it was time to promenade in the Park this evening, and of course I told him that was just nonsense. So, he challenged me to an early morning ride this morning, and I accepted, although I must look positively hagged."

She lowered her lashes and waited. To Tally's irritation, Jonathan responded on cue.

"Nonsense, my love. As usual, your radiance shames the dawn."

A delicate flush spread over the Beauty's cheeks.

How does she do that, wondered Tally rancorously.

"But, dearest," breathed Clea, "whatever are you doing here?"

Jonathan smiled fondly.

"I, too, issued a challenge of sorts last night. Lady Talitha revealed that she is used to riding out early at her home in Cambridgeshire. Since my own custom is much the same here in the city, I asked her to join me. If I had any notion that you would be stirring so early, I would have asked you to join us."

For the first time Clea turned to look at Tally, and as her gaze moved over the form-fitting old riding habit, the tiniest of frowns creased the ivory perfection of her brow.

"But aren't you going to introduce me?"

It was the voice of Lady Belle's riding companion, who had raised his quizzing glass for his own inspection of Tally's attire.

"But, of course," exclaimed Clea, "how remiss of me! Lady Tabitha—Burnwood, is it? Allow me to present my cousin, Miles Crawshay."

Murmuring her correct name through stiff lips, Tally extended her hand to Crawshay, who bent to grasp it with practiced ease.

He was a tall man, and, though slender, gave the appearance of being formed of spring steel. His eyes were of a curiously light brown, set beneath coppery hair cut in a short, military style. With his aquiline nose and sharp features, he bore the appearance of an elegant fox.

"So very pleased to make your acquaintance, Lady Talitha." His lips brushed her fingertips. "I take it you are newly arrived in the metropolis?"

"Y-yes," breathed Tally, flustered by the man's unexpected gallantry. "I am—visiting friends. The Thurstons. In Half Moon Street."

Crawshay bowed again.

"I look forward to waiting on you there."

Though his words were commonplace, something in the way his glance strayed first to her mouth, then to the place where her riding jacket buttoned tightly across her breast, caused Tally's heart to thump, and she unconsciously edged her horse a little closer to Jonathan's Horatio.

"Oh, my dear," Clea burbled at that moment, "Miles has been telling me of a new gaming house which has just opened up in Henrietta Street. It's owned by a Madame de Robitaille. There are rooms for roulette and faro, and her dinners are superb. It sounds marvelous, doesn't it? Of course, only the best people are seen there. I want to go, Jonathan. Will you take me?"

Jonathan's lips tightened.

"I've heard of Madame's establishment, and I don't think it's at all the sort of place you'd care for, Clea."

Lady Belle's laughter gurled engagingly.

"But it sounds *just* the sort of place I'd care for. Please?"

"Really, my dear, I think not," Jonathan responded quietly. "The play is very deep, and rumor has it they fuzz the cards."

"Surely not," Crawshay interposed in a shocked voice. "I've been there several times, old chap, and I assure you I've seen nothing that would indicate any sort of shady dealings."

"Mmp, perhaps not, but," the viscount addressed Clea, "I still must regretfully refuse to accompany you there, my dear. Surely you can find enough play to amuse you in the endless round of balls and routs in which we seem to indulge."

Clea's lovely mouth hardened into a mutinous line.

"You know I hate playing for chicken stakes. Jonathan, I want to go to this new place!"

The smile had left Jonathan's eyes.

"We'll discuss this another time, my love. In the meantime, what do you mean to wear to Lady Talgarth's ball? I should like to send flowers."

But Clea was not to be placated. With a vicious jerk on her reins, she turned away. "I'm not sure I shall be attending Lady Talgarth's ball. Come, Miles."

In a swirl of dust, she was gone, and Crawshay, with a jaunty wave, galloped after her.

An awkward silence seemed to crawl toward eternity before Jonathan said with a rueful chuckle, "Clea is not at her best early in the morning."

"She is very beautiful," murmured Tally, somewhat at a loss for words.

Jonathan's eyes followed Clea's voluptuous form as the riders disappeared from view. Really, thought Tally in some irritation, one almost expected him to lick his lips.

"Yes, she is, isn't she?" he sighed. "I still can't believe my good torture. I thought I had lost her forever, and now—it is like a long cherished dream come true, knowing that she . . ."

He seemed to come to himself with a start.

"Forgive me. I don't know how I came to prose on like this. I don't usually open my budget on such short acquaintance."

To this Tally could find no answer. Fumbling for an-

other subject, she returned to the discussion that had
been occupying them before Lady Belle's unfortuitous
appearance.

"It is getting late, and I must return home. May I
ask you to consider my suggestion once again? About
conducting our business meetings at Cat and Richard's
home?"

"I have done so already, and I believe you are right.
It's the only viable alternative. I shall send you a few
chapters of *Town Bronze* by messenger today. Let me
know when you have completed your illustrations for
them, and then we can meet."

Tally drew a deep breath. She could hardly believe
that her life as a professional artist was about to begin.
She wheeled her horse about for the return home, and
as she paced slowly beside Jonathan, she could not help
but envision cozy afternoons with her head bent close to
his.

Chapter Seven

Tally returned to the Thurston home to find Cat waiting impatiently for her in a third-floor salon which had been transformed into a sewing room. On a sturdy work table reposed a small mountain of pattern books and fashion magazines, over which poured Cat and her dresser, an intimidating female known as Fosdick.

"Tally!" cried Cat, "At last. You have breakfasted, haven't you? Good, then we can begin. Now," she continued purposefully, "I think our best plan would be to make some choices from these." She waved a hand at the mountain, which threatened to topple to the floor at any moment. "Next, we shall make the rounds of the modistes, so that we can choose a few things to be delivered immediately. Then . . . What in the world are you laughing at, Tally Burnside?"

"Nothing," said Tally with a chuckle as she sank into a nearby chair. "Except that I think you should be sent to the Peninsula, for I'm sure you would be of much more use to Wellington than any of the generals he has now."

Cat lifted her nose, refusing to be drawn.

"As I was saying, after we have chosen some gowns that can be delivered right away, we shall go round to the linen drapers and merciers and purchase the material for the ensembles we have picked out from the magazines. Then I shall send word round to my sewing-woman to come make them up."

She handed Tally a recent issue of *La Belle Asemblée*.

"I want you to look at the evening dress in here—it's the first gown pictured. Fosdick and I both agree that it would suit you beautifully. I especially like the stomacher á la Venus, although I think you would show more to advantage in a pale peach rather than the rose shown there."

Tally turned to the page indicated and gazed at a tall maiden who stared haughtily at the world from beneath a headdress á la Turque, adorned with pearls and a diamond crescent. She was encased in an underdress of white satin, over which flowed a drapery of rose-colored figured satin, edged with silk floss trimming. The low-cut bodice was draped with white spotted lace, and the sleeves, made of the same fabric, fell to her wrists, where they were caught up by more rose-colored satin.

"Cat, I'd look like Christmas beef in this outfit. It's much too . . . too."

"You would *not* look like Christmas beef, you widgeon," retorted her friend. "And it is not 'too . . . too' . . . It is elegant, and it will be vastly becoming. Well," she amended, "except for the headdress, perhaps. The headdress is a little much. But," she hurried on as Tally opened her mouth, "the gown is elegant, and you will look a dream in it."

Tally closed her mouth.

"Now, then," continued Cat, pressing her advantage. "Look at this opera dress. I think in a jonquil Chinese crape, don't you, Fosdick?"

The dresser pursed her lips thoughtfully and nodded. She then pointed out that a trimming of lace worked in the Dutch style would finish the gown admirably.

"Yes, that would be just perfect. And see here, a Regency cap to add the finishing touch."

Tally sat silently, beginning to think she had faded from view as Cat and her henchwoman conferred over page after page of ball gowns, morning gowns, carriage dresses, opera dresses, and demi-toilettes.

Finally, she cleared her throat loudly.

"Excuse me," she announced.

". . . and what do you think, my lady, of this India muslin scarf to go with . . ."

"I said," repeated Tally in a loud voice, "excuse me." Two heads swung toward her.

"Excuse you for what?" Cat asked confusedly.

"Excuse me for interrupting this high-level conference, but I would like to put in a word—or two."

Cat simply stared blankly, but Tally, satisfied that she had her friend's attention, continued.

"I would like to make sure you understand that, while I am prepared to accept your very kind offer of a loan, I have no intention of buying out every shop in London. One or two moderately priced gowns should do for a start. Then, when I have my own money, we'll see about India muslins and Chinese crape."

Cat exchanged an exasperated glance with her dresser, then turned to her friend with an indignant stare.

"Tally, you are being such a peagoose about this—a silly, tiresome, stubborn peagoose. If you will only . . ."

Here, not unexpectedly, Tally uttered a spirited rejoinder, and within seconds the discussion degenerated into what could only be called a brangle. After a few moments Fosdick lifted her hand, in the manner of a nanny restoring order to a nursery, and the ladies subsided.

"I'm sorry," said Cat in a voice of forced calm. "I should not have said that. *But*, if you will consider a moment—dearest—you will see that one or two gowns will not remotely approach what is needed for even a short sojourn in Town. However," she went on in a slightly louder tone, as it became apparent that Tally was about to reopen hostilities, "I shall agree to stifle my inclinations."

This last produced such a ludicrous picture in Tally's mind that she giggled despite herself. In a moment the two friends were enjoying a hearty laugh, and Miss Fosdick permitted herself a faint smile.

A short time later the ladies sallied forth in Cat's town coach and were soon tenderly deposited on the doorstep of Madame Poquette, arguably the foremost among the fashionable modistes of Mayfair. And, thought Tally, the most expensive. She gasped at being told the price of a jaconet muslin round dress that she admired for its elegant simplicity.

Madame Poquette, upon receiving a steely glare from Mrs. Thurston, one of her most valued patrons, abruptly called to mind that she had confused the price of this gown with that of another one, which, though more heavily embroidered, was not nearly as becoming as the jaconet muslin.

Tally was then induced to examine an evening dress of apricot silk. By coincidence, the price of this gown was also most reasonable, so that Tally was able to add to her selection, with a fairly clear conscience, another walking dress, two morning gowns, a robe suitable for evening wear, and a ravishing ball gown of amber satin, ornamented with slim bands of acorns and oak leaves embroidered in raised gold thread.

As they were assisted again into the carriage, Cat briskly directed the coachman to Leicester Square, the headquarters, she explained, of Newton's, her favorite linen-draper.

"Um," began Tally hesitantly, "Aunt Sophronia used to patronize Grafton House. The prices there are much less dear than—"

"Really, Tally," cried Cat in appalled accents. "Perhaps we should simply go to Cranbourne Alley and buy off the rack. Grafton House, indeed!"

"I fear," Tally sighed, "that my hands will be shaking with age and unable to hold a pencil before I can repay you in full, Cat."

"In that case, I shall probably be too old to care by then, so we needn't worry about it."

Despite her misgivings, Tally could only smile affectionately at the young woman who was, indeed, dearer than a sister to her.

In the draper's shop, Tally's eyes grew round as Cat drew her into a dazzling world of silks, satins, gauzes, muslins, and laces in all the colors of nature. Glittering spangles and rosettes, luxurious fringes and embroidered bandeaux jostled for space on the shelves with rainbows of ribbon, silk floss, and beaded trim.

"Look," exclaimed Cat, "here is that jonquil crape we need. And, you know," she added, as inspiration struck, "I have a perfectly exquisite shawl that would add just the right touch. It's a lovely, forest green, with the tiniest bit of scarlet, and some of this same deep yellow. I bought it last year, but then Richard gave me one very similar for my birthday, and, of course, that's the one I always wear."

"Oh, Cat, I couldn't," began Tally.

"Nonsense. I'm grateful that it can be put to some use

before it simply crumbles away in a dark drawer someplace."

Tally felt there was a flaw somewhere in this reasoning, but knew she was waging a losing battle. Thoughts of the crumbling shawl brought to Cat's mind dozens of other accessories which, for one reason or another she was unable to wear herself, but was sure they would suit Tally admirably.

"Not," she added swiftly, "that I am just using this opportunity for ridding myself of all my castoffs. You don't feel that, do you?" Cat's eyes were anxious.

"I definitely do not feel like a charity case, it that's what you mean." Tally bestowed a fond smile on her friend. "My dear, I know you far too well to suspect you of any but the best and truest motives. Besides, I should imagine there is not a fashion-conscious matron in Mayfair who, if the truth be told, wouldn't be tickled to death to receive Cat Thurston's castoffs."

It was very much later in the day when the two ladies returned to Half Moon Street, their coach laden with so many parcels that the combined efforts of three footmen were required to transport them into the house under the watchful eye of Bates, the butler.

After directions were given for the removal of the packages to the sewing room, Tally and Cat made their way upstairs to restore their strength with a nap before dinner.

In her room Tally found on her dressing table a package, upon which her name was inscribed in a bold scrawl. She reached for it quickly, eager for her first look at Jonathan's novel. A quick knock at the door interrupted her, and she turned to find her maid, Lettie, entering the room with two enormous bandboxes, bearing the name of Madame Poquette. These, the girl announced breathlessly, had been delivered only moments before Lady Talitha and Mrs. Thurston had returned home.

No sooner had Lettie placed, with the utmost tenderness, the apricot silk in Tally's wardrobe, as well as a second gown, this one a pomona green walking dress, than another knock sounded announcing Cat, accompanied by her little maid, Teresa. The two lurched into the room, staggering under the burden of an incredible assortment of tippets, scarves, gloves, bandeaux, feathers, laces, and every other sort of feminine accessory.

"I see what it is, Cat," remarked Tally, her arms akimbo. "You have robbed the most fashionable shops of every item on their shelves, and we may look to see you taken up by the Runners before dinnertime."

"Ooph!" Cat dropped her bundle on Tally's bed. "Don't be absurd. Actually, this was a splendid idea. When I started going through my things just now, I had no idea that I had accumulated such a number of odds and ends that have turned out to be of no possible use to me. I begin to see the justice of Richard's complaints about my spending. In fact," she continued piously, "Richard will probably heap thanks on you for bringing me to a sense of my own, er, foolishness."

Tally's shout of laughter was cut short as Cat drew from the pile an exquisite Zephyr cloak, trimmed with silver embroidery. Against it she laid a wreath of palest pink rosebuds.

"What do you think?" asked Cat. "Wouldn't it do nicely for the ball gown we selected from *The Ladies' Magazine*—the pink lace with the satin underdress?"

Tally's mouth formed a silent *O*, as she gazed in awe at such splendor so carelessly displayed.

Cautiously she stepped to the bed and allowed her fingers to trail over the creamy richness of a Norwich silk shawl. She picked up a small chicken-skin fan, its ivory ribs delicately pierced, gilded, and painted with dainty medallions. A white silk cap, glittering with spangles and adorned with a curling feather next caught her eye, and she placed it on her head, turning to Cat for approval.

"That reminds me," said Cat, twisting the cap to a more becoming angle, "Monsieur Panchon, my hairdresser, is coming tomorrow. He is a perfect wonder, Tally, and he will create something fabulous for you!"

By now, Tally knew better than to raise any more objections to her friend's plans. In truth, she found her resistance to Cat's efforts slipping. She glanced into the mirror to observe that Cat had tucked most of her hair beneath the silk cap. That did look much better. Was it possible, she mused, that she was not plain as a pump handle? Could Papa have been wrong? Perhaps she really did have—potential.

She stood submissively as Cat and her maid wound more scarves, shawls, and fringes about her. She felt as though she were being wrapped in a golden dream in which she floated at the center, exquisitely gowned and coiffed, graciously accepting inflated compliments from hordes of men vying for her favor. And watching from afar, stunned admiration reflected in his gray eyes, was . . .

Tally returned to reality with a start, to find that Lettie was folding the last of Cat's largesse into a drawer. The largesse provider, with a final conspiratorial wink, whisked herself from the room.

Thoughts of gowns and furbelows scampered from Tally's mind as she moved quickly toward the fat packet on her dressing table. Once more she was foiled by a knock on the door. It was Lettie again, this time come to assist her mistress in preparing herself for dinner.

Glancing in the mirror when Lettie had finished, Tally felt an unfamiliar stab of dissatisfaction as she absorbed the full horror of the gown in which she was garbed. How could she have failed to notice how badly it fit?— or how sallow that particular shade of brown made her look? She experienced a stir of anticipation as she thought of the transformation in store for her.

Conversation among the three friends was light and general that evening, and it was not until dinner was nearly over that Richard bethought himself of a piece of information he had been mulling over all afternoon.

"I had a note from Chelmsford today at my office," he announced. "He wishes to visit us tomorrow evening to discuss a matter of 'some import.' Have we any plans, Cat?"

Cat shook her head, her face alive with curiosity.

"Is that all he said?" she demanded. "But how provoking. What could he possibly have to discuss with us?"

Richard professed himself to be mystified, and Cat promised to send a message that evening requesting that he dine with them the next night. Tally, her heart thudding, said nothing.

Thoughts of the handsome viscount continued to drift in and out of her thoughts for the rest of the evening, until, at long last, she finally found herself alone, seated at her dressing table. With trembling fingers she opened the package and drew forth a sheaf of papers.

The words, "TOWN BRONZE; THE ADVENTURES OF CLIFFORD AND CLIVE IN THE METROPOLIS" were printed across the top of the first page. Taking a deep breath, Tally began reading.

Chapter Eight

Tally came to her surroundings only when her candles began to sputter out one by one. She glanced at the little clock on her dressing table and discovered to her surprise that it was well after midnight, and she had been reading and sketching for two hours.

Jonathan had included with his first three chapters a brief key, revealing the real persons upon whom he had patterned his fictional characters. To her amusement, Tally discovered that the model for the flea-brained young peer, Clifford, was Ceddy Bagshot, notable for his vapid conversation and ornate quizzing glass. Clifford's friend, Clive, a worldly Corinthian, was in reality a certain Mr. George Wendover, with whom Tally had yet to become acquainted. The arrogant Duchess of Wigand, whose sketch had so intrigued Jonathan on the occasion of his collision with Tally, was featured in the story as a leader of society known as Lady Irongirth. Tally chuckled as she read the list of names before her. Many of them were familiar to her; others she would meet at another time.

She looked over the few preliminary sketches she had made. The first chapter was set in that mysterious locale, Cribb's Parlour, evidently a haunt of "sporting coves," to quote Clive the Corinthian. The second chapter was laid in Hyde Park and at the Italian Opera. Mmm. No trouble there, but the third chapter took place almost entirely at a cock fight. Oh, dear. Well, she would just have to ask Jonathan to describe these places to her.

The last of her reading candles were guttering in their sockets when she at last laid aside the pages, but it was some minutes before she rose to prepare for bed. Her brief immersion in Jonathan's London had provided her with much food for thought.

If Tally had held any doubts concerning Lord Chelmsford's writing talent, these had been summarily dismissed. The man's style was sharp and penetrating. His satire bubbled with wit, but it was not unkind. He held his subjects up to the mirror of reality, and proceeded to pluck from them, gently but with deadly accuracy, their pretensions and conceits.

Nor did the problems of the day escape his pen. To Tally's surprise, Jonathan reserved his harshest words for those who preyed on the weak, those who lived a life of ease and luxury on the backs of a suffering underclass.

> Children are born here without love. They grow up
> without kindness. They grow old without care, and
> die in the loneliness of the unwanted.

Tally read the words by the flickering light of her last candle and found herself moved almost to tears by them.

Rising, she prepared herself for bed, the phrases still ringing in her ears. She was more than ever determined to do justice to Jonathan's brilliant satire with her drawings, and as she settled herself under her feathery comforter, her head filled with ideas for the sketches she would continue tomorrow.

Late to bed made her late rising, and when she hurried into the breakfast parlor, she found Cat there before her.

"Good morning, slug-a-bed," was Cat's greeting. "Choose from the sideboard, and I'll ring for coffee."

When her plate was laden with a fragrant selection of eggs, toast, and York ham, Tally joined her hostess at the table in a sunny nook overlooking the Thurstons' tiny back garden.

"I hope you have no plans for this morning," said Cat through a mouthful of kippered herring. "We must be up and about as soon as you've finished here."

"But we shopped all day yesterday. Surely, there cannot be anything left in London that we need to buy."

"Only a length of amber stain to make up that gown with the embroidered trim. I don't know how we came to forget it when we were in Leicester Square yesterday, but we must have it for the Talgarths' ball. It's next week, you know, and all the world will be there."

"But," Tally began again, "I had planned to do some

sketching this morning. I really must begin, you know, for . . ."

"Dearest, I promise this will be our last excursion, for a while, at least. You can begin your drawing immediately after lunch. Oh, but no," Cat caught herself. "Monsieur Panchon will be here first thing this afternoon to do your hair. After that, Tally, you shall have the rest of the day to yourself. Until dinner, that is. Don't forget, the Viscount Chelmsford will be dining with us." She speared another sliver of herring and glanced at Tally. "You don't have any idea why he is visiting us tonight, do you?"

Tally's eyes widened in what she hoped was an innocent stare. "Me? Whatever can you mean? How could I possibly have any knowledge of Jo—the viscount's activities?"

"Because you nearly jumped out of your skin when Richard mentioned him last night. You can't fool me, Tally Burnside. You never could, you know. Now, tell me this instant what is going on."

Tally smiled.

"I believe you are part witch, Cat Thurston. Yes, you are right, I am aware of the reason for the viscount's visit. It has to do with—with something we discussed yesterday. But it is not my place to tell you about it, so you'll just have to contain yourself for a few more hours, Madame Nosy Parker. Now," she continued hurriedly, "tell me about this satin ball gown. I don't remember your mentioning it before—or the Talgarths' ball."

Cat sighed gustily.

"Very well, if you don't mean to tell me, I shall have to be content to wait, but I *do* think you might confide in your best friend. You're being quite beastly, you know. I forgive you—only because, as you no doubt recall, I have a very noble nature."

With this she rose and announced that she must change for their outing. With a rustle of silken skirts, she swept from the room, her nose in the air, not deigning to notice Tally's rich chuckle.

As Tally had suspected, the search for amber satin turned into a lengthy expedition in which Cat selected a figured silk for herself, after which she recalled a need for matching gloves and slippers, and of course new plumes for her headdress.

All the while Tally's mind was busy with plans for her projected sketching session later in the day. Should Clifford and Clive be introduced full face, or in three-quarter profile? What would a very green peer wear on his first day in town? To Cat's requests for her opinions on the merits of a feathered cap over one draped in scallops, she answered in the most distracted of tones.

They arrived home just in time to partake of a hasty luncheon before Monsieur Panchon was announced. After a brief conference with his fashionable patroness, he motioned Tally to a chair with the air of a kindly conjurer, ready to work his magic. He would not allow her a glimpse in the mirror until, with a flourish and a snip of scissors in the empty air, he gestured to a waiting maid, who brought a small looking glass to Tally.

By now Tally's muse was beckoning to her in deafening accents, and she hardly glanced at her reflection. She paid little attention to Cat's ecstatic comments, but mumbled a hurried thanks to the beaming Monsieur Panchon and left the room quickly before her friend could come up with any more time-consuming ideas for her betterment.

She spent the rest of the afternoon closeted with her drawing materials, and raised her head only at Lettie's knock. "Will you wear the new apricot silk for dinner, my lady?" asked the little maid eagerly.

She nodded an acquiescence and stood in silence while the girl slid the gown over her shoulders. A few moments of buttoning and tucking, and she was pronounced ready.

At that moment Cat poked her head into the room. She joined a bemused Tally at the mirror and gasped at what she beheld there.

The gown fell softly over Tally's bosom, outlining its delicate curve. The silk caressed her slim waist and the alluring swell of her hips, and the warm color of the fabric seemed to emphasize the delicate blush that flooded her cheeks. Her head, released from its burden of long, frizzed hair, swayed delicately atop her slender neck. Monsieur Panchon had swept her hair into a simple Clytie knot, from which a few tendrils escaped to float deliciously about her cheeks.

"Oh, Tally," breathed Cat. "Didn't I say you have potential? Wasn't I right?"

Tally was unable to tear her eyes from the mirror. "I do look—nice, don't I?" she whispered.

She laughed aloud suddenly and turned to hug her friend. "Oh, Cat, how can I thank you? I can't believe it's really me!"

Her gaze returned to the mirror, and she executed a shaky pirouette. She was not a beauty, of course. An image of Clea's face floated before her. Tally knew she could not hope to compare to such flawless perfection, but at least she could face the world now in the knowledge that she was not quite the plain provincial she had always considered herself.

"Our guest will be arriving soon, Tally." Cat drew her friend gently from her daydream. "We must go downstairs."

Tally's breath quickened. Their guest—Jonathan! What would his reaction be to the new Lady Talitha? Suddenly, the fluttering feeling was back in her stomach, and she twisted her little ring nervously as she followed Cat from the room.

To her vast disappointment, however, Jonathan's expression on greeting her, beyond a certain puzzlement as he kissed her hand, indicated nothing more than a courteous pleasure at seeing her once more.

Conversation during dinner was amicable and easy. Tally was surprised to learn of Jonathan's familiarity with the workings of the Foreign Office. Apparently, Lord Whittaker, Richard's supervisor, considered the viscount an invaluable player in the game of diplomacy that was waged on a daily basis by his office.

Richard chuckled. "He's still talking of the splendid job you did in convincing Count Weidenback to weigh in on our side in his recent discussions with Metternich."

"Ah yes," replied Jonathan solemnly. "The result of my keen wit, my superb diplomatic skills, and the fact that the count is my uncle—a distant uncle, but a relative nonetheless."

"A very handy thing, having a relative, however distant, who's an intimate of Metternich's. We need all the help we can get in convincing that wily old fox to come to side with Britain against Napoleon."

"Well, I don't know how influential I was with the old trout," sighed Jonathan, "but one does one's humble best. By the by, how is your new aide working out?"

Richard sighed. "Oh, Shipworth's doing all right, but it will be some time before he acquires the knowledge and experience that made Ridgeway so invaluable."

"Ridgeway?" echoed Cat. "Isn't he the young man who—?" She stopped short, glancing at Jonathan in confusion.

"Yes," replied Richard smoothly. "The young man who hanged himself last year."

"Oh!" Tally breathed the word.

"Yes."

It was Jonathan who spoke, his voice a little strained. "He had been going through a consuming infatuation for Clea, and it was assumed that was his reason for ending his life. Clea was devastated—though I have told her over and over that the tragedy was not her fault. She never gave the cub the slightest encouragement."

Cat made a noncomittal sound, and Richard dropped his eyes.

Talk turned to other matters then, and it was not until dinner was over and Richard and Jonathan had joined Tally and Cat in the little salon on the first floor that Jonathan stood before the fireplace to face his host and hostess directly.

"I understand," he began hesitantly, "that Lady Tally rather surprised you with her reason for visiting London at this time."

Richard and Cat glanced at each other before Cat raised her eyes to Jonathan's in a limpid stare.

"Why, no, my lord," she replied. "We have been begging her for this age to visit us here. We were delighted when she finally tired of the fastness of Cambridgeshire and decided to come to us. We hope her stay will be a long one."

Jonathan laughed, his even teeth a white blaze against his bronzed skin. He turned to Tally.

"You were right, 'Miss Burnside.' Your friends are apparently the soul of discretion." He addressed himself once more to Richard and Cat.

"No, I was referring to the lady's embarkation on a career as a caricaturist."

Had Jonathan disappeared before their eyes in a puff of smoke, Richard and Cat could not have looked more astonished. They whirled in unison to face Tally, who could not suppress a chuckle.

"It's all right, my dears. Jonathan—that is, Lord Chelmsford is privy to my dark secret."

"But—but . . ." sputtered Cat, while Richard still sat in bemused silence.

Jonathan drew a deep breath and continued in a more serious vein. "I have a secret of my own to impart to you. It is not one which I ever intended to share, and I hope you will not think me presumptuous if I ask you to promise that you will not reveal it."

He turned to Richard and smiled.

"Please do not think I am asking you to conceal anything illegal—or even immoral. It is important only to me."

Tally rose to seat herself next to Jonathan on the small confidante. "And to me," she said simply.

Richard gave Cat's hand a squeeze and lifted his own in a gesture of promise.

"Do you recall," asked Tally, "that I told you that the author of *Town Bronze* is a peer who wishes to remain anonymous?"

Richard and Cat nodded blankly, but as Tally paused, astonished comprehension gradually crept over their faces.

Richard's gaze swiveled to Jonathan.

"You don't mean . . . ?"

Cat chimed in immediately with, "You're not—you can't be . . . ?"

Jonathan said nothing but ran a finger around the inside of his collar, as though it had suddenly become too tight. He nodded awkwardly, and Tally stared at him in wonder. Never had she thought to see the Viscount Chelmsford, the epitome to her of all that was self-possessed, so ill at ease. Why, she wondered for the umpteenth time was Jonathan so fearful of exposure as the author of *Town Bronze*? Was he concerned about the controversy? Surely, his consequence was more than sufficient to face down the handful of persons who might be outraged at having been pilloried in a piece of trivia. What was his concern?

Richard and Cat were assuring Jonathan of their undying silence and support.

"Of course, old man," Richard was saying. "You're more than welcome here at any time. I often work at home, so you may feel free to visit at almost any time of day without rousing suspicion."

"Yes," Cat chimed in. "We can fit up that little room next to your study, Richard. Tally and Jonathan can work in there."

She turned to Tally. "There is a door between the two rooms. Lord Chelmsford can go into Richard's study, as though to confer with him, and can easily slip unseen into your studio."

She beamed at the small group around her, pleased at her arrangements.

"Dear lady"—Jonathan laughed—"what an admirable conspirator you make. If I were you, Thurston, I'd hire her on at your department."

"What a splendid idea," responded Richard, sweeping his wife into the curve of his arm. "Perhaps we should put her in charge of Plots and Schemes, junior division, of course. But," he continued, "do you suppose we could be Cat and Richard to you from now on? I have a feeling, my lord, that we are likely to find ourselves on a somewhat familiar footing in the days to come.

"Another splendid idea—Richard, if in return you will drop that infernal 'my lord.' My friends call me Jonathan, you know."

The rest of the evening was spent in pleasant conversation, and it was late when Jonathan took his leave. At the doorway Tally laid a tentative hand on his sleeve.

"My l—Jonathan, I read the chapters you sent."

"And . . . ?" he queried, the corners of his mouth lifting.

She shook a finger at him in mock severity.

"I have no intention of pandering to your already swollen consequence, my lord, so I shall simply say that your work is . . ." She capitulated with a shy smile. "It's the best satire I've ever seen."

Jonathan's response was not the pseudomodest disclaimer she expected. Instead, his eyes lit with pleasure.

"I think it's pretty good, myself," he replied, with a grin, "but it's always nice to hear one's good opinion of one's work confirmed. I'm glad you like it," he added, suddenly serious. "Your opinion matters to me, Tally."

Tally felt the blood rush to her cheeks and hastened to change the subject. "I do have one small problem, and I'm afraid I'm going to have to ask for your assistance."

"Ask away; I'm at my collaborator's beck and call."

Tally described her difficulty with the locales described in *Town Bronze*, and Jonathan promised to visit the Thruston home on the next day.

Having provided herself with a plentiful supply of candles, Tally worked far into the night to prepare several sketches for Jonathan's perusal on the morrow.

When she finally laid down her pencil, she stretched cramped fingers and leaned back in her chair, idly riffling the vellum sheets of Jonathan's book.

I tell you, Cliffie, sometimes I think London is not a geographical location, but the product of someone's fevered imagination.

The words fairly leapt from the page with the familiarity of an old friend. How had she missed that phrase on first reading? And why was it so familiar?

She turned another page, and frowned thoughtfully as she reread the words that had so moved her the night before.

Children are born without love. . . .

Surely, she had seen these words before as well. She straightened suddenly and moved to a small secretary in which she kept the small collection of favorite books she had brought from home. She selected one and returned to her chair.

The book was entitled *Back Streets of Shame*, by one Christopher Welles. It contained a number of searing essays on the wretched conditions in which so many of London's citizens were forced to live. She ran her fingers over pages soft with use, and her breath quickened. Yes, there it was! Her lips moved as she read the same phrase again, word for word. Suddenly cold, she dropped the book into her lap. Quickly she searched out another volume, this one a collection of political commentaries culled from the columns of one of London's most prestigious newspapers, and signed simply "Clement." Here again, she recognized the words and phrases which bore an unmistakable relationship to the prose in *Town Bronze*. Tally felt a horrible suspicion confirmed.

No—no, it couldn't be! The Viscount Chelmsford was nothing but a cheat—a plagiarist, no less! And a careless one at that. Both Welles and Clement were pseudonyms of respected men of letters. She and her father had spent many pleasant hours discussing their works. How could Chelmsford have hoped to copy them without discovery?

Sickened, Tally climbed into her nightdress and crawled between her bedcovers. It was all ruined—her dreams of a new life turned to ashes, for of course she could not continue her collaboration with Jonathan, knowing him to be a thief of other men's talents. No wonder he was so careful to cloak his identity!

Not, she told herself despairingly, that she was surprised. She had already known that beneath his handsome exterior, beyond the apparent warmth and charm, lay a different sort of person altogether. If the man she had chatted with so easily in the Park seemed incapable of such a deception, she could well imagine it in the character of the arrogant brute who had laughed at her humiliation four years ago.

She almost cried as she recalled the anticipation with which she had looked forward to tomorrow's meeting with Jonathan. Now, the thought of it filled her with a mixture of anger, grief, and dread.

Chapter Nine

Jonathan hesitated for a moment before mounting the stairs to the Thurston home. It was rather too early for paying calls, and he stood in the morning sunshine musing on the unaccustomed eagerness with which he looked forward to his first working session with Tally.

Of course, this was not a social visit, but more on the order of a business appointment. His relationship with Tally was, naturally, to be purely professional. On the other hand, last evening had been one of the most pleasant he had spent in a long time. He rarely found himself in a relaxed, family atmosphere, for he spent most of his time with Clea. He ignored the tug in his mind caused by the implications of that last and hastily changed the direction of his thoughts.

He had hardly recognized Tally when she entered the room the night before. He had been aware that the girl was badly clothed, but the lovely young woman who greeted him in her gown of apricot silk had astonished him, and had stirred something within him—something simple and clear in his nature that he had all but forgotten. He had delighted in her sincere and open appreciation of his work.

He smiled now and tapped on the door. A warm greeting formed on his lips as he was ushered into Richard's study, but it froze there, unspoken, as he beheld Tally standing at the workroom entrance. Her expression was that of a particularly annoyed avenging goddess, and he cautiously closed the door behind them.

"Good morning, my lord," she said distantly.

Jonathan was bewildered by this sudden about-face, and somewhat affronted. He bowed slightly.

"And good morning to you, Lady Talitha." He raised

a quizzical eyebrow. "What have I done to deserve a return to the status of 'my lord'?"

He made as though to hand Tally the envelope he had brought with him, containing another installment of *Town Bronze*, but she pushed his hand away furiously.

"What in God's name . . ." began Jonathan, but Tally interrupted him.

"I'm afraid I must inform you, my lord, that I will be unable to assist you in your—your little project."

"What?" His voice was a blend of astonishment, disbelief, and anger.

"I would have you know, my lord, that I am an avid reader."

This apparent nonsequitur caused Jonathan to frown in blank puzzlement.

"Two of my favorite authors," Tally continued in a rapid monotone, "are gentlemen who write under the names of Christopher Welles and Clement."

Jonathan stiffened, and his features assumed a rigidity that matched Tally's own. "I am familiar with their works," he said warily.

"That perhaps explains," finished Tally, whose throat was now so tight that she feared she might not get the words out, "why the prose of those men bears such a marked similarity to your own."

Jonathan remained perfectly still for several moments. Tally stole a look into his face and found that his eyes, now the color of glacial rock, were boring into hers as if they would peer into her very heart.

"What are you saying, Lady Talitha?" The words were uttered softly, but there was no mistaking the menace in them.

"I think my meaning is perfectly plain, sir." Tally's heart was beating in great panicky thuds that she feared must be audible.

"Not quite plain, my lady," Jonathan said. "Please tell me exactly what you mean. Why do you find it impossible to provide me with illustrations?"

Dear God, why must he make it more difficult than it already was? Tally knew an urge to simply flee from the room and let the man draw his own conclusions. Instead, she straightened her shoulders and stared coldly back at him.

"Because your talent is a lie. You have stolen someone else's words to cover your own inadequacy as a writer, just as a thief would purloin a coat to conceal a threadbare suit. I cannot work with one who would stoop to plagiarism."

There, she had said it. She released her breath in a sound that was almost a sob and looked once more into Jonathan's face. To her astonishment, his eyes had returned to their customary shade of autumn smoke, and his lips were curved in a rueful smile.

"Bravo, little spitfire. Spoken like an avenging angel. I cannot think of another woman of my acquaintance who would dare face me so." He turned to pace the room for a moment before he stood before her again, so close that she became intensely aware of his faintly spicy scent.

"I find your sad reading of my character rather discouraging, but since our acquaintance is of such short duration, I suppose I must not take exception. Tell me, does no other explanation for that similarity occur to you?"

Tally was so taken aback by his words that for a moment she could not reply. Explanation? What other explanation could there be for his use of those phrases? Unless—oh! Oh, no! Her knees suddenly refused to hold her up, and she sank into a nearby armchair of cherry-striped silk. She could only stare at him, her eyes wide with dawning comprehension.

Drawing another chair close, Jonathan sat down and took one of Tally's hands in his. "I had vowed that no one would ever know this about me," he said in low, intense voice. "It is bad enough that you had to be told about my authorship of *Town Bronze*. Now, I must ask that you keep my other, er, secrets."

Tally felt as though she were a bird, mesmerized by the proximity of a large, handsome, and extremely dangerous cat. She felt the strength of his fingers on hers, and felt—not fear—but a swift exhilaration at his touch.

"*You* are Christopher Welles?"

Jonathan nodded, his eyes never leaving hers.

"And Clement?"

"And several others, some of whom you may have heard of."

With an effort, Tally came to herself and withdrew her hand from Jonathan's. She felt as though his touch had penetrated to her very bones, and she stood abruptly to take her own turn in pacing the carpet.

"But, I don't understand! You have an enormous talent—you are—respected and admired. Why do you have such an aversion to making your name known to the public?"

"For much the same reason, I should imagine, that you prefer to remain anonymous. I would become a virtual social outcast, and, while I might not find that much of a strain, my family would suffer greatly. In fact"—he laughed shortly—"they would no doubt ostracize me. It is not fashionable, you know, for a member of the *ton* to express unpopular opinions. Can you not imagine the sobriquets? 'Rabble rouser' would be the kindest. Or, 'lover of the Great Unwashed.' "

Tally observed with some surprise the bitterness written on his face.

"Would your family not support you in your endeavors? I should think they would be proud of your talent."

Jonathan's smile was a twisted grimace. "You do not know my family. I learned to read very early, and I can scarcely remember when I first discovered the pleasures of putting my own thoughts and emotions to paper. One day, my mother found me at my nursery table scribbling a story of high drama concerning a mouse I had seen scurrying from the wainscoting pursued by our fat, whiskered Puss. Mother expounded at some length on the undesirabilty of such a pastime. I should be, she pointed out sweetly, out on my pony, or learning to shoot the gun dearest Papa had bought for me only the day before.

"When I was ten years old, my father hired a tutor for me, only to dismiss him without a reference when it was found that the man had actually encouraged my writing efforts. Then he rounded on me and bellowed that by Heaven I wasn't going to turn into a limp-wristed milksop while he still had breath in his body! It seemed to make no difference to him that I thoroughly enjoyed riding and shooting and hunting and all the other endeavors thought proper for a young peer. The fact that I loved writing above all was enough to cast me into outer darkness."

Throughout Jonathan's narrative, Tally kept her eyes

fastened on his face. She, who had received nothing but love and encouragement of her talent from her father, was wrung with pity for the small boy who had met only harsh disdain from those who had no doubt meant everything to him. Unthinking, she laid her hand softly on his sleeve.

Jonathan turned to her.

"Please forgive me. I had not meant to bore on about my misspent youth. I—I have never spoken about this to anyone, you see. I did not realize I had such a fund of spleen built up."

His smile warmed as he noted her dismay.

"Do not pity me. I made a concerted effort to excel in those areas deemed important by my father, and his pride in me was only slightly diminished by the knowledge that his oldest son cherished unmanly pretentions as an intellectual."

Tally could not hide her indignation as she retorted hotly, "I do not wish to speak ill of your family, Jonathan, but I think they behaved like—like barbarians! I am *so* glad you went behind their backs to continue your writing, and I think it would serve them right if you put them in your book in a chapter all about ignorance and stupid prejudice!"

The expression of sadness on Jonathan's face was suddenly replaced by one of light and warmth, as he gave a shout of laughter.

"What a splendid champion you make, Tally! As a matter of fact I did include a short reference to my sister, Arabella. When I was seventeen, she made my life a living hell when she discovered some very bad poetry I had written to the neighborhood flirt."

Picturing the humiliation of an adolescent in the throes of first love, Tally bristled. "How could she have been so cruel—to her own brother! Did she tell your father? Was he very upset?"

"Oddly, Father was a model of parental forbearance on that occasion. Apparently, it is considered acceptable for young fools to write verse to the objects of their desires."

"As long as it is very bad verse," finished Tally with a sympathetic grin.

"Precisely."

Tally considered for a moment.

"But surely your fiancée has been of support to you. It must have been a great comfort to you to have Lady Bellewood to confide in."

"Clea?" The unmixed horror on Jonathan's face was almost ludicrous. "Good God, she's the last person in the world I would tell. She must never know. You must promise faithfully you will never tell her, Tally."

"Of course, but . . ."

"Clea—that is, Lady Bellewood, is of a delicate and retiring nature. She would be devastated by the uproar if it were to become known that I pen scurrilous essays and articles. I—she—we would be banished from Society, and she would never forgive me."

"I see."

She did not see. She could hardly believe her ears. How could he not share the deepest secrets of his soul with his beloved? Good Heavens, one would think the man had embarked on a career of piracy on the high seas! Besides, if she were any judge, Lady Belle's nature was about as delicate and retiring as that of a Billingsgate fishwife.

"I see," repeated Tally, coming to the conclusion that the cause of Jonathan's extreme reluctance to acknowledge his renown as a writer centered more on Lady Bellewood's sensibilities than those of his family. Though certainly he had been conditioned by their abhorrence of anything that smacked of intellectual pursuit.

Resolutely, she put these thoughts aside. Turning to the large table Cat had set up for her use as a drawing board, Tally picked up the little pile of preliminary drawings she had sketched the night before and handed them to Jonathan.

"Yes, these are just what's needed." Jonathan chuckled. "I especially like your rendition of Sir Clifford. He's as green a tulip as one is likely to meet. I can just see him on the toddle in Bond Street. Now, what about Sir Toby Potwell? I had in mind Lord Beddoes for that hard-living old party."

"Yes, I saw him in your key. But, so far, he has only appeared in Cribb's Parlour." She hesitated. "I have a confession to make."

Jonathan waited, an amused twinkle lurking in the back of his gray eyes.

"I know I told Mr. Mapes that I was familiar with the London scene, but," she finished in a rush. "I have no idea what a Cribb's Parlour might be."

"I should hardly think so, my girl," he replied solemnly. "No gently bred young lady would have any knowledge of that haunt of sporting men.

"The owner is the ex-boxing champion of England, Tom Cribb. Devotees of the Fancy flock through its portals for the opportunity to mingle with the Pets and Bruisers, and in the hope that they might be given an invitation to join Cribb in his private parlour. It is a privilege extended to only a select few, you know."

"Have you ever been admitted to this Holy of Holies?" asked Tally with a mischievous smile.

"I shall modestly admit to the honor. I have sparred with Cribb from time to time, and I work out regularly with Gentleman Jackson at his gymnasium."

Tally's eyes slid over his muscular torso, evidently the product of those workouts, and she found it necessary to take a deep breath.

Abruptly, she turned her attention back to Jonathan's description of other taverns owned by prominent Pets of the Fancy. As he talked, Tally took notes. He went on to describe the Cock Pit near Westminster, the Fives Court, the subscription room at Brooks's, and the aspect of the more unsavory gin and brandy shops crowded together in places such as St. Giles, Seven Dials, and Tothill Fields. In none of these locales, he informed her severely, should she so much as consider placing her dainty feet.

"If you need any other information on the London scene outside the purlieus of Mayfair and Oxford Street, come directly to me," he directed.

Tally instinctively bridled at the viscount's autocratic manner. "If I should require your assistance, sir," she uttered coldly, "I shall be sure to ask for it."

Jonathan stood silent for a moment, an appreciative grin on his face. "While I applaud your spirit of independence, my dear, please accept my advice on this. There are areas of our fair city where an unaccompanied woman is considered fair game for all sorts of unpleasantness."

He moved to place his hands on her shoulders, and
the warmth of his fingers spread to the very core of her
being.

"Please let me help you if you need more information
on Cliffie and Clive's favorite haunts."

Breathlessly, Tally stepped back.

"Thank you, my l—Jonathan, for your help in describing them. I shall render them to the best of my ability.
And now, I have promised to lunch with Cat, and she
will be waiting for me."

She bowed him from the house with all possible speed.

Returning to the little work room, she sat for some
minutes at her drawing table, pencil poised, her eyes directed, unseeing, not at her tablet, but into the sunny
garden outside the window.

Chapter Ten

Lettie was nearly bside herself with admiration. "Oh, my lady," she sighed. "You look—splendid. Like you just stepped out of a story book."

Tally did not respond. She stood staring as though mesmerized at her reflection in the mirror. Lettie had brushed her chestnut curls until they glowed with warm, russet highlights, and piled them high atop her head, leaving a few tendrils to dance about her cheeks.

Her eyes, seeming even wider than usual, were candle-light on brown velvet, and her lips, touched with the lightest of pink, curved in a soft smile. Smooth, round shoulders rose from a gown of amber satin, which fell in heavy folds from just under her breasts to the floor. Gold thread, woven into a delicate leaf trim, shimmered as she moved. Against the sweet curve of her bosom lay a topaz necklace, its luster reflecting the candlelight which surrounded her.

"Thank you, Lettie," she whispered.

She could hardly believe that the young woman who gazed back at her from the mirror was herself—plain, country Tally Burnside. But she was not plain, was she? She could not qualify as a genuine beauty, but the girl in the glass was undeniably attractive.

Downstairs, Richard's cheeks puffed in an appreciative whistle when she entered the drawing room.

"Well," he said slowly. "Well, and well, well. I shall be the envy of every man at the ball, when I make my grand entrance with two absolute stunners on my arm."

Tally responded with a shy smile, and Cat, herself ravishingly attired in a petticoat of pink figured silk, over which floated a cloud of silver net, moved to take Tally's hands in her own.

"My dear, you are positively dazzling! You will not lack for partners tonight!"

"Why?" asked Tally demurely. "Have you already co-erced another consignment of young men to steer me about the dance floor?"

"There will be no need for coercion tonight, my girl."

Cat's words proved to be prophetic, for, while the males assembled at the Talgarth ball were not precisely thunderstruck, *en masse*, Tally found her hand claimed for a Boulanger almost as soon as she emerged from the ladies' cloak room.

Her partner was an extremely shy young man, and Tally soon forgot her own diffidence in setting him at ease. So successful was she, that in a matter of moments, the youth, who introduced himself as Mr. James Wilmot, not long down from Oxford, was regaling her with anec-dotes of his journey home from school. To his blushing delight, he was rewarded with a trill of Tally's clear laughter.

By the time the orchestra had wended its way through the final chords of the dance, the young man was beam-ing at Tally in naked adoration. He relinquished her hand only when she had promised him another dance later on, and begged that she would make time for a stroll with him on the terrace before the evening was over.

Tally felt a surge of exhilaration at this unfamiliar dis-play of admiration, and passersby were treated to the sight of an uniquely attractive young woman in their midst, her cheeks delicately flushed, and her eyes aglow.

Thus, Tally found herself with a plenitude of partners, and a few hours into the evening, she found it necessary to recoup her strength at the refreshment table.

"Tally! What a pleasure to see you here. I trust you have saved a dance for me?"

She whirled and found herself facing the Viscount Chelmsford, who looked impossibly magnificent in the dark evening coat that shrugged over his wide shoulders.

"Jonathan! I had no idea you would be here this evening."

"And miss the saddest crush of the Season? We wouldn't think of staying away."

We?

Tally followed the direction of Jonathan's amused

glance, and there was Lady Belle, in the center of her usual court. Tonight she graced the assemblage in a gown whose underdress of wine satin clung lovingly to every seductive curve. Over this lay a tunic of pale pink gauze, sewn with hundreds of tiny spangles, so that with every graceful movement, she shimmered like the enchanted princess of a lover's fantasy. Her guinea gold hair was caught in an airy puff of curls, and, nestled in their silky depths, a headdress of her favorite diamonds winked in the candlelight.

How fortunate, Tally thought wryly, that she had viewed the vision in the mirror earlier in the evening with a healthy dose of reality. For, if she had cherished any dreams of being the belle of the evening, those hopes must be most cruelly dashed. As she watched, Miles Crawshay bent over Lady Belle's hand and then swept her into the waltz that was just beginning.

"And now, that dance, Tally." It was Jonathan, his arm extended to lead her onto the floor.

"Oh, I am sorry, Jonathan, my card is full." Tally spoke the words with genuine regret, tempered by the pleasure it gave her to be able to say them.

"In fact," she continued, "if I am not mistaken, here comes my partner now."

She motioned to the figure of a portly dandy, approaching with purpose.

"Hah! Chelmsford," the gentlemen bellowed jovially. "Haven't seen you since the Bessemer mill. Hope you didn't place any blunt on Stubbs."

"Not I, Lord Mellenthwaite." Jonathan laughed. "I am far too downy a bird to wager on any opponent of Bessemer's whose reach is as short as young Andy's."

"Hah," his lordship barked once more. Then he turned with a courtly bow to Tally.

"My lady, I believe this is my waltz."

But, as he extended a chubby hand to Tally, Jonathan deftly interposed himself.

"I beg leave to claim a prior privilege, Mellenthwaite. You see, Lady Talitha and I are old friends and haven't seen each other in dogs' years. So much to catch up on and all that."

So saying, he whisked Tally onto the dance floor,

under the astonished—not to say, outraged gaze, of the plump peer.

"Jonathan, how could you?" gasped Tally. "Of all the rappers! 'Old friends,' indeed. Why, we haven't known each other a fortnight!"

"A fortnight? Come now, we've surely known each other for much longer than that."

Tally jerked spasmodically in Jonathan's light grasp. She stole a look upward into his face, but his expression was unreadable.

"Indeed?" she quavered.

"Mm, yes. You remind me dimly of someone I met several years at—at a come-out ball, I think it was."

Tally froze. She cast frantically about in her mind for another subject to throw into the breach, but Jonathan was continuing.

"You, however, are much more attractive than that other young woman. I notice, by the way, you have a new way of doing your hair. Most becoming."

By now, Tally wished she could simply collapse to the floor and dissolve there. He did remember that awful night! And he was teasing her! Well, she would show him that she was not to be humiliated a second time!

She raised a disinterested face to his. "I can't imagine what you are talking about." Quickly she nodded toward a couple dancing nearby. "Is that Mr. Wendover? I have not met him, but I overheard someone addressing him as such."

"Yes, that's George. Don't you think he will make an excellent Clive?"

Tally watched the gentleman, whose carelessly tied cravat, tumbled curls, and muscular physique marked him as a Corinthian. He had obviously been imbibing rather heavily, for he stumbled as he steered his embarrassed partner about the floor. No one could call him attractive, indeed his surly features were arranged in a most haphazard manner, and there was about him an insolent air of self-assurance that she found displeasing. Yet, she supposed, some might find a certain charm in his studied nonchalance. Yes, such a man, worldly and evidently ripe for any spree, would no doubt appeal greatly to young Clifford, fresh from his country estate.

Jonathan obligingly drew near to the erratically weaving couple, and Tally committed to memory Lord George's splayed nose, his thin smile, and the arrogant tilt of his head as he bent to pay a compliment to the young lady he held in his arms.

"Yes," agreed Tally. "Perfect. I shall commit him to paper this very night."

She gave herself up to the enjoyment of the dance. Oddly, she felt at ease in Jonathan's arms. Her body seemed precisely constructed to fit against his, and she felt as though she were receiving the rhythm of the music through his muscular frame. Her feet seemed to move of their own volition, following his steps without effort, and the throbbing of her heart soared above the strains of the melody. She was floating—she was flying! She had not known dancing could be so exhilarating!

Jonathan smiled at the animated little face before him. Tally's cheeks were pink with excitement, and her eyes fairly blazed as he whirled her through the steps of the waltz. What a difference from the last time he had danced with her. He smiled suddenly, remembering the icy composure she had maintained all through the seemingly endless patterns of that long-ago waltz.

Had he done the right thing in reminding her of that occasion? He had wished only to assure her that she now bore no resemblance to the unattractive maiden she had been, having emerged from her plain, ill-fitting chrysalis into a charming butterfly.

Jonathan's arms tightened around Tally invountarily, and as her soft curves fitted themselves to him, it was as though the rhythm of her heart sang through his blood. Startled, he bent his gaze to hers and held his breath in recognition of what he saw there.

The music stopped, and Tally stepped breathlessly back from Jonathan's arms.

"Oh, that was lovely!" she cried. *What was that in your eyes, Jonathan? Merely a reflection of my delirium?*

"But, how unfashionable, my dear." His voice betrayed nothing of what had just occurred, beyond a faint roughness.

Tally's glance flew to his face.

"To be seen actually enjoying yourself," he continued. "It's simply not done, my dear. You will, of course, wish to convey to your partner that you have been invited to every social function of the Season, and have thus become too, too bored with the whole thing."

Her eyes still dancing, Tally allowed her lids to droop. Her small nose lifted in disdain, and the corners of her mouth twisted in an exaggerated picture of ennui.

"Gracious, my lord," she drawled, "Have you ever seen such a dismal crush? I vow, I quite wonder why I came—so very dull, don't you think?"

Jonathan threw back his head in laughter. "Perfect! You are just like every other insipid young woman in the room tonight. Now, stop it please, and be Tally again."

"Since I find it impossible to be anything else—" she began, only to be interrupted by the sound of a cool chime of laughter behind her.

"Jonathan!"

It was Lady Belle, shaking her finger at her fiancé in mock reproof. Beside her stood Miles Crawshay, impeccable, if slightly overdressed, in a waistcoat of Italian brocade, and a velvet coat.

"Jonathan," Lady Belle repeated, her blue eyes sparkling mischievously. "You promised to dance the first waltz with me. Fortunately for you, Miles was nearby and rescued me from the ignominy of having to sit with the matrons while you abandoned me for another."

She turned to Tally and sent a puzzled glance skimming from the top of the shining curls to the hem of the amber satin gown.

"Lady Talitha, how—nice to see you again."

Tally smiled courteously and turned to respond to Mr. Crawshay's greeting, which was somewhat warmer than Clea's.

Jonathan and Crawshay merely nodded to one another. Tally was left with an inescapable impression of mutual antipathy.

Jonathan smiled fondly on his betrothed. "The picture of you sitting amongst the matrons," he said laughing, "is too ludicrous to bear thinking of, my dear. There now, they're playing another waltz." He reached for her hand. "Come, allow me to make retribution."

Clea giggled in capitulation, and was soon swept away in Jonathan's arms.

Tally eyed Miles Crawshay in some misgiving. Despite

his air of polished courtesy, she felt uncomfortable in his presence.

"You seem to be enjoying the ball, Lady Talitha."

It was an innocuous enough statement. What was there about Mr. Crawshay's manner that insinuated awareness of all that one would like to keep secret? His knowing smile seemed to imply a shared conspiracy, leaving Tally with the unreasonable, but uncomfortable feeling that he knew all—whatever all might be.

She assumed an air of nonchalance she did not feel. "Yes, indeed, Mr. Crawshay. It is my first ball since I returned to London."

"Returned?"

"Why, yes. This is not my first visit, of course, but it has been some four years since I enjoyed the bustle of the metropolis. And you, Mr. Crawshay?" she asked in an effort to turn the conversation away from herself.

"Ah, four years ago I was a soldier, ma'am, serving in the Peninsula. I took a ball in the shoulder at Corunna and was sent home. I cannot lift my arm above my shoulder, you see." He grinned deprecatingly. "I told my superiors that I'm still fit enough to lead a charge, but they would have none of it."

Tally's eyes widened. Corunna! She recalled the reports she had read of the bloody fighting there. Why, the man was a hero!

"In what unit did you serve, Mr. Crawshay?" she asked diffidently, hoping that her question would not bring back unpleasant memories.

But Mr. Crawshay apparently had no difficulty in discussing past glories. "I was with the Eighty-second Foot. It was just outside the city where I received my wound. We had been ordered to hold our position by the river, but we were outnumbered three to one. A group of our fellows became cut off from our party, and I tried to make my way over to them. The last thing I remember about that day was a horse rearing in back of me. I had turned at the noise he made—then the pain in my shoulder—then—nothing."

"I have heard it was dreadful beyond words," she said softly, the picture of the battle filling her mind. "Several families in our village lost sons and husbands there."

"But surely"—Crawshay smiled brightly—"this is an

unfit topic for such a gay occasion. Shall we join the dancers, Lady Tally?"

But Tally, referring again to her card, was obliged to decline, and in a few moments found her hand claimed by a large gentleman who had asked most earnestly earlier in the evening for a cotillion. As she and her partner bounced down the floor in the lusty rhythms of the country dance, she did not notice that she was followed by the speculative gaze of Miles Crawshay.

Some moments later, Tally stood breathlessly on the sidelines, accepting a flowery bouquet of compliments from the large gentlemen. Her eyes crinkled in laughter. No, *surely* she did not resemble a wisp of thistledown windblown across a meadow as she flew through the steps of the dance. Nonetheless, she confessed guiltily to herself, the large gentleman's blatant flattery was as welcome as rain on a parched garden. She could not remember when anyone had so much as told her she was presentable, much less that she was a vision of fairylike beauty.

Practicing, she gazed upward through long, thick lashes, and was rewarded by a returning stare of unmixed infatuation.

"Guard yourself, my lord," spoke a voice from behind Tally. Cat's white hand came to rest on her shoulder. "It is my sad duty to inform you that Lady Talitha is the most arrant flirt of my acquaintance."

The words were uttered with a twinkle of mischief, and Tally's erstwhile partner merely blushed and grinned.

"But now," continued Cat, "I beg to deprive you of your vision, as I require her services." She turned to Tally. "Alvanley is wearing that monstrous signet ring of his tonight, and during the last set, it caught here in the lace at my wrist."

She held up her arm to display a length of torn trim trailing from her sleeve. "I cannot mend it with one hand, Tally. Would you mind assisting me?"

"Of course not," responded Tally quickly. "I have pins in my reticule, and it won't take a moment."

Excusing themselves, the ladies made their way to a salon adjacent to the ballroom. Cat preceded Tally into the room, but as Tally prepared to follow her, Cat stopped suddenly. Tally peered over her shoulder to see what had caused her friend's quick intake of breath and a sudden stiffening of her form.

Unbelieving, Tally stared at two figures who stood close together at the far end of the room, bathed in the glow of a single candle. Richard stood with his head bent attentively over that of Lady Belle, whose slim hands were placed intimately on the lapels of his coat. Her eyes clung to his, and, as she whispered urgently, Richard's hand came up to close over hers.

Chapter Eleven

Late morning sun filled the Thurston breakfast room. Tally, her sketch pad wedged between her plate and her coffee cup, leafed through its pages as she nibbled eggs and York ham in a distracted manner. Occasionally, she added a line here, removed one there.

She was finding it difficult to concentrate on the frivolous doings of Clifford and Clive, for despite her best efforts, her thoughts insisted on returning to the words Jonathan had spoken the night before. She had tried to believe that he had merely been making small talk, that in truth she did remind him of someone else. But then there was that wicked glint in his eye as he spoke. No, he had deliberately provoked her.

She straightened her shoulders, determined to be all business this morning. Jonathan was due to arrive momentarily (they had agreed that morning visits were liable to prove the least noticeable of any time of day) and she had a neat packet of drawings ready to show him. She had, she felt, adequately transformed the swarthy features of George Wendover into the essence of Corinthian Clive.

She gazed in self-congratulation at a drawing of Clifford and Clive at the Fives Court, which she had created from Jonathan's description of that haunt of the sporting set. The two scapegraces stood at the outskirts of a crowd surrounding a boxing ring in which a pair of pugilists enthusiastically pummeled each other black and blue. She had included every class of society in the disorderly mob that cried encouragement to the fighters; sailors and navvies jostled elbows with clerks and butchers and peers. From balconies above the ring, dandies raised quizzing glasses to inspect the proceedings.

She smiled in anticipation of Jonathan's compliments.

He had been extraordinarily appreciative of her work, and she basked in his praise. In fact, she had found the hours spent with him over the last week most enjoyable. Their conversation had roamed far beyond the confines of their collaboration. Twice, he had stayed far into the evening, and they had chatted companionably, talking of every subject under the sun.

To her dismay, she was finding it increasingly difficult to maintain her image of Lord Chelmsford as an insolent dandy, the catch of the marriage mart and an insensitive clod. He had displayed none of these loathsome attributes to her, and she certainly could not claim that he was simply making himself charming to her. For he had no reason to cozen her. In truth, she felt oddly comfortable with him, as though there had never been a time when she did not know him. If only . . .

She looked up as Cat entered the room, and the two exchanged greetings.

"You are looking well," remarked Cat, "after your night of dissipation."

"I had a wonderful time," Tally admitted with a grin. "And I owe it all to you, oh best of my friends."

"Nonsense. I shall readily take the credit for nudging you into shedding your ill-fitting chrysalis. But the beauty of the butterfly that emerged was all yours, Tally. I swear, you fluttered into some heretofore impregnable hearts last night. Have you seen the flowers already piling up in the drawing room?"

"No! Really?" Tally's face lit with pleased surprise. "Who would be sending me flowers?"

"Oh, Lord Brindfield, for one. And Philip Shoulton. And there's young Charlie Brendenwood, who must have bought out every flower woman in Covent Garden."

Tally remained silent for a moment. Surely, a new gown and a new hair style could not be responsible for this glorious upheaval in her life.

As though reading her thoughts, Cat mused aloud. "Of course, it is not your new feathers that has brought these gentlemen to your doorstep, Tally. It is—oh, I don't know—a new air of confidence, I guess. When last you stood before the portals of the Polite World, you hardly had two words to say for yourself. It was as though you were a captive, mute and miserable inside those awful

clothes. Richard said the same thing last night, just before we retired."

"Ah," said Tally, mischief sparking in her eyes. "And
how is our wandering lad this morning? Still quivering
from his ordeal?"

"Not nearly so much as he would have been were he
not in the act of prying Clea's dainty little claws from his
coat when we peeped in on him."

"Honestly"—Tally's laughter bubbled—"the look on
his face when he turned away from her and saw us in
the doorway. I never saw such a pitiful expression of
relief in my life. And Clea! I'll wager this is the first time
in her career that a man has ever withdrawn in haste
from a tête à tête with Lady Belle."

"Yes," replied Cat complacently. "I expect I shall
savor her expression of chagrin for some months to
come. Although I must confess it was all I could do at
the time to keep my hands from her lovely white throat.
Did you hear her? 'Oh, dear me, Mrs. Thurston! I pray
you do not think anything amiss! Richard insisted I accompany him to the window at this side of the house to
observe the lovely full moon just rising.' " Cat's magnificent bosom rose on a wave of indignation. "The wicked,
lying bitch! She'd better take care not to creep around
my husband again. 'Lovely full moon,' indeed! Richard
told me she wafted up to him on the dance floor and
said that there was someone who very much wished to
meet him in private, but when he entered the room behind Clea, there was, of course, no one there."

"I don't know what she could have been thinking of,"
replied Tally. "All London knows that Richard is fidelity
personified. He worships you, for heaven's sake!"

"No." Cat chuckled. "That he does not. Nor would I
want him to. I can think of few fates more dismal than
to be placed on a pedestal and adored from afar, for all
the world like a lump of sculptured marble."

Tally laughed, but her thoughts drifted, as was their
annoying tendency, to Jonathan. That was the look in
his eyes, when he watched Clea, wasn't it? Adoration?
Tally had the feeling that Lady Belle very much enjoyed
accepting the homage of her worshipers from atop a pedestal. But surely, adoration was not a very good basis for

a lifelong relationship, was it?—even if the idolatry were mutual, which Tally somehow felt it was not.

Uncomfortably, she pushed her chair away from the table and picked up her sketchbook. Bidding good-bye to Cat, she made her way to her newly created workroom next to Richard's study to await Jonathan.

Once alone, however, the words Jonathan had spoken last night began their merciless repetition in her mind. "Someone I met several years ago—years ago—years ago." She put her hands over her ears and shook her head to no avail. "Someone who looked like you—ooh—ooh," the din continued.

There was no escape. Jonathan had recognized her as the social reject he had made sport of so many years ago. And he had made fun of her—again! How could he! He must have known how she had suffered on that occasion. How could he have been such an insensitive boor!

But wait a minute. Not once in the brief time she had known him since she returned to London had he given any indication of being other than a warm, sensitive, caring human being. Was it possible that she had misjudged him?

Once more her thoughts returned to the fateful night of her come-out ball. For the first time she considered what the effect might have been if, as she cringed in the black reverberation of those hurtful words, Jonathan had offered an expression of sympathy, or said nothing at all—or had simply turned on his heel and walked away.

Why, Tally thought slowly, she would have been utterly undone. She would have raced from the room in tears, thus adding to her humiliation by making a complete fool of herself. Had Jonathan known that? His brusque demeanor had turned her shame into an enveloping rage, resurrecting the tattered rags of her pride. Had he acted so by design?

So deep was she in her reverie, that when Jonathan slipped into the little room a few moments later, she stared at him blindly. For a moment, he seemed to her the reflection of her thoughts, taken solid form.

"Did you really say those dreadful things on purpose?" The words flew out of her mouth without thought, and she would have given anything to have them back.

Oddly, Jonathan answered her question without hesitation, as though his thoughts had been running parallel to hers.

"Of course I did," he said simply. "I could not think what else to do." His dark brows lifted questioningly. "Surely, you realized what I was about—at least, later, when your very understandable rage had dissipated."

Jonathan moved to grasp her shoulders lightly, and he was instantly transported to that night. The Viscount Chelmsford of that long-ago time was certainly no rescuer of wounded doves. It seemed as though Clea had absorbed what few gentle emotions he possessed. But he could not stand by and watch another human being disintegrate before his eyes, particularly one so terrifyingly vulnerable. For years the vision of those great brown eyes had stayed with him. Why had something not told him at the time that . . . He dropped his hands abruptly.

"You were—what, seventeen?" he asked. "You cannot think I ripped at you for the sake of hurting you even further? Good God, what sort of a monster have you thought me all these years?"

Tally forced a smile to her lips, but the deep breath she drew was shaky. "I can only say that I have misjudged you, and—and, I'm glad I now have the opportunity to know the real Viscount Chelmsford."

Jonathan's expression was unreadable as he stood back several paces to look at Tally, long and searchingly. He said nothing further, but, as though having made his mind up about something, he gave a little nod and smiled.

Stepping to the table upon which Tally had been working, he picked up the packet of sketches and began scanning them. To Tally's dismay, a frown shadowed his forehead, which grew steadily deeper as he perused them further. He looked up, finally.

"Tally, these are very good. That is, the characters portrayed are excellent, but the background is all wrong."

"But I have drawn them just as you described them."

"No, no—look here at the Fives Court." He spread the sheets out. "The ring is much too small. And there is no balcony such as the one you have drawn."

"But you said there was an upper tier which runs around the perimeter of the room."

"Well, yes, but it is not an open balcony. It is more like the walls to a second floor—a mezzanine, if you will, but it has walls, into which are set windows—"

He stopped short, as Tally simply stared at him in confusion.

"An enclosed balcony—with walls?"

"Well, no, not precisely."

Jonathan picked up one of Tally's pencils and attempted to modify the sketch, only to render it completely useless as an illustration.

He set it aside in dismay and turned to another drawing, this one of the Cock Pit. Tally's pencil had caught the cruelty of the sport. One of the fowls was in the process of disemboweling the other, as the spectators, eyes glittering greedily in the lantern light, urged their favorites to greater carnage.

"Yes, but Tally, there are no windows in the Westminster Cock Pit. And look at that fellow in the basket. He looks like a prize piglet about to be tucked under the arm of the farmer's wife and taken off to the fair."

Tally stared at him in growing apprehension.

"It's not supposed to be a real basket, don't you see? It's more like a little cage, actually. And the fellow's smiling! Don't you remember? I told you that when someone wagers, and then can't pay the bet, he's hoisted up in the basket until he makes arrangements to pay. Now, would the fellow be happy about that?" He shook his head. "I don't know, Tally. Your drawing talent is extraordinary, but you simply don't know the territory."

Tally stiffened. Was he saying that he couldn't use her drawings? She felt herself grow cold as she saw her hopes for a career as an artist go aglimmering.

"No!" she cried, placing her hands over the drawing in an instinctive gesture. "You are quite right—about not knowing the territory, I mean. But I can fix that!"

"How? I described these places as best I know how. I suppose we could go through every drawing line by line, but that would take forever, and it probably wouldn't answer, anyway."

"I don't know," responded Tally desperately, "but I'll think of something. Just give me a day or two. I'll think of *something*."

Jonathan regarded her uneasily. "You would not consider going to any of those places yourself, would you?"

"Of course not. At least—no, of course that would not be possible. Would it? I mean, if you were to come with me—"

"No," replied Jonathan flatly. "A gently born female would no sooner be seen in any of those places than she would sign on for duty in a sultan's harem."

"Mmm." Tally's brow furrowed in thought. Catching Jonathan's extremely dubious eyes on her, she brightened and smiled disarmingly. "Well, if that won't fadge, I shall just have to work out something else. And I shall, you know. You'll see."

Jonathan took his leave then, and mounted his curricle outside the Thurston home with some misgiving. He wondered what plot Tally might be hatching. In his short acquaintance with that resourceful damsel, he had learned to appreciate her determination to make her own way in the world. He very much feared that if she had decided that it was necessary for her to visit the Fives Court, and the Cock Pit, and Cribb's Parlour, and all the other males-only locales patronized by Clifford and Clive, that would be precisely what she'd do.

As he guided his team deftly through the heavy midday traffic of Mayfair, he mused on his new partner. Certainly, she was unlike any other female of his acquaintance. He smiled as he recalled the painfully shy, uninteresting little dab he had met those many years ago. Now, she had acquired her own coating of town bronze and had been transformed into an enchanting pixie.

Strange, how much he enjoyed her company. It was as though they had known each other for years. He thought of Clea and wondered that he had never been able to converse with her as he did with Tally. It was well-nigh impossible to imagine an evening spent with Clea by the fire in lively conversation. But then, Clea was nothing like Tally. Clea was a glorious, golden goddess. Tally was wholly of this earth—a vibrant little creature of laughter and surprise. Clea was his deity, and Tally . . . He was puzzled and not a little alarmed at the feelings that were developing within him toward his new friend.

Yes, that was it! Of course, that was it. What he felt

for Tally was friendship. He had not recognized it as such because he was unused to feeling in such complete harmony with a woman. His relationship with the fair sex had been full and varied, but always on the most physical of levels. Except for Clea, he hastily assured himself. His feeling for Clea was deep and spiritual—of course. A picture of her honey blond loveliness swam before his eyes. His pulse quickened as he envisioned satiny skin molded into enticing curves that, at last, welcomed his caress. His lips curled in an ironic smile. Well, perhaps not altogether spiritual.

Tally was new to his experience. How wonderful it was to be so completely at ease with an engaging imp who entered into one's deepest dreams and desires and treated them almost as her own.

He continued on his way, secure in the knowledge that he need have no fear in continuing his exploration of the many facets of the imp's personality.

Chapter Twelve

Two days later, Jonathan cantered easily along a secluded bridle path in Green Park. He scanned the grassy slope for Tally's slight figure, for she had promised to meet him here for another early morning ride. This was their third such outing, and he found, with some surprise, that he looked forward to her appearance as he rarely did to any other of his acquaintances, male or female.

The reason was, he supposed, that it was so enjoyable to be able to speak his mind simply to Tally on any subject. Unlike every other female in his social circle, he must not confine his remarks to the latest *on-dits*, or to inflated compliments on her gown, or to her fine eyes. His enjoyment at being able to share his literary ambitions with her was almost palpable. To her he could describe his triumph over a difficult passage; he could discuss with her a point of characterization. Her response was always honest and intelligent, and more often than not, witty.

He sighed with pleasure. How satisfying to have found such a delightful friend, one who was as enchanting as she was companionable. He smiled as he thought of the sessions to come in the little studio at the back of the Thurston home.

Then he frowned. What if she were unable to get the backgrounds right in those otherwise brilliant illustrations? She had promised a solution with airy assurance, but . . .

His reverie was broken off as a small, cracked voice caught his ear.

"Vi'lets, guvnor? Buy some vi'lets fer yer lady fair on this fine mornin', yer worship?"

Jonathan sighed and turned his head to behold one of London's ubiquitous flower women gesturing to him with her blossoms. What in the world was she doing out and about so early—and in the park, at that? Life must be treating her badly if she were scrabbling for business at such an unlikely hour.

Reaching into his pocket for coins, he bent down to accept the violets from her trembling hand. To his astonishment, the old woman snatched the blooms away, and with a sprightly dance step, whisked off her gray, somewhat greasy wig. She swept him a low bow, the ends of her tattered shawl nearly scraping the ground, then straightened to smile impudently into his eyes.

"Tally!" The word fairly exploded from Jonathan. "What—what in God's name are you doing in that—that disgraceful getup?"

"Not Tally, my lord." She had replaced her wig and the grimy bonnet which perched on it, and she allowed her shoulders to sag in a self-deprecating slump. She paraded before him in an arthritic hobble, her flower basket held wearily on her hip. "Granny, perhaps—yes, Granny Posey. That has a nice ring, doesn't it?"

Jonathan dismounted slowly.

"But . . . what . . . why . . . ?"

"Don't you see? Lady Talitha Burnside cannot visit the Fives Court or the Cock Pit, but Granny Posey can sidle into those places without drawing a second glance."

"Tally!" The word burst out again. "You cannot be serious!"

"But, of course I am. You did not recognize me, did you? Nor would anyone else of my brief acquaintance in London. I think I look quite splendid—thanks to Addie's nephew, Charlie. Miss Adlestrop is my old governess, you see, and Charlie is an actor. He was kind enough to provide me with this, er, costume, and to help me with my makeup."

She pirouetted before him, her dusty skirts billowing.

"Are you telling me, Lady Talitha Burnside," began Jonathan in an awful tone, "that you plan to travel the streets of London in that filthy garb?"

Tally nodded brightly.

"And snug in your disguise you think to infiltrate the places we have been discussing, unprotected and alone amidst the most dangerous crowd of thugs one would be likely to encounter on the entire planet?"

Tally nodded again, perhaps a shade less brightly.

"Tell me, my girl, do you fancy yourself living between the pages of one of Mrs. Radcliffe's romances? I never heard of such lunacy in my life as this plan of yours!"

"Lunacy!" Tally's eyes blazed. "It is a very good plan, as you would agree if you could see beyond your male sensibilities. There are hundreds of old women who make their way around the city looking just like this. Dressed in these clothes, and with a few wrinkles and spots added to my face, nobody will pay any attention to me at all. I am obviously too poor to make robbery worthwhile. I am certainly no threat to anyone, so no one will even think of harming me. I shall," she finished proudly, "be able to gain admittance to any gin shop in London with no questions asked."

At this Jonathan dropped his head into his hands and gave way to laughter. "A worthy goal for any gently bred maiden," he gasped. His frown soon returned, however, and he continued with unabated resistance to Tally's grand plan.

"Really, my dear, you must see that it will not do."

"But how else am I to see these places for myself so that I can get your wretched backgrounds correct? Jonathan, I am perfectly serious about this, and I mean to carry it through."

Jonathan stood silent, gazing into her earnest countenance. He had never felt so completely at a loss. How could he explain to her the danger she faced in exposing herself to the underside of London? In her innocence, she simply could not conceive that anyone would want to harm a defenseless old woman, and did not realize that there lurked in those dark back alleys scum who would maim, or even kill for tuppence. He cast about desperately in his mind for words that would sway her.

Even as he opened his mouth, he could see in Tally's eyes the futility of argument.

"You cannot forbid me, you know," she cried mutinously.

"I would not be too sure of that," replied Jonathan with a glint in his eye that made Tally uneasy. "However, perhaps it need not come to that. I shall make you a bargain."

Tally said nothing, but raised her brows dismissively. Jonathan raised a gloved hand.

"No, hear me out, Tally. I will agree to let you—that is, not to stand in the way of your plan, if you will allow me to accompany you."

Tally looked at him swiftly. "But, you could not . . ."

"I don't mean that we should travel together. We would simply be in the same place at the same time. I shall meet you somewhere near the Thurston home, and we will go by carriage to whichever haunt of vice you plan to invade. We will enter separately, and when you feel you have soaked up enough atmosphere, we'll leave in the same manner."

"Really, Jonathan," began Tally angrily, "I do not need to be guided around town like an unruly sheepdog on a leash. I am quite capable . . ."

"I have no doubt that you are capable of many things, but fighting off a large attacker is not one of them. Please, Tally. Let me do this for you."

Under that smoky gaze, Tally suddenly felt her breath catch in her throat. Did he realize how unfair his tactics were? That all her independence and determination would simply melt in the sincerity of his concern?

Striving to conceal her sudden trembling, she answered coolly. "Very well. I shall do as you ask, but I trust you will not try to interfere needlessly, or tell me where I may and where I may not go."

"Agreed," said Jonathan, the corners of his mouth twitching only slightly.

Thus it was that some hours later, a certain aged flower woman could be seen making her way into the King's Arms public house, at the corner of Duke and King streets. This was the establishment belonging to Thomas Cribb, and through its portals streamed the cream of the sporting world and those who wished to be a part of it.

Spying a vacant stool in the corner of the taproom, close by the fire, Tally settled herself in the shadows. Unobtrusively, she drew out a small sketch pad and went to work. She recognized none of the habitues of the tavern but saw that they came from every rank of society. She noticed the respect accorded certain brawny individuals by the haughtiest of Corinthians as they made their jovial way to the parlour. She also noticed that it was only the more favored of Mr. Cribb's patrons who were ushered into that room, Cribb's special territory.

Edging close to this sanctum sanctorum, Tally peeked inside, and in a few strokes of her pencil, she captured the essence of that mecca of Pets and peers alike, Cribb's Parlour.

She signaled to Jonathan, who was enjoying a heavy wet with the champion himself and several cronies whom he had encountered upon his arrival. By the time she had crept to the door and made her exit, he, too, had made his departure.

On the way home, Tally was loud in gleeful self-congratulation.

"You see?" she chortled. "It simply could not have gone smoother! From the time I shinnied down the tree outside my window till I found you waiting in your carriage, not a soul saw me. Although, I must admit it was hard to stay awake so long after the household had gone to sleep. I shall be absolutely worthless tomorrow! Not that I can allow myself to slack off. I have three drawings to complete featuring Cribb's Parlour, and this time I know they'll be right. Oh, Jonathan, isn't it exciting?"

In the darkness Jonathan smiled. How like a child she was in her enthusiasms. It seemed as though the interior of the carriage was lit not from the flicker of the lamps and flambeaux they passed, but from the sparkle emanating from the absurd little flower woman sitting beside him. He knew a moment's impulse to draw her to him—to warm himself at the glow that surrounded her.

The friendship between Jonathan and Tally grew rapidly, and in a matter of days, they were on the easiest of terms with each other. Jonathan found himself spending more and more time at the home of his friend, Richard Thurston.

The Thurstons were pleased at this turn of events. Richard and Jonathan's casual friendship soon deepened into a comfortable camaraderie, and Cat smiled as she observed Tally's growing acceptance among the *ton*, for which the Viscount Chelmsford's attention, no matter how platonic, was at least partially responsible.

One person, however, was not at all pleased by the budding relationship. The Countess of Bellewood watched the visits to the Thurston menage and the rides in the park with a frown that grew angrier by the day.

Not being very wise, Clea showed her displeasure in a series of waspish outbursts that made Jonathan uneasy. In his eyes she could do no wrong, but never in his long infatuation with her had he seen that luscious mouth thin to such a hard line or those limpid blue eyes freeze to a crystalline glitter.

"But, my darling, I have business with Richard Thurston. We are working on a project that may facilitate Lord Castlereagh's negotiations with Metternich. I have distant family connections in Austria, you know, and—"

"I care nothing for Castlereagh or your connections in Austria, Jonathan. All I know is that you are making me a laughingstock with your attentions to that little Burnside chit, and I will not have it!"

To Clea's fury, her betrothed refused either to reaffirm his undying devotion to her or to discontinue his attentions to the little Burnside chit. Venomously she cast about for a means of revenge, and when her cousin—her distant cousin—Miles Crawshay presented himself in her drawing room for a morning visit, she greeted him with a request. His reaction was not promising.

"You cannot have thought, pet. Chelmsford would more than likely call me out."

Clea trilled her silvery laugh.

"But you have never avoided a challenge, Miles."

"Not a quarrel of my own making, no. But I have an aversion to putting my precious hide in jeopardy over one of your whims."

"Don't be silly. Chelmsford challenge you to a duel? I don't think he's ever considered such an action. Besides, you know he cannot stay angry with me."

Crawshay appeared unmoved, but his eyes flicked over Clea's face in speculation.

"Just what is it you are up to, my lovely schemer? It cannot be simply your addiction to gambling. Why are you bent on putting Chelmsford in a rage? If I were you, I should be careful what I was about. He is not one of your painted puppies to be whistled to order."

"Pooh. He may not be painted, but he can be whistled to order at any time of my choosing. And I am *not* addicted to gambling—I simply enjoy my little flings, and

I do wish to try my luck at Madame de Robitaille's house. Will you take me? Please, Miles?"

Crawshay smiled cynically, and flicked Clea's cheek with one slim finger. "Very well. I cannot say I would mind causing my lord an uncomfortable moment. I have always found him to be distressingly high in the instep. But," he continued, his expression hardening, "take care, my precious gamester. It would do neither of us any good to alienate Chelmsford. Do I make myself clear?"

Clea turned an offended shoulder. "You needn't concern yourself, Miles. I know what I am about, and I do not fear his anger—his very temporary anger. It will serve only to attach him to me more strongly than ever. You'll see."

The next morning brought rain to London and an unwelcome visitor to the town home of the Viscount Chelmsford. It was the mission in life of Mr. Wilton Delberforce to provide, like the shower now in progress, a steady infusion of nourishment to a society always greedy for gossip.

He arrived at Chelmsford House just as Jonathan was sitting down to breakfast. The viscount sighed inwardly and invited his guest to partake of his sirloin and eggs; then he waited for the inevitable downpour.

But Mr. Delberforce was not to be rushed. He indeed had a thunderbolt to drop on the viscount's head, but there was form to be followed in these matters. He settled his corpulent form in a chair across from Jonathan and proceeded in the most delicate manner to regale his host with the latest *on-dits*. It was not until he was well into his second tankard of ale that he approached the reason for his appearance.

"I say, my lord," he wheezed in a tone of utmost confidentiality. "Have you perchance visited the town's newest hell?"

Jonathan responded with a disinterested shake of his head.

"But Madame de Robitaille's place grows more popular by the moment. One may meet everyone there."

"So I have heard." Jonathan yawned, inspecting the platter of sirloin through his quizzing glass.

"Yes, indeed," continued Mr. Delberforce slyly. "Last night the Countess of Bellewood spent several hours there. I believe she was accompanied by her cousin, Miles Crawshay."

If Mr. Delberforce had anticipated a violent reaction on the part of the viscount, he was doomed to disappointment. Beyond a momentary stillness, he might have not heard his guest's words.

Mr. Delberforce persisted, his eyes glittering avidly. "Unfortunately, her luck was not in, I hear. She lost rather heavily, I understand."

"Mm, yes," Jonathan responded mildly, "the countess does enjoy a fling at the tables. Perhaps next time she will recoup her losses. It frequently happens that way."

Mr. Delberforce sank back into his chair, disappointed. Petulantly, he refused an offer of more toast and marmalade, and in a few moments had taken himself off.

It was many moments later before Jonathan rose from the table, and when he did so, he moved with a controlled anger that would have been easily recognizable to any of his friends. Certainly his valet had no difficulty in perceiving that his master was in the foulest mood he had encountered in a very long time. By the time his lordship was dressed to go out, the man was exceedingly relieved to see him out the door.

Not many minutes later Lady Bellewood was startled to behold her betrothed in the doorway of her boudoir. She was reclining on a chaise longue of palest blue, her favorite color, and at Jonathan's entrance she started visibly. For an instant she observed him warily through a curtain of thick, curled lashes, then opened her eyes wide to display a look of mischief, nicely blended with one of contrition.

"Jonathan, dearest," she purred. "How is it that you are out so early, and on such a wretched day?"

"It is, indeed," agreed Jonathan grimly. "I thought we had agreed that you would not visit Madame de Robitaille's gambling establishment."

"*You* agreed I should not go there," Clea responded with a toss of her shining curls. "I made no such promise."

"Very well, then. I asked you not to go, because I care for you, and I wish to guard your reputation. I told you what kind of place it is, and you completely disregarded my wishes. And you went in the company of Crawshay."

Peeping at him again through her lashes, Clea felt a stirring of uneasiness. She had never seen him so angry. Was that contempt she detected in his gaze? Abruptly, she changed tactics. She widened her blue eyes and extended a trembling hand to him.

"Ah, Jonathan. Do not be angry. I . . . I was lonely. You have not taken me to a single gathering this week. And I was bored." She curved her mouth into an appealing smile and allowed a few tears to bedew her great blue eyes. "As for Miles, you know he means nothing to me—he is my cousin, after all."

"Mm, yes, so you have told me."

"Well, he is my friend, as well. Surely you understand how precious a good friend can be."

She smiled inwardly. *We must all have our little friends to play with, mustn't we, love?* Glancing at Jonathan, she perceived that his face was still darker than the thunderclouds to be seen from her boudoir window.

"Besides," she continued, smiling even more winsomely. "I have been punished enough for my transgression. I lost dreadfully last night, and I shall have Faversham bleating at me again."

"Martin Faversham is your man of business, Clea, and he does a superb job. He has your interests at heart; you would do well to listen to him."

Clea sighed tremulously and rose to stand before Jonathan. "You are right, of course, my dearest love. Oh, Jonathan, I am such a giddy creature. I need you to keep my feet on the straight and narrow, and"—she rose on tiptoe—"right now I most desperately need a kiss."

Jonathn stared down at her for a moment, then, with a sound that was almost a groan, gathered her into his arms and kissed her with a desperate passion.

As he drank in the intoxicating honey of her lips, his wrath was forgotten, and his only thought was of the exquisite beauty who was the fulfillment of his dreams, and for whom he had waited so long.

Chapter Thirteen

Tally squinted against the early morning sunlight and pulled the bedclothes around her shoulders. She really should be up and away to her studio, but, oh, just a few more minutes of sleep would be heaven. Last night had been very long, starting with a musicale at Devonshire house, and continuing later with another prowl through the alleys of London with Jonathan. The evening's excursion had included two gin shops and a dog fight.

She squeezed her eyes shut and turned her face into the pillow, but sleep would not return. And she knew the reason very well.

"You stupid chit," she scolded herself, "all because Jonathan . . ." She sighed.

Jonathan had been in an odd mood all evening. He had arrived at Devonshire House with Clea on his arm, and a whisper had gone around the room. All the *ton* had heard of Lady Belle's indiscretion at the tables and wondered what would be Chelmsford's reaction. There was a certain air of disappointment in the gathering when it became evident that no perceptible rift had occurred. Jonathan appeared to be as enchanted as ever with his beautiful fiancée, and Clea behaved toward him with unusual attentiveness. Indeed, the two had remained close together the whole time, and Tally had experienced an odd pang as she watched Clea flutter lovingly about the viscount.

Still, there occasionally crept into his eyes a most peculiar expression as he gazed at his love. Tally could have sworn he looked almost baffled. Later, when Tally had joined Jonathan in the darkness of his carriage, her disguise securely in place, he had appeared distracted and out of sorts. Once she observed him watching her, with that same expression of puzzlement.

She had found the dog fight to be an exercise in human degradation. In a cavernous old building overlooking the river, a match was taking place between a mastiff, half mad with terror and rage, and a monkey, which, it was said, had been imported from Italy. What it lacked in brawn, the monkey more than made up for in quickness and cleverness, and the dog was soon covered in saliva and gore. From her corner Tally sketched the watchers of the carnage. Some waved money in their fists, and others screamed exhortations at the combatants. All seemed to have been reduced to a blind, animal lust for death. The battle ended only when the mastiff had been left a motionless, bloody bundle of fur on the earthen floor.

Afterward, Jonathan berated himself for having subjected her to such a scene, but she shakily assured him that she was not a simpering miss, after all, and had witnessed many a wrangle among the animals at Summerhill. Jonathan had squeezed her shoulder, and his smile had been warm.

"Pluck to the backbone, aren't you, little one? Any other female of my acquaintance would have gone into strong convulsions less than two minutes after the match began, assuming she could have been coerced into poking her dainty nose in such a place."

Tally had basked in his praise. And then it happened. A large man, dressed in the clothes of a navvie, and much the worse for drink, lurched out of the building. Evidently he had wagered badly, because he was in a towering rage. As she turned away from Jonathan, Tally inadvertently brushed against the man, and with a roar, he swung his arm against her, catching her on the side of her head with his fist.

When Tally opened her eyes a few seconds later, she was lying on the ground, cradled in Jonathan's arms. A few feet away, her attacker lay stretched out in an unconscious stupor. A large bruise swelled his jaw. Tally lifted her head and moaned a little at the unexpected pain. Jonathan drew her against his breast, and she was instantly aware of the strength of his arms around her, as she had been at the moment of their collision those few weeks ago.

She knew she should withdraw and rise to her feet,

but she was lost in the dizzying wonder of his embrace. If she were to tilt her head upward—just an inch or two—his lips would be nearly resting on hers. The impulse to do so was almost overwhelming, but she remained still, unwilling to risk destroying the moment.

"Tally," Jonathan was whispering hoarsely, "Tally, my dear, are you all right?"

His fingers brushed her cheek with the lightest of touches and moved to touch her mouth. Her breath caught, and she was struck by the realization of what was happening. Ignoring the pain, she jerked her head away, and as she did so, she met Jonathan's eyes. She read a sudden awareness there, followed by embarrassment, and in another moment, she had jumped to her feet. She turned her face away so that he would not find the shame she knew must be written there.

"Are—are you all right?" Jonathan repeated awkwardly.

"Yes, I'm fine. Really, I am not injured at all."

In her rush to get away from him, she almost broke into a run toward the carriage. She had already wedged herself into the farthest corner of the vehicle when he seated himself.

"Thank you," she muttered through stiff lips, "for coming to my assistance."

Jonathan merely nodded, and neither of them referred to the incident again. Something had been changed between them though, Tally realized. The easy camaraderie that had marked their relationship up to this point was gone, and the gentleman who escorted her home as dawn began to creep over the chimneypots of London was a cool, correct stranger.

Now, as she squirmed among the bedcovers, she castigated herself once again. Why had she behaved like such a ninnyhammer, clutching at him in a fevered swoon. What must he think of her? It was only, she told herself, that she was unused to finding herself in the embrace of a handsome man—or any man at all, for that matter.

She recalled with a shudder of distaste her only previous experience along those lines. Squire Mayhew's oldest son had come upon her in the cloakroom at a local assembly one evening. He had been more than somewhat in his cups, and his sweaty fondlings had turned her stomach. She had planted an instinctive and very hearty slap across his plump cheeks, and he had never repeated the endeavor.

There had been the vicar's nephew, of course, but he had never carried his sentiments beyond an occasional bashful glance. The only other males, she reflected ruefully, who had displayed any designs on her immediate person were young men whose interest lay in her father's title.

"The only thing to do, Tally Burnside," she told herself firmly, "is to put the whole thing out of your mind."

This she was able to do with less difficulty than she had anticipated, because two days later Cat's morning callers brought the intelligence that the first installment of a scandalous new novel had that day appeared in Hatchard's Book Store.

"It's called *Town Bronze*," twittered Mrs. Drummond Burrell, who had arrived with her good friend, Lady Sefton. They were both patronesses of that bastion of propriety, Almack's in King Street. Tally had already been granted vouchers for the subscription dances, but Cat had impressed upon her the importance of remaining in the good graces of these august personages.

"It's simply disgraceful!" continued Mrs. Burrell, her narrow cheeks aquiver. "Nothing but a piece of trash, of course."

"Yes," agreed her companion, with a mischievous sparkle in her eyes that belied her words. "But such delicious trash! I declare, I should imagine George Wendover is simply livid this morning. The author's portrayal of him as the personification of Corinthian arrogance is quite wicked!"

"Who is the author?" asked Cat in her blandest manner. "Is he anyone we know?"

"I should think that will prove to be the mystery of the Season." Lady Sefton laughed. "For, like his illustrator, he writes under a *nom de plume*. What was it, now? Hash or Bash or some such. Rumor has it that he is a peer, since no one else could be so conversant with the ways of the *ton*."

"Really, Maria," Mrs. Burrell said repressively. "It could be any one of a number of persons—a servant in a great house, perhaps, or someone's man of business."

Cat glanced at Tally, whose heart was thundering so

loudly in her ears that she was barely able to follow the conversation.

"We must procure a copy at once, don't you agree, dearest?"

Cat's voice held only the piqued interest of a bored lady of fashion, and Tally, twisting her little ring about her finger so that it fairly spun, nodded mutely.

The two ladies, after graciously assuring Mrs. Thurston that they looked forward to seeing her and her charming guest at next Wednesday's gathering in King Street, took their stately leave. Tally sank into the nearest chair and noisily expelled a long pent-up breath.

"Cat," she breathed in an awed voice. "You were magnificent!"

Cat bobbed an impudent curtsey, then giggled unaffectedly. "Oh, Tally, that was such fun. I begin to believe Richard was right. I was born to be a conspirator."

"But did you hear what Mrs. Burrell said? I know for a fact the first chapter of the book came out only yesterday, and she had already read it!"

"Along with half of London, apparently. And did you hear Maria Sefton? 'Delicious trash,' indeed! Mark my words, Tally, you and Jonathan have, like Byron, awaked to find yourself famous!"

Cat's words proved to be true beyond Tally's wildest dreams. At the Italian Opera that night, the usual buzz of conversation that nearly drowned out the performance was all *Town Bronze* and the mystery of its authorship. One dandy went so far as to bring a copy with him to the theater, where he remained immersed in the work all evening long, studiously ignoring the players on the stage, and emerging only occasionally to level his quizzing glass at certain other members of the audience with a knowing smirk.

From her seat, Tally had a clear view into the box occupied by Jonathan and Clea, but after one glance, in which she found her gaze returned with a swiftly uplifted eyebrow, she forebore to look at him again.

In the corridor between acts, Tally strolled with Cat and Richard past the boxes of friends and acquaintances. Cat was enjoying herself immensely, taking part in the lively discussions that were taking place concerning *Town Bronze*.

"Do you not think that Branwell Shovelsnuff is Petersham?" she was saying to the Duchess of Bedford. "After all, who else is so obsessed with that unpleasant habit?"

The Duchess laughed.

"If it were not obviously he from the description given in the book, his portrait in the illustration would certainly give him away."

Richard glanced at Tally and rolled his eyes toward the ceiling. Tally watched, smiling, as he fell behind to chat with Lord Whittaker, his superior at the Foreign Office. She noticed Clea Bellewood standing close by, and in a moment, when Lord Whittaker had turned away, she approached Richard, bumping into him as though by accident.

Under Tally's indignant gaze, Clea proceeded to bestow upon Richard the full treatment, complete with waving eyelashes and beguiling smile. Tally could not hear their talk, but it became apparent that Lady Belle was well on the way to another conquest. *Walk away, Richard!* she fairly shouted inside her head. *Just turn away, and leave!*

But Richard did not leave. Instead, he remained in rapt conversation with Clea for several minutes before recalling himself to his obligations, upon which, he lightly kissed Lady Belle's fingertips and hurried off to Cat, who was by now at the other end of the corridor.

Tally simply stood, rooted to the carpet. Her mind raced. Surely Richard was not inclined to embark on a flirtation with Clea. Had he not made it clear in the alcove off Lady Talgarth's ballroom that he was not interested in any woman other than his wife?

She gave herself a little shake. She was making too much of what she had seen. If Richard chose to play the gallant for a few minutes to a lovely woman, that did not mean he intended to betray his wife. Did it? Resolutely, she put the episode from her mind and hastened back to the Thurston box for the beginning of the opera's last act.

Well satisfied with her few minutes' work, Clea sauntered into her own box and settled herself beside Jonathan.

"Any new gossip making the rounds, my love?" Jonathan asked idly as Clea put up a graceful hand to tuck in a stray curl.

She yawned. "It's really too tiresome. No one is speaking of anything but that wretched book. *Town Bronze*, you know," she answered in response to his questioning look.

"Ah," replied Jonathan lightly. "I heard of it just this afternoon. Have you read it?"

"But of course." Clea laughed her throaty chuckle. "I just said, everyone is talking about it. One must keep *au courant* with whatever is the latest rage."

"And what did you think of it?"

Clea shrugged her lovely shoulders.

"Oh, it's just what one would expect. A faradiddle, and nothing more, but it is fun to try to discern the various characters. It was easy to spot George Wendover, and Ceddy Bagshot, of course. I'm sure Lady Irongirth is Cornelia Wigand, but some of the others I'm not so sure of. I must say I'm a little disappointed."

"What do you mean?" asked Jonathan, puzzled.

"I wonder why I am not portrayed in the book."

Jonathan simply stared at her, at a loss.

"You cannot mean you would wish to be featured in such a work?"

"We-ell, after all, the most prominent personages in the Polite World seem to be in it."

"Yes, but they are all—that is, doesn't the author hold those people up to ridicule?"

"Only those who are ridiculous." Clea smiled smugly. "Primrose Promise, for example, is portrayed as a sweet young thing to whom no one could take exception. If I appeared in the book, I'm sure it would be as a lady who simply enjoys her position in Society."

She turned her head to watch the stage, and Jonathan stared at her as though he had never seen her before.

A pale, thin moon had risen some hours later, when Tally and Jonathan set out together on yet another foray. This time Tally was to become acquainted with the interior of the taproom in Limmer's Hotel, in St. James's Street, a favorite watering hole of military and sporting gentlemen.

Jonathan's greeting was casual and bore, to Tally's

heightened senses, only a residual awkwardness from the incident of two nights ago.

Limmer's was located near Mayfair, in an area of select gentlemen's clubs, and might have been supposed to maintain some gentility in its standards. Tally found this to be far from the case, however, and after selling a few of her flowers, she found a settle near the kitchen door. Shaking out her grimy shawl, she tucked her skirts under her and began to work. Since this taproom was similar to others she had visited in the last few days, it took her very little time to sketch the essentials of the place. She was about to tuck her pencil and pad in her pocket, when she observed a tall man enter the room. Tally recognized him as Miles Crawshay, Clea's cousin. With him was an unsavory person, short and squat, with a furtive manner. The two seated themselves not far from Tally's perch.

Idly, Tally limned a swift drawing of the two with their heads bent together over mugs of ale. Suddenly, her fingers stilled as a fragment of their conversation was carried to her. It was the short, dark man who spoke, and Tally caught her breath in astonishment at his words.

"But what if Thurston won't bite?"

"He is already quite besotted with the countess," replied Crawshay. "I foresee no difficulty in . . ."

Here the voices of the two men dropped to a whisper, and Tally drew closer to them.

"My dear fellow," Miles spoke with a sneering laugh, "believe me, Thurston finds her irresistible, as who would not?"

Once again the swarthy man uttered an expression of doubt. Crawshay's reply was cut short as both men looked to the other side of the room where an altercation had broken out. Their attention returned immediately to their discussion, but now they were almost completely drowned out by the noise of battle.

In a far corner Jonathan searched frantically for Tally. Where was she for God's sake? He had told her—she had promised to stay within his sight! There! There, busy in her corner and totally oblivious to the danger she was in. When he got his hand on her again, he would slowly, and with great care, strangle the infuriating little chit.

Tally saw Jonathan beckoning wildly to her, but was loathe to leave before hearing more of the disturbing conversation she had stumbled upon. She edged even closer to the two men but was unable to hear anything more.

The melee had by now reached Homeric proportions, and Tally found that her path to the exit was blocked by two extremely large gentlemen, evidently bent on dismembering each other. Jonathan was nowhere to be seen. Fearfully, she scuttled around the end of the room, only to find herself facing a stout cudgel, held menacingly by yet another large combatant. Tally was not the hulk's target, but he came perilously close to the gray wig as he swung his weapon in a wide arc.

She tried to move out of harm's way but found herself hemmed in on all sides. Once more the infuriated fighter hefted the cudgel, and Tally shut her eyes tight and covered her head with both hands.

Suddenly, she was picked up bodily. She turned her head to find her nose inches from Jonathan's, who with his free arm created a path toward the door. In a few moments they were outside, and Tally drew in great gulps of night air.

"Oh, thank you. . . ." she began, but Jonathan was not listening. Gripping her arm he pulled her along the street, his expression grim, and when they reached the carriage he thrust her unceremoniously inside.

Eyes wide, Tally simply gaped at him. He turned to her and grasped her roughly by the shoulders. "You little idiot," he began furiously. "Don't you realize you could have been killed in there?"

"Yes, but—but—"

"You promised me," he continued as though she had not spoken, "that you would remain close under my eye any time you were out in that unspeakable disguise of yours."

"But, Jonathan—"

"This is the last time I will allow you to indulge in this—this lunacy. After this, you will confine your artistic efforts to Vauxhall Gardens or—or the maze at Hampton Court. I knew this was a flea-brained idea to start with, but you . . ."

Tally did not hear the fear behind Jonathan's hoarsely spoken words, nor did she see the frantic concern evident in the blazing gray eyes. By now she was in a royal rage.

"What do you mean, 'allow'?" she stormed. "You have nothing to say about where I go or what I do!"

"I told you it would be unwise to try me," he grated. "If you cannot see that you are putting not only your reputation in jeopardy, but your safety as well, I will take steps to put a stop to your foolhardy activities."

"And just how do you propose to do that? Lock me in the Thurston cellar?"

"The idea is appealing, but I was thinking more along the lines of a large footman, complete with livery and brass buttons to dog your every step."

"You wouldn't!" gasped Tally, white-faced with fury. "Oh, I *knew* you were an arrogant bully!"

Jonathan pulled her close to him.

"*I* arrogant! You tell me that? You are the most . . ."

Tally gazed, transfixed, into the autumn smoke of his eyes, and the fire that leaped from their depths. Jonathan stopped suddenly, and with a startled intake of breath, bent his head. His mouth was hard and angry as it covered hers, and Tally experienced a shocked sensation of pure delight. The feeling was as new as it was pleasurable, and when Jonathan withdrew his lips, only to kiss her again, slowly and searchingly, Tally brought her arms about his neck without volition. She pressed her body against him as though she would melt into his very being.

Then, from the depths of her consciousness, sprang an appalling knowledge.

Chapter Fourteen

Tally sat at her little work table, gazing in consternation at the sunny garden outside her window. How could this have happened? How could she have been so stupid as to fall head over ears in love with a man who would never return her feelings?

Once more, she relived the kiss in the carriage the night before. Once more, she pictured Jonathan's face when he had finally released her. He had been obviously appalled at his actions.

"I—I'm—please, forgive me, Tally. I don't know what happened, there. I didn't mean . . ."

Tally pulled away from him, and it felt as though she were peeling part of her flesh away. She held herself carefully, so that the misery that threatened to engulf her would not show in her face.

"There is nothing to forgive." She was vaguely pleased that her voice gave no hint of the turmoil that raged within her. "It was merely the—the heat of the circumstances. Please, say no more about it."

And he hadn't. Not about that or anything else on the brief ride home. When they reached the corner of Half Moon and Curzon streets, which was their customary point of embarkation, Tally had slipped from the carriage with a whispered, "Good night." Jonathan had reached out as though to touch her hand, but withdrew it quickly and bade her a muted farewell.

Obviously, thought Tally bitterly, the kiss that had been pure magic for her meant nothing more to the Viscount Chelmsford than a momentary whim, which he instantly regretted.

And why shouldn't he? Her thoughts continued indignantly. What kind of a man becomes engaged to a diamond of the first water, and then goes around kissing persons with whom he is on the most platonic of terms. Particularly when those persons are covered with wrinkles and dust and a wig sliding down their nose.

And how was she to face him again, she wondered dismally. How does one greet a man who has just turned one's life to ashes?

"Oh, good morning, my lord. Yes, it is a lovely day, isn't it? Why, thank you I'm very well, except, of course, for this jagged crack in my heart through which my life's blood seems to be oozing away down the street and into the gutter."

Telling herself not to be absurd, she returned her attention to the illustration she was trying to complete. It featured a repentant Clifford and Clive in the Bow Street Magistrate's Office, to whence they had been unceremoniously hauled after a misspent night that had culminated in boxing the Watch.

Tally smiled to herself as she remembered the afternoon she had visited Bow Street under Jonathan's watched auspices. It had been much easier for Granny Posey to creep unnoticed into those rather dingy Halls of Justice than it had for my lord Chelmsford, whose expression had swung from studied disinterest to one of unease that he might be mistaken for a pickpocket. So harassed had he looked at the end of her sketching session, that Tally had longed to reach up and smooth the lines from between his dark brows.

Now, stop that!

It would simply not do to dwell on Jonathan, and his smile, and his broad, muscled shoulders, and his . . .

No!

She would concentrate on her work, and—yes—on the endless round of social obligations in which she had suddenly been plunged. That was more like it. For the fact was that she had become a social success, and had she chosen, could have spent almost every hour of every day at some rout, or ridotto, or breakfast or soirée or any of the other functions the *ton* managed to pack into the few months when the *Beau Monde* was at large in town. Now, when she attended a ball, her card was nearly always filled, and Cat's morning parlor always contained a full compliment of smitten young dandies.

Tally had, to her astonishment, learned to flirt. With

her new feathers had come an almost instinctive ability to send glances through her long, thick lashes to devastating effect, and to bestow wide, innocently provocative stares that one enamored swain had compared to "the spice-brown gaze of some shy forest nymph."

Why, for heaven's sake, could she not have fallen in love with one of those nice young men? Why had she lost her heart to a man who was in love with the most beautiful woman in London, possibly all of England? Jonathan's adoration of his Clea was patent, and Tally could find nothing in herself with which to lure Jonathan away from that fascinating beauty.

She turned to her drawing once more, and as she did so, she heard noises that indicated Richard's presence in his study next door.

Richard!

In her abstraction, she had completely forgotten the snatch of conversation she had heard in Limmer's tap-room. Was it possible that Richard had actually embarked upon an affair with Clea? It couldn't be! But if it were, the two people who meant the most in the world to her, Cat and Jonathan, would be devastated.

She stood in thought for a moment, then squaring her shoulders, she knocked firmly on the door that separated her studio from Richard's study. "I must talk to you," she stated baldly when he ushered her into the room.

Briefly she recounted to him the conversation she had heard between Miles Crawshay and the stranger. Then, after a moment's hesitation, she told of watching him apparently succumb to Clea's blandishments at the Italian Opera.

To Tally's surprise, Richard displayed neither guilt nor anger. Instead, an odd smile played across his lips, and he bade Tally sit down.

"Where in the world did you run into those two?" was his first question.

Caught off guard, Tally mumbled something about seeing them as she strolled one afternoon in the park.

Richard lifted a quizzical brow, but said nothing. After a brief silence, he continued quietly. "Tally, you know I love Cat with all my heart."

"I thought you did, at any rate."

"Believe me, I do." Richard's voice was low and intense. "I must confess I am interested in talk of a totally imaginary relationship between the Countess of Bellewood and myself, but I am at a loss to explain it."

Tally returned his gaze gravely. She did not know Richard very well, but she had liked him instinctively on first meeting. She did not think him the sort of man to play his wife false—but then, what did she know of the world? Jonathan was betrothed to a beautiful woman whom he loved desperately, yet he had kissed another, apparently with no more compunction than a gentleman would in pinching the bottom of a buxom chambermaid. He probably did a lot of that, too, she sniffed inwardly.

"I want to believe you, Richard," she sighed, "and I want to trust you, but you must admit the whole thing looks very smokey."

"Like a plugged chimney," he admitted cheerfully. "But there is no accompanying fire."

"All right, I'll accept your word, but I will tell you this," she added fiercely, "if you do anything to hurt Cat I'll—I'll slice out your liver!"

Richard's crooked grin spread wide across his face. "And I'll help you do it," he promised. He became serious again. "Tell me again about this stranger who met with Crawshay—in the Park."

"Well, he was—oh, wait!"

Tally ran to her work table and returned with the little sketch she had made of the pair. Richard studied it intently, then asked her to repeat again everything she remembered of the conversation between the two men.

"Mmm." Richard stood motionless for several seconds. "Do you think you could incorporate this drawing into one of your illustrations for *Town Bronze*?"

"Of course. Nothing could be simpler. May I ask why?"

"Oh—just an idea that came to me."

Richard said nothing more, and after a moment, Tally sighed. "Very well, I shan't plague you any further."

Richard placed his hand on her arm. "You really have no cause for concern, you know," he said softly. "About any of this."

He held her gaze for an instant, then turned away abruptly. "And now, if you will excuse me, I have an appointment."

In a moment he was gone, and with a sense of foreboding, Tally returned to her little studio. She sat down again at the table, but, once more, simply sat staring into space, chewing absently on the end of her pencil.

At lunchtime, she was still engaged in this unprofitable activity. She dined in solitary splendor, Cat being absent on a round of obligatory morning calls, but when she had finished, she stood abruptly and went in search of her bonnet. Armed with her sketch pad and pencil, she left the house and proceeded to the end of Half Moon Street and crossed Picadilly. She was soon seated on a bench in Green Park, her fingers flying as she drew the likeness of two youngsters rolling hoops along the path. So engrossed did she become in her work that she did not see the pair of strollers who approached.

"Why, Lady Talitha, what a charming surprise!"

Tally started so precipitously that the pad slid from her lap and her pencil flew from her fingers, landing at the tips of a pair of dainty half boots. She looked up to see Clea Bellewood smiling roguishly at her from under a lacy parasol. Beside her stood Miles Crawshay, quizzing glass at the ready.

Tally gasped, horrified at having been caught at her nefarious vocation. "Lady Bellewood! Good afternoon. And Mr. Crawshay."

She dropped her hands into her lap to still their trembling, and began twisting her ring in a familiar gesture.

Crawshay bent gracefully to retrieve her sketch pad and raised his glass to inspect the drawing she had made. She had set down only a few preliminary lines, and he returned the pad to her with the merest show of polite interest.

"But how is it you are in the Park all alone?" Lady Bellewood asked, scanning the smooth lawn in all directions. "Did you not bring your maid with you?"

Her tone implied assignations in the shrubbery, and Tally flushed to the roots of her hair. She knew she had committed a solecism in leaving home unaccompanied, but the ritual of the obligatory escort when in London had always been most irksome to her.

Gripping her ring even tighter, Tally assumed an air of nonchalance. "No, I did not. The poor thing has the

toothache, and I did not wish to take any of Cat's other
servants away from their duties merely to guide my steps
in the Park. I am not so fortunate as you," she continued
smoothly, "in having a relative to see to my, er, needs."

Clea's tinkling laugh could have etched a mirror, but
her simper remained fixed.

"Yes, I am indeed fortunate," she agreed smugly.
"Miles and I have always been close, and with Jonathan
out of town, I appreciate having him near."

"Jo—Lord Chelmsford has left London?" Tally asked,
shock tightening her voice.

"Why, yes, he left early this morning for his seat in
Warwickshire. Did he not tell you?" Clea's blue eyes
were wide with innocent surprise.

"N-no. That is—there is no reason why the Viscount
should discuss his plans with me."

"You are quite right, of course. I merely thought,
since you have become such friends . . ." Clea's voice
trailed off in quiet malice.

"Oh, no—I—we—it's just that . . ."

"Come, my dear," Crawshay interposed in an amused
tone, "withdraw your dainty claws, so that Lady Talitha
can stop abusing that pretty little ring, and let us be on
our way. If you will remember, we were on our way to
Hatchard's to be the first to purchase the new installment
of that wretched novel."

"Oh yes, *Town Bronze*." Clea's face brightened.
"Have you read it, Lady Talitha?"

"Oh! Yes—yes, Cat purchased the first installment
some time ago, but we have not yet read the second."

"So delicious, don't you agree? But then, you are no
doubt unfamiliar with most of the persons so cleverly
pilloried in the book. The description of Lord Beddoes
as Sir Toby Potwell was priceless, and that wicked drawing of him was the finishing dash of pepper to the broth!"

"I have met Lord Beddoes," replied Tally carefully,
"and, as you say, he seems most accurately portrayed. I
found him all the more interesting because the book also
describes his efforts to alleviate the suffering of those
incarcerated in the 'Jerusalem Hospital', which I collect
refers to Bethlehem, or Bedlam as I believe it is called."

"Oh, stuff." Clea wrinkled her classic nose. "I skip
over the boring parts."

"And has anyone discovered the identity of the author of this acclaimed satire?" Miles queried.

"No." Clea laughed. "But one hears the most absurd theories. Why, yesterday someone put forth the name of the Prince Regent as the most likely candidate! Can you imagine?"

Tally faintly declared herself incapable of imagining such a thing.

"Well, I intend to find out," Clea continued brightly. "It would be such a coup to discover the author's name before anyone else. I shall have to set my spies to work."

In response to Tally's startled intake of breath, Miles lifted an airy hand.

"Lady Belle simply means that she has as her consultants a network of the most unrelenting gossips in town. I shouldn't wonder if the unfortunate fellow, as well as his illustrator, were not exposed to the glare of public opinion in less than a fortnight."

"As he deserves to be," sniffed Clea. "If he is a peer, as people say, this Dash person will be quite ruined when he is found out—penning scurrilous broadsides as if he were some low scribbler of penny-a-liners. It is not to be countenanced!"

Tally turned cold. Jonathan was right; if Clea found out about his secret career, she would abandon him like a bad memory.

With another of her metallic laughs, Clea placed her hand in the crook of Crawshay's arm. "We really must be on our way. Such a pleasure, Lady Talitha."

Nodding her head in a haughty gesture of dismissal, she drew Crawshay along the path toward Piccadilly, and was soon out of sight of the girl on the bench.

"Well, pet," murmured Crawshay appreciatively, "I'd say you have her firmly on the ropes."

"Don't be absurd, Miles. She is not of the slightest consequence to me. Now, what were we discussing? Oh, yes. Dearest, can you not possibly see your way to lending me a few guineas?"

"A few guineas? My dear, I would hardly call three thousand pounds a few guineas. You have me confused with Golden Ball."

"But you have access to . . ."

"No," Crawshay replied sharply. "You know that

money is earmarked for an entirely different purpose. Besides, if I am not mistaken, that amount will settle only the most pressing of your gaming debts."

Clea turned to bend on him the full force of her wide, blue gaze. "But, Miles, what am I to do? You know I would not turn to you if I were not absolutely desperate."

"I am sure you will think of something," replied Crawshay, unfazed. "What about Chelmsford?"

"Jonathan?" Clea's lovely mouth twisted in an ugly grimace. "If Jonathan were to discover the extent of my—my difficulties, he would—well, it simply doesn't bear thinking of."

"Of course. Well, I suppose you'll have to unburden yourself of more of your expensive little trinkets." He drew close to her and gently wrapped one of her shining curls about his finger. "Poor beauty in distress. Don't worry, love, it will all come about. When this business is done, I shall shower you with guineas."

Clea swayed toward him. "Ah, Miles—" she began, but he forestalled her by laying a finger across her lips.

"Tell me about Thurston," he commanded casually. "How stand matters in that quarter?"

Clea lips curled in a sly smile. "As you would expect. He was quite—responsive at our little rendezvous this morning. By this time next week . . ."

"Excellent, my dear. Our friend will be pleased."

Tucking her arm once more in his, he turned again toward their destination.

A hundred yards or so behind them, Tally still sat on her bench, furiously berating herself for having turned into a veritable *blanc mange* at Clea's sly dagger thrusts. She jumped to her feet and started for Half Moon Street. On the way, she pondered the news she had received from Lady Belle.

She had no right to be upset that Jonathan had gone away without informing her, but she was. Was he so appalled at last night's incident that he couldn't even face her? Given Jonathan's reputation with the fair sex, that hardly seemed likely. A quick kiss in a darkened carriage hardly qualified as an earth-shaking event in the life of a London man about town.

Yet, it had not seemed like a casual kiss. She recalled

the blazing anger with which Jonathan had crushed her mouth against his, an anger that had moved swiftly into an aching tenderness. The memory created a treacherous warmth that spread from the pit of her stomach into regions whose existence she had heretofore been hardly aware of. Surely, such a kiss could not have left Jonathan unaffected.

No, she thought abruptly. No. Jonathan was filled with his love for Lady Belle, and there was no room for anything but the most minor affection for her. What had happened in the carriage was—was nothing.

Tally trudged wearily through the Thurstons' front door and inquired of Bates as to the whereabouts of the lady of the house. She was told that Madame had returned from a round of visits an hour or so ago. She had gone directly to her room and had not yet come down.

Puzzled, Tally climbed the stairs to Cat's room and knocked gently on the door. It was not until she had knocked a second time and softly called Cat's name that her friend bade her enter.

She found Cat seated at her dressing table, staring at her reflection in the mirror. Pale stains on her cheeks gave evidence to tears shed and dried, and now she simply sat silently.

Tally rushed to her and sank to her knees beside the dressing table stool. She flung her arms around her friend. "Cat, what is it? What's the matter?"

Cat turned to look at her, her usual vivacity replaced by a look of stunned shock. "I paid a morning call to Cassie Wentworth. She recently gave birth to a daughter, you know. She lives in North Audley Street, and on the way home, I decided to stop in that little shop in Oxford Street—you know, the one where we saw that bonnet with the apple green satin ribbons."

Tally watched her in bafflement, and Cat continued in a shaky voice.

"There was some sort of carriage accident up ahead, so my coachman made a detour up Duke Street and turned onto Henrietta Street." Cat glanced quickly at Tally, the tears bright in her eyes. "A new gambling house opened there some weeks ago, run by some Frenchwoman. I understand it has become a favorite of Clea Bellewood's. The carriage became stalled in traffic for several minutes and stopped just at a small mews which opens out into Henrietta Street. Set into that mews is a side door to the Frenchwoman's house." She paused, and lifted her hands in a forlorn gesture.

"As I sat in the carriage, idly glancing into the street, the side door opened, and Clea stepped out. She was followed by R-Richard!"

Tally went rigid. No! Richard could not have behaved so basely. He had given his word! She laid her hand on Cat's.

"Oh, my dear. It—it must have been the merest chance. I mean, in the middle of the day, and all."

"Precisely," said Cat in a dull voice. "Why would anyone visit a gambling house in the middle of the day? Madame does not start her festivities until very late in the evening. Besides, I have not told you all. Richard kissed her hand in the most intimate manner before turning away, and when he walked off, he was whistling! Tally, Richard and Clea are having an affair!"

Chapter Fifteen

"No!" Tally replied in horror-stricken tones. "Oh no, Cat! Richard loves you! He would never . . ."

Cat rose to pace the floor, her face a mask of pain.

"That's what I thought. I believed his explanation of what happened at the Talgarth ball, and thought I had nothing to fear. Even when I caught a glimpse of the two of them at the opera last week, and he was laughing down into her face, I told myself I was reading something into his behavior that was not there. But today . . . Oh, Tally, if you could have seen them!"

Tally lifted her hand to her friend, but Cat, with a strangled sob, brushed past her and ran from the room. After a few moments, Tally, her head bowed, made her way to her own chambers.

An hour or so later, she descended the stairs for dinner, but found the small salon empty. Bates informed her austerely, that neither Madame nor the Master would be dining that evening.

There followed what was the longest evening Tally had ever spent. She had hastened upstairs to tap at Cat's door, only to be told in a remote but firm voice through the polished wood paneling that Cat wished to be alone. Tally did not seek out Richard, which was just as well, because she later discovered that he had strode from the house with the information that he planned to spend the night at his club, and had been seen no more.

In the days that followed, Tally watched in despair as the atmosphere in the Thurston home changed from one of warmth and gaiety and love to one of chill bleakness. Richard returned home eventually, but he and Cat behaved to one another like strangers who occasionally met in the corridors of a hotel, with a murmured greeting and lowered eyes.

Tally bled for her friends, but found her thoughts drifting to her own heartache. She had not heard from Jonathan since he had retired to his home in Warwickshire, beyond a short note informing her in businesslike terms that he had completed the last chapters of *Town Bronze*. He would, he said, send them by post, hoping that she would be able to complete the final drawings by the deadline issued by Mapes, and he was hers most sincerely etc., etc.

Tally stared dismally at the little piece of paper. Apparently, their entire friendship was to fall victim to a single kiss. Had her reaction been so obvious? Did he realize, she wondered in horror, that she was in love with him and feared that she would hang on his sleeve? That she would sit at home, wearing the willow and pining away to a thread for the sound of his voice?

She jumped to her feet in sudden anger. Well, he would find that he was very much mistaken in his assumption. She strode purposefully to Cat's room where she found her friend, as usual, sitting by the window with her chin in her hand. Grasping her by the wrist, she pulled her abruptly in her feet.

"Cat Thurston, we have had enough of sighs and megrims in this house."

Cat simply blinked at her in stunned confusion.

"How long are you going to sit in your darkened room like Patience on a monument? I know you are, er, upset with Richard—perhaps with good reason, perhaps not . . ."

" 'Perhaps not?' " squeaked Cat. "Tally, I told you—"

"I know what you told me, and I know what Richard told me, and I know what you told each other, and I am frankly weary of the whole thing, as I should think you would be, too. Are you simply going to cease existing? I'd think you'd have more pride. You are one of Society's leaders, and here you sit, like—"

"Yes, I know, like Patience on a monument. Tally, it's all very well for you to talk, you've never been in love, but—" She stopped short to stare, as Tally paled noticeably and dropped her eyes to her lap, where she began twisting her ring.

"Tally?"

Tally merely shook her head and furiously dashed

away the tears that had sprung with appalling readiness to her eyes.

"Oh, my dear," said Cat gently. "I had no idea. Who is it? Why have you not said anything?" She stopped abruptly and eyed her friend in sudden perception. "It isn't—oh, it can't be—Jonathan?"

Still wordless, Tally continued to twist her ring in agitation.

Cat sighed. "What an awful thing to have happened," she continued sympathetically. "But I suppose it might have been foreseen, with the two of you living in each other's pockets for the past weeks. I am sorry, my dear. Life plays cruel jokes—on those who least deserve them, it seems."

There was a moment's silence, broken at last by Cat, who managed a rusty little laugh. "I believe you came in here to persuade me to rise up off my backside and get on with my life. Apparently you could do with the same good advice."

Tally shook herself and gave her friend a watery smile. "You're right, as always," she replied briskly. "What do you say to a few morning calls, plus a side trip to Bond Street. I understand Cecile's is displaying a new line of bonnets."

Afterward, Tally decided ruefully that it would have been better to lengthen the shopping trip and shorten the time allotted for visits, for at the third home on their itinerary, Chesterfield House, one of the guests gracing the drawing room was none other than Lady Belle.

Tally, entering behind Cat, stopped short at the threshold, but it was too late to draw back. She seated herself as far away from Clea as she could, but in a matter of minutes, the countess had risen to make her leisurely way across the room.

"How nice to see you again, Lady Talitha," she breathed. "You have not been out and about lately, I believe."

"No," replied Tally discouragingly, but Clea was not to be deterred.

"Have you been out of town?"

Tally merely shook her head and made as though to turn away to converse with the person seated on her other side. Clea would have none of it and laid a restraining hand on hers.

"I was just saying to Jonathan this morning, that I wondered where our sweet Lady Talitha had got to. Yes," she twinkled in response to Tally's swiftly raised glance. "He returned late last night and visited me very early this morning. He said he could not do without his morning kiss from me for one more day."

Her laughter tinkled obtrusively in the quiet buzz of conversation surrounding them, and Tally felt herself turn hot and then cold. She cast an agonized glance at Cat, who in another moment rose to take her leave, apologizing prettily for the shortness of their visit and murmuring something about an appointment with her interior designer. The two women made their exit, leaving Clea to gaze after them in triumph.

Her pleased expression lasted only as long as it took for them to make their departure. If only, the countess thought bitterly, Jonathan had really said those words to her. In actuality, his visit had lasted no more than five minutes. He had been distant, not to say curt, and had disclosed the purpose of his visit as a request for Clea to produce the bracelet he had given her so that his man of affairs could see that it was properly insured.

Clea had informed him regretfully that the bracelet was not at the moment in her possession, since she had taken it to the jeweler's just yesterday to have its faulty catch repaired. Oh, how sweet of him to volunteer to collect it for her, but she really couldn't remember to which jeweler's it had been brought. Her maid, you see, had taken care of it, and she was out of the house at the moment.

When she had seen Jonathan from her home, Clea had sunk into the little brocade sofa by the fire, cold and shaking. Even now, thinking back on the incident, she felt perspiration dampen the palms of her hands. Oh, God, what was she to do?!

On leaving the home of his betrothed, Jonathan had leapt into his curricle with a light step. For the first time since he had left London so precipitously, he perceived a ray of hope in his situation. How could he have been such a fool, he asked himself for the hundredth time in the past few days. He had been blind as a schoolboy in the throes of calf love, bewitched by a lovely face and a seductive form. If it had not been for the advent into his life of one small elf with brown eyes, he might have entered into a life-long partnership with a woman whose unearthly beauty he now realized was as shallow as her soul.

Was it really Tally who had opened his eyes? Surely, he had never known such enjoyment in the company of a woman, or could have believed that simple conversation with one who shared one's interests and aspirations could be so satisfying. But, what was there about Tally that had caused him to take her unknowingly into his heart?

He laughed softly, picturing glossy chestnut curls, rumpled by ink-stained fingers or skewered with well-gnawed pencils. He thought of a turned-up nose and a soft mouth curved in a wide, genuine smile. Tally was without artifice. She may have learned the age-old feminine craft of flirtation, but her beguilements were open and joyous, and were never used with an eye to what she could get out of a man. Tally was, he concluded, unique to his experience, and he was eternally grateful to have acquired her for a friend.

He frowned. Who was he trying to cozen? That kiss in the carriage had not been one of simple friendship. Not on his part, certainly. It had taken every ounce of self-discipline he possessed to release her from his arms that night. The urge to press her soft curves against him, to continue drinking in the dizzying sweetness of her lips had been almost overpowering. What must she think of him, he wondered. He had behaved like the veriest schoolboy, dropping her off in the street in the middle of the night without a word, and then scuttling out of town as though the bailiffs were after him, with no message to her beyond that priggish little business note.

Was he in love with Tally? He was a little uncertain of the meaning of the word, after his experience with Clea. Certainly, he felt no inclination to mold his character and redirect his life to fit Tally's expectations, as he had with Clea. There was no need for that; he had shared every secret of his heart with Tally, and she had empathized with his aspirations. With her he had felt no shame in indulging his talent; rather she encouraged pride in his accomplishments. All he knew, really, was that Tally had become a part of him, and he could no more envision continuing his life without her than he could imagine doing without fresh air to breathe.

Such was his distraction that it became necessary for his tiger to point out to the most notable whip in London that his reins were slackening perilously.

Tally peered anxiously at Cat. During the course of their excursions, her friend's spirits seemed to have lifted somewhat, but upon their return home, it was as if she had removed a rigidly cheerful mask. The bright smile fell from her lips, and she seemed to wilt visibly. In an effort to dissuade her from retiring to her room for another afternoon of gloomy reflection, Tally drew her into the small salon for some light conversation.

"Did you hear Lady Fox this morning? She was rattling on about *Town Bronze* at a great rate, and her conversation was not about its author, but about the illustrations! I cannot tell you how set up I am in my own estimation."

Cat smiled wanly. "I've heard more than one comment on 'those wicked sketches', Tally." She became more animated. "I think everyone has become just as interested in them as they are in Jonathan's work. Have you nearly finished with them?"

"Almost. I'm expecting the last batch of chapters to arrive by post any time."

"Jonathan will not bring them himself?" asked Cat idly, but with a sharp glance at her friend.

Tally began a minute study of her fingernails.

"N-no. I—I don't know whether Jonathan will be coming here much from now on—particularly since work is nearly finished on *Town Bronze*."

"No other collaborations with him in the future?"

"Good Heavens, no! I really think it would be best, all in all, if the Viscount Chelmsford and I part company."

Cat sighed. "What a pair we are! Moping like a couple of weeping willows. Oh, Tally"—she put up a hand to brush away the tears that threatened once again—"I never thought I would be put in the position of betrayed wife!"

Tally rose to sit beside her on the small confidante

placed by a sunny window. "Cat," she began diffidently. "Do you think it is possible you might be wrong? Richard did deny any involvement with Lady Belle, and, truly it doesn't seem like him. He asked you to trust him; can you not do so?"

"I know what I saw, Tally. You should have seen the way he was kissing her hand. I hope she counted her fingers when he was through! And, of course, he denied it. My mother told me that when she made the mistake of facing Papa with his infidelities, he swore up and down he was innocent—at first, anyway. Later, he raged at her for prying into matters that did not concern a wife. That's when she learned the value of complacency—and compliance." Her voice broke. "But, oh—I don't know whether I shall ever be able to absorb that lesson. Oh, Tally, I do love him so."

The tears had begun in earnest now, and Tally watched in dismay as Cat hurriedly left the room.

So much for her efforts to cheer Cat out of doldrums, she thought sourly. With dismal clarity she realized that she had failed to extricate herself from them as well. At least Cat had known herself loved and known herself to be worthy of that devotion. Tally had no such knowledge with which to console herself. The idea of Jonathan's forsaking the fascinating Lady Belle for the uninspiring Lady Talitha was ludicrous—or at least it would be, if it weren't so painful.

She was still occupied with her unpleasant musings when twilight began to descend, and she looked up with a start as Richard entered the room, his day's chores at the Foreign Office completed.

After one startled glance at the room's occupant, he prepared to withdraw, but Tally forestalled him. She rose quickly and moved to face him. "Richard, I want to talk to you."

"Not now, Tally. I'm tired and I want my dinner."

"Well, you're not going to get it until you explain your actions."

Richard stiffened, and eyed her angrily. "I owe you no explanations, Talitha Burnside. You may be a guest in this house, but you have no right to meddle in my affairs."

"I'm not meddling in your affairs," she snapped. "I'm

meddling in Cat's. You told me Clea Bellewood was less than the dust beneath your feet, and not two hours later you were nibbling her fingertips in Henrietta Street!"

"I told you—"

"No, you didn't! You refused to tell me anything, and now Cat is upstairs crying her eyes out. Richard, if you had some good reason for what happened with Clea, couldn't you—?"

"No," he replied coolly. "As a matter of fact, there is a very reasonable, and extremely innocent explanation for my meeting with the countess—and for my, er, behavior."

"Well, then?"

To Tally's astonishment Richard replied simply, "I have chosen not to tell her."

Chapter Sixteen

Tally gaped at him.

"You *what*?" she gasped. "Richard, what on earth can you be thinking of—to—to deliberately put Cat through hell. Why . . . ?"

Richard gripped her arm and sat her back down unceremoniously on the little confidante, and glared down into her face.

"Because I possess the absurd desire that my wife trust me."

"*Trust* you! After the exhibition you have been putting on with Lady Bellewood? Richard, she may be desperately in love with you, but she is not stupid! When a woman observes her husband practically in—in—*in flagrante delicto*, how much trust is she expected to display?"

Richard thrust a stubborn jaw forward. "I told her there was nothing between me and Clea Bellewood. No matter what she saw, or thought she saw, that should be enough. Love isn't just moonlight and cuddling; it involves trust where everyone else would disbelieve you."

Tally shook her head in wonder.

"That's true, but there are limits, for the dear Lord's sake! Tell me, if the situation were reversed, would you be so willing to believe? If on more than one occasion you saw Cat accepting the attentions of one of the smarmiest men of your acquaintance, and at last surprised them in a distinctly compromising position, would you then say to Cat, 'Ah, but of course, my dove. If you say there is nothing between you and Sir Quiverlips, I am perfectly willing to abide by your declaration. More tea, my precious?' "

A startled expression came into Richard's eyes, and he shifted uncomfortably. "I—umpf—well, I would certainly

be willing to discuss it with her," he mumbled
defensively.

"Quite." Tally's smile was triumphant, and she deemed
this a good time to leave. Nodding wisely, she departed
the room with a satisfied swirl of her skirts.

She decided to put in an hour at her sketching before
it was time to dress for a dinner party she was pledged
to attend with Cat and Richard. She wished ardently that
she could excuse herself, as it was surely going to be like
dining out with a pair of effigies on a tombstone.

As she passed through the hall, she found a package
addressed to her in Jonathan's dark scrawl. The final
portion of *Town Bronze*, no doubt. Tally picked it up
listlessly and brought it with her to her worktable and,
lighting her candles, sat down to read.

Despite herself, she was soon caught up in the antics
of Clifford and Clive. One of the last chapters told of a
contretemps between Clifford and a rather outspoken
lady of the evening near the Royal Opera House in Covent Garden. The pretty bird of paradise, it seemed, had
discovered that Clifford had underpaid her on his last
visit and was determined to see that matters were made
right. It was only with the arrival of Clive on the scene,
that young Clifford's embarrassment was relieved with a
roll of soft.

Covent Garden, mused Tally. She had attended the
opera there, of course, but had not had the opportunity
to make much of a survey of the market area. She made
a few scrawls on her sketch pad, but realized after a few
moments that her knowledge of that infamous haunts of
sharps and ladybirds was woefully inadequate.

She pondered for several moments, chewing furiously
on the end of her pencil. There was simply no way out
of it. She must return to Covent Garden for a look at
the place at night, when its denizens were out in full
force under lamplit shadows.

Jonathan was in town, but asking him to escort her
was out of the question. It would look as though she
were seeking an excuse to see him again, and she could
not bear to be humiliated if he were to refuse. True, she
had promised to refrain from going abroad in her disguise
without him, but she appeased her conscience by pointing
out that the circumstances were different this time.

She could plead a headache to get out of the dinner party. Then, it would be a simple matter to slip into her wig and rusty old skirt and shawl. Thank Heaven for the tree outside her window!

Upstairs, Richard gloomily made preparations for the evening's festivities. He and Cat had taken turns in the last several days fulfilling their social obligations, each giving various excuses for the absence of the other. Tonight was different. Lord Whittaker's dinner party was being given in honor of his oldest daughter, who was making her come out this Season. Only those of his associates for whom he held the most affection and respect had been invited, and a refusal by either of them to attend on any other grounds beyond a cataclysmic upheaval in the household or a terminal illness would have been deemed an insult.

He had just shrugged into the shirt of snowy lawn proffered by his valet, when a soft knock sounded at the door. Scribster opened it to admit Cat. His eyes lowered immediately in comprehension, and the next moment the man had bowed himself unobtrusively out of the room.

Cat stood for a long moment at the door, her eyes locked with those of her husband, whose hands had frozen at the buttons of his shirt. At last, she stepped into the room and took a long shuddering breath.

"Richard," she said simply. "Would you tell me again? Please, look me in the eye and tell me again that there is nothing between you and Clea Bellewood. You see, I do want to trust you—I want to so very much."

Richard reached his wife in two strides and then stopped short. He placed his hands lightly on her shoulders and looked deeply into her eyes. "Cat, forgive me. I should have explained—"

"No. No, you need not if you think you shouldn't. Just—just tell me again, so I can see."

"Cat, my dearest—my loveliest, my own darling Cat. I love you—now, and forever, and no other woman in the universe, including Lady Belle, could interest me in so much as her little finger. I promise you this with all my heart."

Cat sighed as though a burden had been lifted from

her slight shoulders, and like a tired child, she laid her head on her husband's breast.

"Please," he murmured into the satin darkness of her hair, "let me explain, as I should have done before. But you must agree to tell no one what I have to say."

She smiled mistily up into his face.

"Of course, dearest. And I am all ears for it, but first . . . oh, but first, my love, the rest of me needs attending to."

The next instant the two were locked in a kiss that lasted for many satisfying moments. Richard's hands moved along the soft curve of her back and stroked her deliciously rounded derriere.

"Do you think, my sweet," he whispered, as he led her toward the bed, "that Lord and Lady Whittaker would take it amiss if we were a few minutes late for dinner?"

Cat's laugh was low and husky. "Perhaps more than a few, dearest."

In her room, Tally practiced an expression of wan lassitude before her mirror. By the time she had it perfected, the hour was far advanced, and she wondered why there was no stir in the house of impending departure. In fact, it was not for another forty-five minutes that she heard Cat's step in the hall and her knock at the door.

One look at her friend's countenance, and she realized this was not the same Cat who had dragged herself so lugubriously from the small salon earlier in the afternoon. Her face fairly glowed, and she laughed joyously as she stepped into Tally's room.

"Aren't you ready yet, slowcoach? We should have been on our way long ago!"

"Cat!" cried Tally. "You look—that is, have you and Richard . . . ?"

Cat threw her arms about the girl in a rib-cracking hug, and she laughed again.

"Yes, you are quite right. Richard and I have, um, settled our differences."

"Oh, Cat, I am so glad."

"We're rather pleased about it, too. But, what is this, puss? You're not ready for the Whittaker's party."

Tally hastily assumed her air of pallid lethargy and raised a limp hand to her forehead.

"I have such a wretched headache, Cat. I think I'll just stay home tonight, if you don't mind."

Cat did not mind in the slightest, displaying what Tally mischievously described as a blatant eagerness to keep her husband all to herself on the carriage ride to and from the Whittaker's.

With admonitions to rest quietly, and recommendations of burning pastilles and a poultice to her head, Cat hurried away to her evening's entertainment.

Waiting for another half an hour, to assure that she would remain unobserved as she slid down her tree, Tally quickly donned her disguise and made her escape.

Covent Garden lay little more than a mile from Half Moon Street, but in atmosphere, they might have been a thousand leagues apart. By the time Tally had crossed the Haymarket and made her way past Leicester Square, she had ventured from the manicured affluence of Mayfair into a sordid warren of grimy dwellings and shops surrounding the unsavory environs of the market square.

As her path took her deeper into the smells and sounds of London's underbelly, Tally knew more than one moment of unease. Faster and faster flew her feet, and she looked neither to the right nor to the left, until at last she emerged, panting but unscathed into the broad piazza called Covent Garden.

She paused for a moment in the portico of St. Paul's Church. When she had caught her breath, she moved into the throng that flowed and swirled in a dark tide of humanity, and eventually found herself tossed up on the other side, near the gleaming rear facade of the Opera House.

Scanning the area, she took up a vantage point in a shadowed angle. She seated herself quietly, and drawing her pad from the depths of the frayed old shawl, began her night's work.

It seemed as though in whichever direction she turned, she found fascinating material for her imaginary file. In an arcade across the cobblestones, two roisterers stumbled from a gin shop and were immediately set upon by an elderly beldam who exhorted them to examine the tray of rather soiled ribbons she had been purveying up

and down the street. Nearby, a wrinkled old man sawed
on a scarred old fiddle as a small dog waltzed on his hind
legs, tongue lolling from the side of his mouth. The man's
wife circulated among passersby with a brightly stitched
hat, hopefully rattling the few coins it contained.

In the center of the square, near the now-quiet market
stalls, a small crowd surrounded a hawker of broad-
sheets, while a young boy, surely no more than seven
years old, could be seen briskly picking the pockets of
the unsuspecting customers.

While all this was going on, a steady parade of vehi-
cles, from fashionable curricles to hackney carriages,
trundled around the perimeter of the piazza, picking up
and discharging passengers, or pausing while their own-
ers stopped to chat with pedestrians, or to harangue
those who blocked their own passage.

Tally smiled to herself, wondering what the nuns
whose vegetable garden had given the square its name
several hundred years before would have thought about
these profane doings.

A ripple of activity nearby caused Tally to whirl toward
the Opera House, where elegant carriages with their accompanying footmen were beginning a slow procession
toward Bow Street. Goodness, surely she had not been
sitting here that long! Tonight's performance must be
over. She hurried through a narrow alleyway to the front
of the gleaming new theater, where she was just in time
to observe the glittering throng leaving the building.

She crouched unobtrusively in the shadow of a column
in the portico and began sketching. She had no sooner
begun, when another group of Covent Garden habitues
strolled into view.

Tally had heard of the nightly parade of Cyprians outside the theater, but she had not dreamed they would be
so audacious. Sauntering in gaudy replicas of the exquisite gowns worn by their betters, they called raucous invitations to the gentlemen leaving the building. Some even
proffered business cards! Tally's fingers flew over her
sketch pad as she recorded the antics of the demi-
mondaine, and the reactions to them of the *haut monde*,
male and female alike.

Suddenly, Tally was distracted by a high-pitched squeal
emanating from a point just over her shoulder. She

twisted around and observed to her horror that Clea Bellewood stood on the top stair of the portico, pointing a trembling finger at her.

Tally's first stricken thought was that Clea had somehow pierced her disguise and had chosen to denounce her in the most crowded spot she could find. But what was it that Clea mouthed in her piercing screech?

"My bracelet!" The words streamed toward Tally in menacing shafts. "There! She's the one who took it—that old crone there."

The flash of jewels at Clea's breast brought Tally to the awareness that the countess was wearing the magnificent sapphire necklace Jonathan had given her as a betrothal gift. In the next instant, Tally realized that the wrist being waved so distractedly by Lady Belle was bare. The bracelet which she most certainly would have worn as well was nowhere in evidence.

"She took it!" Clea's voice had now reached a pitch guaranteed to shatter glass. "I know she did! Someone arrest her!"

Tally was not at all sure of what was going on, but at these words, she leaped to her feet, casting her sketch pad to the ground. She must get away! Like a deer pursued by hounds, she bolted into the crowd, but rough hands caught at her. Her arms were gripped by two burly passersby, and she was marched ungently to where Clea waited in triumph with a group of her friends.

"Search her," she commanded Tally's captors.

This, however, the two men, apparently a pair of navvies on an evening spree, were unwilling to do. Viewing the pathetic figure cringing before them, they opined that it might be better to wait for the appearance of someone from Bow Street, just down the street.

The wisdom of this course of action soon became apparent as a gentleman of official mien hove into view. He disdained a show of credentials, relying on his authoritative bark to proclaim his office.

Dear God, thought Tally, a Bow Street Runner. She tried to force her mind to some coherent plan to extricate her from this nightmare, but her brain seemed frozen in a fog of sheer terror.

"Orright, now, orright," brayed the Runner, a portly

gentleman arrayed in a voluminous frieze coat. "Wot's the matter 'ere?"

Clea waved her hand. "This filthy harridan has stolen a bracelet from me—a very valuable bracelet, and I want her arrested!"

The Runner paused portentously and withdrew from one capacious pocket a worn pencil stub. From the other, he took a small notebook and thumbed through its grimy pages until he came to the desired place. Wetting the pencil with a large pink tongue, he rolled an eye toward the countess.

"A bracelet chersay? What kinder bracelet, and how d'yer know this wretched old besom took it?"

Clea drew a breath of pure outrage. She was not accustomed to having her orders questioned, particularly by officious minions of the law.

"My good man, I am the Countess of Bellewood, and I am telling you that this—this person stole my bracelet. It was of sapphires and was the companion-piece to my necklace." Here she removed her zephyr gauze scarf, allowing the Runner an opportunity to make what some might have considered an overly conscientious examination of the precious bauble and its splendidly exposed resting place.

"Just as I was leaving the theater," continued Clea in a shrill voice, "I felt a jerk on my wrist, and when I looked down, the bracelet was gone. And there was this old witch, hobbling away as fast as her scrawny legs would carry her."

The Runner peered closely at Tally, who shrank in the grasp of the two stalwart passersby. She could only be thankful that the dim light prevented the law officer from observing that the wrinkles so liberally etched into the aged face before him were completely false.

"And what have you to say fer yerself, old lady?" the Runner bellowed.

Here was a fresh horror. Tally had never had occasion to speak in her role as flower woman. She had no idea whether or not she could convincingly manage the accent of such a person.

"I di'nt do nuffink," she whispered hoarsely in a barely audible voice.

The Runner swelled importantly. His day-to-day duties

often involved confrontations with persons of the old lady's station in life, but he rarely had an opportunity to display his prowess before a member of that class commonly referred to as "toffs."

"Orright, then, let's 'ave a look."

To Tally's utter consternation, he bent to grasp her wrist. Ignoring her humiliation and fear, he subjected her to a swift but thorough search, in which her pockets were turned out, her shoes removed, and the rest of her briskly patted down.

Clea watched the proceedings with a small smile on her lips. When the Runner's activities produced nothing more than a well-gnawed pencil, she seemed oddly unsurprised.

"Well, of course, the first thing she must have done was to pass the bracelet to a confederate. I demand that she be taken to jail until she confesses with whom she's working."

"I hardly think that will be necessary, my dear." The deep, quiet voice spoke out of the crowd, and hearing it, Tally went limp with relief.

"Jonathan!" Clea cried, seeing him. Her rouge appeared garrish in the ghastly paleness of her face.

"Yes, it is I, my love." Jonathan stepped up to stand before her. "We seem to have missed each other all evening long, haven't we? I must offer my humblest apologies for not having arrived at the theater in time to watch the performance with you. As for the bracelet that seems to be the center of some controversy—is this the one you're seeking?"

So saying, he pulled a shimmering handful of blue fire from his pocket and swung it before the astonished Runner.

Clea uttered a single cry of shock and fear. Tally swayed and gritted her teeth with the effort it took not to give way to the trembling dizziness that threatened to overcome her. She had never swooned in her life, and, she told herself fiercely, she was not about to start now.

Chapter Seventeen

The roaring in Tally's ears faded, and she lifted her eyes to find a pair of smokey gray ones peering intently into hers. Jonathan had moved to her side to steady her, and as he did so, he whispered in her ear, "The carriage is behind St. Paul's Church."

After he had made sure she was able to stand unaided, Jonathan turned to Clea with a rueful smile.

"I am sorry, my darling. I was several steps behind you as you left the theater, and saw your bracelet lying on the ground where it must have fallen from your wrist. I was still well behind you when I scooped it up and was detained in conversation with friends. I had no idea such an altercation was taking place outside the building, or I would have made my appearance sooner."

He turned to the Runner, who was opening and closing his mouth like an offended haddock.

"Now then, sir," Jonathan continued quietly. "Since this unfortunate misunderstanding has been cleared up, I'm sure you'll want to release this poor woman. She has obviously done no wrong."

The Runner harrumphed at some length, but apparently having decided that discretion was the better part of getting on the wrong side of an obvious swell, he waved a hand at Tally.

"Orright, then, be off wi' ye, Granny."

Tally needed no encouragement. Remembering just in time to accommodate her step to her supposedly advanced years, she faded into the night at a frantic hobble.

In a few moments, the Runner took himself off with much bowing and scraping, and within another short space of time, the crowd had dispersed, leaving Clea and Jonathan alone on the stairs in front of the Opera House.

Jonathan turned to his fiancée. For a moment, he simply stared at her, watching bemusedly as she assumed an expression of pretty gratitude.

"Jonathan," she began, "I am so—so pleased that you recovered my bracelet. What a silly mistake. I could have sworn that old besom had taken it. Where ever did you find it?"

She reached for the jewelry, and Jonathan slipped it casually into her uplifted palm.

"I retrieved it from your cousin's pocket," he replied calmly, "though it took some persuasion before he finally disgorged it. I fancy he may not be so eager in the future to act as your tool."

"I—I don't know what you're talking about, Jonathan. How could Miles possibly have come into possession of my bracelet?" Clea said tightly. "Please, let's just go home. This has been a perfectly wretched evening for me."

Jonathan laughed shortly. He felt as though he were watching a bad play, one in which he had invested heavily and was about to close with the finality of a snap.

"But not," he replied softly, "as wretched as it must have been for the harmless old woman you chose as a pawn in your little charade."

"Charade!" exclaimed Clea, suddenly going on the offensive. "Surely, you're not implying that I would—would contrive an episode like this. Jonathan, how could you think such a thing?"

Jonathan watched detachedly as her lovely blue eyes shimmered with tears, and one slim hand fluttered to rest against the classic perfection of her throat. His only reaction was one of dismal appreciation of the art which had kept him on the end of her tether for so long. He laughed shortly.

"Very well done, my dear. Once, such a gesture would have sent me to my knees in a quaking mass of guilt. How, I wonder, could I have been such an ass?"

"Jonathan!"

"No, please do stop now." He sighed wearily. "Clea, it's over. All over."

How very transparent she was, he thought, when one's eyes were opened to her true nature. As clearly as though she were speaking her thoughts aloud to him, Jonathan was made aware of Clea's panic at losing the rich prize standing before her. In the next instant, he watched her indomitable ego slide into place. God knew that he had given her every assurance that no man, particularly not the Viscount Chelmsford, who all London knew worshipped the very ground whereon her dainty slippers trod, could withstand her seductive charm. Now, her lips opened slightly, and she moistened them with the tip of her pink little tongue. When she laid her gloved hand on his sleeve, he knew an urge to shake it off, as one would an importunate child. Her eyes widened in an expression of touching vulnerability.

"My love, I don't understand. Is this some kind of joke? What do you mean—over? I know you cannot . . ."

Jonathan removed her hand gently, but with finality, and studied her for a moment as though she were an exotic but totally incomprehensible life form.

"A few days ago," he began conversationally, "I received a visit from one of the senior members of the staff at Rundell and Bridges, where I purchased the bracelet. I have done business with the man for a number of years, and we are on excellent terms. He wondered if I were cognizant of the fact that a lady had brought the item into the store not long afterward to have a paste copy made of it."

Jonathan observed Clea grow very still, but she said nothing.

"By the merest coincidence," he continued, "this excellent fellow heard of a bracelet being offered for sale which sounded identical to the one I had purchased, and when he looked into the matter, he discovered that it was, in fact, the sapphire bauble which I had given you a few weeks earlier. He purchased it in the hope that I might be interested in rebuying it, which as it happens, I was."

Clea glanced down at the jewels still sparkling in her hand.

"No," Jonathan said with a faint smile. "The bracelet I returned to you is the one you slipped into Crawshay's pocket as you left the Opera House. I find that, while I am perfectly willing to allow you to retain this skillful reproduction, I am loathe to provide any more expensive trinkets for the adornment of your admittedly exquisite body, or to finance your disastrous gambling career."

Clea drew a ragged breath.

"So," she rasped, "when you told me you wanted to see the bracelet in order to make sure that it was properly insured, you were lying. You merely wanted to humiliate me!"

"I hoped that if you were given an opportunity, you would tell me the truth. Although, to be perfectly honest, it would have made little difference to me by then."

Clea quickly rearranged her features into a facade of artless remorse, and Jonathan could only marvel at the variety in her seemingly bottomless bag of tricks.

"Ah, love, you are right. I have been so foolish. I allowed myself to be drawn in at Madame de Robitaille's, and when I discovered the extent of my debts, I—I didn't know where to turn."

Now the tears were allowed to slip into a silky forest of eyelashes, where they trembled in glittering profusion before sliding down her cheek.

"I know I should have come to you, my dearest, but I could not face your anger—even though I deserved every harsh word I feared you would fling at me. I—just—didn't know what else to do." This last uttered in a forlorn whisper.

"But Clea," Jonathan responded in a bored voice, "how is it that you were reduced to such dire straits? Surely, the three thousand pounds you lost to Madame—yes, I did do some investigating—was as a drop in the pond to one of your wealth. Can it be that this is not the first time you have lost heavily at the tables? That you are, in fact, at *point non plus*?"

"You know I—enjoy gambling," replied Clea evasively.

"Yes, but you were ever so careful, were you not, to conceal from me the extent of your, er, enjoyment? I cannot count the evenings when you were unable to join me for an evening's entertainment, pleading a headache or some such. Did you really think I would not eventually discover that you spent those evenings in some discreet hell?"

Clea stood silently, staring down at the bracelet in her hand as though it would offer some counsel.

"The thing I find most indicative of your true character, however," continued Jonathan, "is the heartless manner in which you drew in a harmless old woman, exposing her to humiliation and the threat of prison, merely to further your own wretched scheme.

"I had business elsewhere this evening and did not arrive at the theater until the audience was filing out. I saw you as soon as you stepped into the portico from the interior of the building, your faithful henchman at your side. I started up the stairs, and had nearly reached you, when I saw you deftly remove the bracelet from your wrist and slip it into Miles's pocket. I saw the nod you gave him as he slid away into the crowd, and I was very near at hand when you began your interminable screeching at T—at the flower woman.

"But she was only an old hag! Although"—Clea paused, a faintly puzzled expression on her face—"there was something about her . . ."

"Yes," said Jonathan hastily, "but she was a human being, not just a cog for your machinations."

Clea sighed and returned to her role of pretty penitence.

"I am sorry to have disappointed you, my love, and I promise I shall try to do better. After we are married, I shall make you a dutiful wife, you'll see."

"Wife!" Jonathan's patience snapped, and the word exploded from Jonathan's lips. "Marriage? Don't you understand, Clea? There will be no wedding. You may consider our betrothal at an end."

Clea fairly rocked back on her heels in shock. Her mouth dropped open and an expression of outraged stupefaction crossed her face. "You—you can't do that! You can't cry off! What would people think? The humiliation! I would be ruined—as would you!"

"I have no desire to ruin either of us. I will allow you the privilege of sending the announcement to the *Morning Post* that 'the Countess of Bellewood has decided that the betrothal of herself to the Viscount Chelmsford is at an end', or however it is they phrase these things."

Clea's face twisted in sudden fury. "You pig! I know what brought about this sudden reversal of your affection. It was the Burnside chit, was it not? Friendship, indeed. I can just imagine what was going on while you were sneaking off with her to the Park and whispering to her in corners. If you think . . ."

For an instant, Jonathan knew a blind urge to strike her.

"That will do, Clea," he growled. "You will not speak Lady Talitha's name. I think we have nothing further to say to each other. Good night, Lady Bellewood."

He turned on his heel and moved quickly down the stairs, leaving Clea to screech after him.

"You will be sorry for this night's work, my lord Chelmsford. I shall make you rue the moment you met Lady Talitha Burnside!"

In a few moments, Jonathan rounded the corner of St. Paul's Church, where he found his carriage awaiting him. Inside, as he had hoped, waited Tally. She had removed her wig and wiped off her wrinkles, and as she sat curled in a corner, huddled in the frayed old shawl, she looked like an abandoned waif.

Jonathan signaled the coachman and climbed hurriedly into the vehicle as it lumbered on its way. He said not a word as he turned to Tally and, in an instinctive move, gathered her into his arms.

When Tally had hurtled back across Covent Garden Square and into the sanctuary of Jonathan's carriage, she had been trembling so violently that her fingers could barely work the door latch.

When at long last she had regained some measure of composure, she straightened and attempted to remove at least some of Granny Posey's more unattractive features. She realized with a start that this would undoubtedly be the last time she performed such an operation, because, career or no, she was never, ever going to set foot in the streets of London by herself in wig and shawl. Much as she hated to admit it, Jonathan was right. The city was fraught with peril for an unprotected woman, no matter how poor and stricken in years.

Her musings took her down the familiar path that led inevitably to Jonathan. She lifted a hand to her cheek, recalling the warmth of his breath as he whispered to her. Even in her terror, she had been intensely aware of his closeness, of his mouth brushing her skin.

She wondered uneasily what his mood would be when he returned to the carriage. Would he castigate her again for her foolhardiness? The blood rushed to her cheeks as she recalled what had happened the last time he had done that. She relived the bliss she had felt in the strength of his arms, and the soft fire of his lips against hers. She reprimanded herself for her wayward thoughts, but to no avail. What was worse, she wanted it all to happen again! She wished for nothing more in the world than to find herself enfolded in the safety and warmth of his embrace, her mouth firmly pressed against his.

When Jonathan at last entered the carriage, it seemed the most natural thing in the world to move into his open arms and to lift her face for his kiss.

His lips were as warm and the sensation as dizzying as she remembered. Her arms went around his neck, and her fingers twined themselves in his dark hair. A low moan escaped her as he drew back from her for a moment, only to bend his head again to hers in a deeper, more demanding kiss.

"Tally, oh, my darling Tally," Jonathan whispered hoarsely, and he drew her even closer to him, as though he would caress her very soul. His hands savored the curve of her back and waist, and he was aware of her full breasts pressing against the pounding of his heart.

It was not until his mouth began a path down her throat and along the threadbare collar of her bodice that Tally came to herself with a horrified start.

"Jonathan! No—I—we cannot . . ." She pushed against him, and, even though he released her at once, his ragged breathing told her that he had been as disturbed as she. He cupped her chin in his hand and looked at her searchingly.

"Tally, are you all right? You weren't hurt back there, were you?"

Tally retreated to a safe distance and waited for the pounding of her heart to subside.

"No, of course not. I was frightened out of my wits, though. Oh, Jonathan, how did you know I was in trouble? How did you find me?"

The recital of the events which had led to the near-disaster on the steps of the Opera House did not take long. When Jonathan finished, he gripped Tally's hand and said in a light tone that did little to mask the intensity of his feelings, "And so, my dear, I find myself *sans fiancée.*"

Unthinking, Tally reached for Jonathan's hand.

"I am so very sorry. This must all have come as a terrible blow to you."

"To discover that my goddess has feet of clay? Well, I suppose it might have, had I not also discovered that I fell out of love with the beauteous Lady Belle some time ago—starting from the time, in fact, when a certain talented and utterly adorable artist came into my life. Oh, Tally"—he gathered her to him again, and his voice roughened. "I do love you so very much. Do you . . . ?"

Their lips met again in a kiss of stabbing sweetness. When she drew back at last, she smiled shyly, her heart in her eyes. "Does that answer your question, my lord?"

Jonathan traced the curve of her cheek with his fingertip, causing a shudder to pass through Tally's body.

"Yes, minx, but I want to hear you say it."

"I love you, Jonathan Ware. I have for some time now, and I suppose I shall keep on doing so until I am a very old lady. Truly an old lady, that is, not one in a wig and funny shoes."

"Thank God you will never have to wear that outfit again, my dearest love."

"No," said Tally in a small voice. "Much as I hate to admit it, you were right, Jonathan. If, in my future artistic endeavors, I am required to depict any more scenes from London's underworld, I shall find some other method of doing so."

He smiled warmly at her.

"I sincerely hope you will confine your future artistic endeavors to charming watercolors of the English countryside—and, of course, portraits of our children, and the odd caricature of my assorted aunts."

Tally raised her eyes to Jonathan's in a swift, questioning glance. "Ch-children?"

Once more, Jonathan's mouth came down on hers, and when he spoke again, it was to murmur roughly, "I was thinking of ten or twelve to start."

Tally laughed tremulously. "I hope you have a very long portrait gallery in your home. I promise to keep my caricaturing to my professional life."

Jonathan's hand, in the act of stroking Tally's hair, stilled. "Your professional life?"

"Why, yes, Mr. Mapes has spoken to me about a series

of sketches he's been thinking about. Something about medical and scientific quackery, I think he said."

Jonathan's dark brows drew together in a baffled frown. "Surely you don't intend to continue drawing on a professional basis once we are married!"

At this, Tally sat bolt upright. "But, of course I do. Whyever would I not?"

"Because you won't need to anymore. I mean, I can understand why, as a single young woman without close loved ones, you had a desire to use your talent to become independent. But, now you won't have to earn your own way."

Tally's fists curled into tight little balls. Was this the man to whom she had given her heart? Was this her friend and confidante?

Suddenly, the wonderful moments of the last few minutes seemed to crumble about her like a precariously stacked house of cards, and a knot began to twist in the pit of her stomach.

"I cannot believe you are saying these things," she said softly. "You of all people. I thought you understood. You certainly don't write because you need the money to stay alive. Surely you must know that I feel the same."

"But you are a . . ."

"Jonathan," she said in a quiet, ominous voice, "if you are going to remind me that I am a female, I think I shall never speak to you again."

"Very well," he replied stiffly. "But you must admit that it does make a difference. You will be a married lady, after all, and . . ."

"And a married lady, of course," said Tally tightly, "must busy herself with her wifely duties, her mind occupied solely with choosing just the right furnishings, and—and nannies for the children she is expected to produce. Haven't you any idea how much my drawing means to me?"

"Tally, you're not being fair."

"At this point," Tally shot back, now totally oblivious to the voice of reason within that told her she was being a perfect ninnyhammer, "nothing would prevail upon me to become a married lady. Now, if you will excuse me, it is time I returned home."

She flung open the door of the carriage, which had stopped its motion some time ago upon completing the short drive from St. Paul's Church to Half Moon Street, and leaped out onto the street, leaving Jonathan to stare after her in dismay.

Chapter Eighteen

The days that followed were the longest that Tally had ever known. Over and over she relived the scene in the carriage, and over and over she vowed that she never wanted to see the Viscount Chelmsford again as long as she lived. Evidently, she thought morosely, he felt the same way. Why had he not come to see her?

Tally strived valiantly to maintain her righteous fury. Unfortunately, there were many times she did a complete about-face, cursing herself for her ungovernable tongue. The man she thought the most wonderful in the world, and the most unattainable had miraculously declared his love for her. And what did she do? She had raged at him like a termagent, thrusting her own views at him without a thought to his feelings.

Her internal arguments swung between those two extremes, until by the end of the week, she felt herself to be a vacillating widgeon, unable to make up her mind or to take a stand on whether or not the sun would rise tomorrow at its accustomed time.

And where was Jonathan?

She finished the last batch of illustrations for *Town Bronze*. Regretfully, since she was unable to find her sketch pad when she returned to look for it early the morning after her eventful night in Covent Garden, she was forced to rely on memory for her final drawing. She sent them all by messenger to George Mapes. She received in return a note of congratulations, and she visited the portly publisher to receive more expressions of good will, as well as a substantial check. Mapes went into some detail on plans for another book, this one a series of satirical verse based loosely on the Mother Goose rhymes which had so enlivened the London political scene more than a generation ago.

Tally listened to the publisher's glowing description of the book as a worthy successor to *Town Bronze* with little enthusiasm, and heard his panegyric on that wildly successful endeavor with such a gloomy expression on her face that Mapes took care to impress upon her that the names of Dash and Mouse were on the lips of every soul in London who possessed the ability to read.

Tally had no need of the publisher's assurances of this fact. When the last installment of the book appeared in the booksellers' shops, the doings of Clifford and Clive were discussed in the streets of commerce, the halls of Westminister, and the drawing rooms of the West End as often as those of Wellington, Castlereagh, and even the Prince Regent. Speculation grew ever more outrageous as to the author and the illustrator of the caustic burlesque.

Despite her heartache, Tally could not help feeling a spurt of exhilaration at having been a part of the novel's success. Once, when her dinner partners on both left and right spoke of nothing but *Town Bronze*, mirthfully discussing the personages exposed in its pages, she had experienced an almost overwhelming urge to reveal her part in the book's creation. For once, good sense prevailed, and she held her tongue firmly between her teeth.

For Tally had found that she was enjoying her newfound popularity. She was invited everywhere and was assured by more than one hostess that her sparkling presence was necessary to any function to ensure its success. She had been told much the same thing by more than one aspiring buck, as well, a circumstance in which she took a certain grim satisfaction on those occasions when she and Jonathan appeared at the same rout or ball.

Not that the viscount gave the merest sign that he took notice of the crush of beaux that always seemed to surround the charming Lady Talitha. In fact, except for the smallest of bows, he scarcely acknowledged her presence at these functions.

"Whatever has happened between you and Jonathan?" asked Cat one morning as she sat in Tally's dressing room admiring a new bonnet purchased the day before at Estelle's Millinery Shop. "I have not seen him here this age."

Tally dropped her eyes. "Now that the book has been

completed, there is no reason for him to come to the house anymore."

Cat sighed. "I was hoping—now that Clea has broken off her engagement to him. . ." She eyed Tally speculatively. "I wonder why the betrothal ended with such a snap."

Tally yawned. "I have no idea." She cast about frantically for a topic with which to change the subject. "Have you any plans for today, Cat? I thought perhaps we might visit the botanical gardens. I have never seen them, and I'd love to do some sketching there."

"Oh, Tally, that's a splendid idea, but I'm afraid I can't. My great-aunt Haverstoke has summoned me today, and she lives out near Richmond. I can't imagine what she wants, except to scold me for not having been near her for months. But let's do that tomorrow. You're more than welcome to come with me today," Cat added, "but I must tell you, she will prose on for hours, and end up giving us a perfectly inedible tea."

"Thank you." Tally laughed. "It sounds a treat, but I think I'll decline. I'll see you at dinner, or are you and Richard going to enjoy another cozy meal á deux upstairs?" She laughed at Cat's rosy blush.

"You know we only do that when you have plans to dine out," she replied with great dignity. "I shall bid you good day, Lady Talitha."

She left the room with a great rustling of skirts, accompanied by Tally's chuckle.

Some hours later, Tally was seated in the little room adjoining Richard's study, pencil in hand. Her worktable was littered with drawings, all of a single subject. Jonathan's face stared up at her from a hundred angles, profile, front-face, and even a few from just over his shoulder. There were watercolors, in which his gray eyes flashed with green, like lightning before a summer storm. There were charcoal sketches in which his black hair swept over his forehead in a smokey curve. And there was one, which she hastily thrust to the bottom of the pile, in which he stood, shirtless, his muscular chest swirled with delicate black pencil strokes, his arms outstretched in an inviting gesture that was purely a figment of her fantasy.

With a sigh, she gathered the drawings into her arms

preparatory to burning them in the fireplace, and was thus occupied when a housemaid tapped at her door with the information that a gentleman wished to see her.

Tally's heart lurched, and her stomach began performing acrobatics. As calmly as she could, she ascertained from the maid that the gentleman awaited her in the small salon, and she willed herself to a calm she did not possess.

To her astonishment and vast disappointment, it was not Jonathan who sat at his ease in the salon, one booted leg swinging gently over the other, but Miles Crawshay. His pointed chin sported a fading bruise, and there was a suspicious darkness over one eye, but he was his impeccable self, dressed in a coat of superfine and a waistcoat of Turkish striped silk, from which depended no less than six fobs.

He rose gracefully as Tally entered the room, and he assisted her in seating herself opposite his own chair. Tally murmured a courteous greeting, but then found herself completely at a loss for words. What in the world was Crawshay doing in the Thurston home? Why would he be paying a call on the person most hated by his beautiful cousin? Particularly after what was no doubt one of the most unpleasant experiences of his life at the hands of his beautiful cousin's ex-fiancé.

As though reading her thoughts, Crawshay coughed deprecatingly and began without preamble. "I should imagine, my dear Lady Talitha, that you are wondering why I have called." Dismissing Tally's automatic disclaimers, he continued smoothly. "I came to return a certain item, which I am sure belongs to you."

As Tally stared questioningly at him, he withdrew from an inner coat pocket a small pad of paper and handed it to her. To her horror, she recognized the drawings it contained as those she had made at Covent Garden. It was the pad she had dropped in panic, the night of her near-imprisonment!

Her mouth was so dry, she could barely speak. "I—I don't understand," she croaked, in what she knew to be a ludicrous attempt at nonchalance. "What is this?"

Crawshay's amused chuckle sounded like a death knell in the cheerful little room. "Why, it is your sketch pad, Lady Talitha. Or, should I say, Miss Mouse?"

The chair on which Tally was seated seemed to heave beneath her, and the surrounding tables and chairs danced and swayed before her eyes. If she had thought confrontation with a Bow Street Runner the worst thing she would ever have to suffer in this life, she was finding herself badly mistaken. She licked her lips. "I don't understand," she whispered, once again.

"You are being extraordinarily obtuse, my lady, for one who, I am told, enjoys a reputation for sharp-wittedness." Crawshay settled back in his chair, as though prepared to enjoy his morning's work. "Very well, I shall try to make myself plain.

"As you are undoubtedly aware, a slight contretemps occurred the other night between the Countess of Belle-wood and a certain flower woman, at the Opera House in Covent Garden."

Tally tried to assume an expression of bored inquiry. "But what has this to do with me?" she asked, examining her fingernails in an offhand manner.

"As it happened, I witnessed a portion of the scene. I saw the flower woman drop her sketch pad on the steps of the theater. As it happened, I, er, left the area rather hurriedly at that point and did not return until sometime later, but I retrieved the pad. After I had perused the drawings, I realized that the artist was none other than the illustrator of that loudly acclaimed satire, *Town Bronze*."

For a moment, Tally thought she was going to be physically ill. With a supreme effort, she lifted her chin and looked down a nose that was singularly ill-equipped for such a procedure. "That's certainly interesting, Mr. Crawshay, but I fail to see what it has to do with me."

"Then I shall have to make myself even more plain." He reached over to tap Tally's knee playfully. She quivered distastefully at his touch and twisted away from him. An unpleasant expression flickered briefly in his eyes, but he said nothing.

"You see," he continued after a moment, "I had noted something oddly familiar about the filthy old creature who had created them."

By now, Tally had almost ceased breathing, and she sat silently, staring at her visitor in growing agony.

"Then it came to me. This person, though dressed in

cast-off tatters, wore an exceptionally beautiful and obviously valuable ring.,"

Tally glanced down involuntarily at her hands.

"Yes," continued Crawshay, his gratified smile widening. "I see you understand now. I had seen that ring on several occasions. It was, in fact, the very same one that you are now twisting in your lap as though you would punish it for your own transgressions."

Tally's hands, cold and rigid as death, stilled, and it took every ounce of discipline she possessed not to cringe back into her chair in tears. Clenching her teeth, she berated herself for being so stupid. Crawshay swung his quizzing glass by its embroidered ribbon and observed her discomfiture with every evidence of pleasure.

"Then my memory was jogged back to an evening some weeks before. I was enjoying a comfortable pipe with an old friend at the Limmer's taproom, when I became vaguely aware of a small gray-haired figure seated not far away. She was busy at something, but at the time I paid no attention. Then, several days later, to my surprise, I found myself pictured as an onlooker at one of Clifford and Clive's more outrageous escapades, along with the friend who had joined me that night."

He leaned forward and fixed Tally with a smiling gaze which chilled her to the marrow.

"You cannot imagine," he said softly, "in how much difficulty I found myself because of that little cameo sketch. However," he continued with a barely perceptible shrug, "I find it quite useless to dwell on what cannot be helped, particularly when there are matters of so much more import to discuss."

Tally rose awkwardly, her knees having apparently turned to pudding. "I think we have nothing further to discuss, Mr. Crawshay," she said with a valiant attempt at indifference. "You have wasted quite enough time with your ridiculous theories, and I wish you will take yourself off."

Crawshay rose also, and caught Tally's wrist in a crushing grip. "Please be seated, Lady Talitha," he grated. "You will hear what I have to say to you, unless the picture of yourself as the publicly identified illustrator of the most scandalous literary sensation London has seen since the days of Swift's *A Modest Proposal* appeals to you."

"You would not!" gasped Tally, her face ashen.

"Without a second thought, my dear." Crawshay spoke with emotionless finality, and Tally at last slumped in defeat.

"What is it you want?" she asked tonelessly.

Crawshay laughed delightedly. "Ah, I do love a woman who comes right to the point." He grew serious and tapped his quizzing glass against his fingertips for a long moment. "As you are no doubt aware, Lady Talitha, your host, Richard Thurston, is employed by the Foreign Office."

Puzzled, Tally nodded.

"You may also be aware that he brings a good deal of his work home with him. You have perhaps observed the dispatch boxes he brings into the house from time to time."

"Yes, of course. He works on their contents in his study. At least, I presume he does. We have never discussed his work."

"Of course. He is quite the perfect civil servant—discreet to the eyebrows. However, it is the contents of those boxes that concerns me. There are persons with whom I am, er, acquainted, who are most curious about certain papers, which Thurston keeps under lock and key in his study."

Tally stared at Crawshay in fearful comprehension. "You're not suggesting—" she began.

"I am suggesting nothing," interrupted Crawshay, his voice filled for the first time with overt menace. "I shall be as plain as possible. You are in a perfect position to slip into Thurston's sanctuary, and you're going to get those papers for me."

Tally stood again, and this time avoiding Crawshay's grasp, she moved swiftly to stand in back of the chair.

"I will not! I would not so much as consider such a— a despicable act. Good God, you're—a spy! You're nothing but a traitor—a slimy Judas! How dare you suggest that I'd help you! I shall tell the authorities of your shameful activities!"

A deep flush spread across Crawshay's vulpine features, and his lips thinned into an ugly line. "Oh, nobly spoken, my lady. Quite the little heroine. But I have watched you, my dear. I have seen your transformation from a country nobody to one of the most sought-after damsels in the *ton*, and it is obvious to the meanest intelligence that your new-found popularity means a great deal to you. However, once it becomes known that it was your pen that provided the illustrations for a piece of scurrilous trash, your position in Society will be considerably altered. With a few carefully placed words, you see, I can destroy you. You will be utterly ruined, my dear—an outcast with not a friend in the world."

He paused to survey her assessingly.

"And what will your family have to say? I hope your brother, Lord Bamfield, is of a forgiving nature."

Tally could only stare at him from stricken eyes.

"As for notifying the authorities," he continued softly, "that would be most unwise of you. My associates are not possessed of as kind a nature as I. I fear they would use rather ruthless means to prevent you from taking such action."

Swallowing the tears that threatened to overpower her, Tally turned to the window to gaze unseeing at the traffic that passed briskly along Half Moon Street.

Crawshay moved to her and stood close behind her, placing his hands caressingly on her shoulders. Tally closed her eyes in disgust as his lips brushed the tip of her ear.

"Are you having second thoughts, my dear?"

Tally shuddered convulsively, but did not answer. She remained unmoving, holding herself rigid.

"Ah, poor child." Crawshay pressed closer, until she could feel the pressure of his body along her entire length. "It is all most unsettling, I agree."

Tally twisted out of his grasp and moved away. "Please leave, Mr. Crawshay. I shall not hear another word of this—unspeakable treachery."

Crawshay contemplated her and shook his head. "Perhaps I did not make myself clear. I am not *requesting* your assistance. I am *telling* you what I require."

Tally moved to the bellpull, but Crawshay forestalled her by once again grasping her wrist.

"Please be still and listen. In his study, locked away in one of his desk drawers, Thurston keeps a file labeled

SECTOR FOUR. The file contains six or seven documents.
You will copy them, so that Thurston will not suspect
they have been stolen."

Tally, still in Crawshay's grip, forced herself to a calm
she did not feel. She faced her enemy scornfully.

"May I point out a flaw in this brilliant plan? Even if
I were to accede to your wretched demands, how am I
to break into Richard's desk? I have no skill as a lock-
pick, and if I take a hammer and chisel to the drawers,
it's very possible he may suspect dirty work."

Crawhay allowed a thin smile to curve his lips. "Your
opinion of me is most unflattering, my dear. Do you
think me a fool?"

As Tally watched in horror, he pulled from his waistcoat pocket several small keys on a chain and handed
them to her. "These will give you access to every drawer
in Thurston's desk. Nothing could be simpler than for
you to steal into his study in the small hours of the night
and find the necessary papers. It should not take you
long to copy them."

"How did you get those?" gasped Tally.

"As I have been trying to impress upon you, my dear,
my associates and I are not fools. They were copied from
Thurston's own. He never even knew they had been, er,
borrowed. We have, you see, a highly efficient organiza-
tion. You would do well to remember that, for if you do
not do precisely as I say, I shall, with great regret, of
course, expose you to the merciless ridicule of the Polite
World.

"And one more item for your consideration. I do hope
the author of *Town Bronze* is not a friend of yours, for
when your secret becomes known, you will no doubt be
hounded mercilessly to reveal his identity."

Tally gasped, as though the breath had been struck
from her body. Dear God, she was completely at this
man's mercy!

Observing her consternation, Crawshay smiled gloat-
ingly. "Do you plan to attend Lady Crewell's masquerade ball next Thursday—five days hence? Excellent. Are
you familiar with the small salon on the floor above the
ballroom? Lady Crewell often receives guests there. Very
good. At fifteen minutes past midnight, you will meet
me there with the papers in hand. Do you understand?"

Tally's heart pounded in great, panicky thuds. She must have time! The costume ball would not take place for five days, perhaps in that time . . . As though from a great distance, she heard her voice whisper brokenly. "Yes."

"Excellent," he repeated. "I shall be costumed, by the by, as Merlin the Magician. An appropriate choice, don't you think? I shall see you then, Lady Talitha."

He turned as if to go, but then swung to face her again. "Perhaps I should add, since you are such a resourceful young woman, that I am extremely familiar with the names and places that will appear in this document. Any attempt on your part to present me with false information will be recognized, and dealt with most severely."

He picked up his hat from where it rested on an occasional table near the door and lifted Tally's chin lightly with one finger.

"No, no—do not trouble yourself, Lady Talitha, I shall see myself out. I look forward to our meeting in five days, my charming little friend."

With a final, brutal squeeze of her shoulders, he released her, and still with that cruel smile on his lips, he bowed himself from the room.

Tally, unable to stand, sank into the nearest chair and buried her face in her hands.

Chapter Nineteen

Jem, the undergroom, was feeling sorely put upon. He had been roused from his bed at an unholy hour to accompany Lady Talitha on another of her unreasonably early rides, and on a morning that was coming on to mizzle if he knew anything of the matter. She had not been her usual friendly self on their canter to the Park, but had ridden with eyes straight ahead and a strained tightness about her mouth, which was ordinarily lovely and smiling.

Now she had dismounted and was walking with the gentleman who had met her among the trees a few minutes earlier. Jem knew him as that toff among toffs, the Viscount Chelmsford, a frequent guest at the Thurston home, as the undergroom was fond of mentioning to his cronies at the Running Footman.

Tally glanced around at the gray mist dripping from the leaves of the little glade in which they paced, and the thought skittered through her mind that the day perfectly reflected her dismal mood.

After Crawshay's departure the day before, she had thought long and hard about what course of action she should take. That she would accede to the man's vile extortion was, of course, out of the question.

After hours of desperate thought, Tally could still see no way out of her predicament, and had at last come to the wrenching conclusion that her short tenure as a budding caricaturist was over. When Crawshay arrived at Lady Crewell's ball for their rendezvous, she would simply not be there. She would not even be in London, but would by then have gone to earth at Summerhill. She imagined it would take little time after that for Crawshay to spread her name through every drawing room in Mayfair.

She must tell Jonathan of her coming exposure. It would not be fair to him to be put through the strain of worrying about his own secret. She would behave with the utmost composure in his presence, assuring him calmly that wild horses would never drag his secret from her lips and that he could consider his position in the *ton* as safe as houses. She would behave as though the passionate scene in the carriage had never taken place, for now a reconciliation with him was impossible. Even if they were to settle their differences, she could not bear to think of him saddled for the rest of his life with a veritable pariah.

After bidding him a dignified farewell, she would sweep out of his life forever to spend the rest of her life in good works. She would forget all about Jonathan and his smokey eyes, and the warmth of his smile, and the feel of his arms about her.

With these staunch resolutions in mind, she held herself carefully as she watched him stride cleanly over the grassy slope. Though it was all she could do to keep from running to him and hurling herself into his arms, she greeted him coolly, allowing nothing to show in her face beyond an expression of calm courtesy.

With an almost unbearable pounding of his heart, Jonathan observed Tally's slender figure waiting still and straight in the mist. After one of the worst weeks of his life, his heart had lifted when he had received her note requesting a tryst at dawn, for he assumed at once that his contrary little love was seeking a reconciliation.

He had done a great deal of soul searching over the past several days. Tally's outburst in the carriage, coming as it did after an admission of her love that had left him shaken and hungering for far more than her kiss, had baffled him. He understood her need to express the talent that fairly bubbled from her fingertips, but how could a woman who professed to love a man place ideas of a career ahead of a traditional marriage in which she would find fulfillment in providing a loving home for her husband and children?

Tally had compared her yearnings with those of his own. He surely had not been prepared to abandon his literary endeavors when he thought himself in love with Clea. He had not burdened her with them, of course; he had merely kept them a dark secret. Turning away from his writing would have been like severing a hand. He realized with some remorse, that the same must be true of Tally's drawing talent. Of course, he thought self-righteously, he had not asked her to give up her drawing. He had merely requested that she not accept remuneration, or allow sketches to be published for the whole world to gawp at. Was that so unreasonable? The next moment, he realized uncomfortably that he would never have been content, now that he had become a figure of some literary renown, to scribble little pieces for the sole edification of his nearest and dearest. No, he mused ruefully, one could talk of art for art's sake, but recognition of one's talent by the outside world was sweet.

Still, she needn't have ripped up at him. Was he some sort of monster that she could not have discussed the matter reasonably with him? It was not until some time later that the thought occurred to him that he had been speaking that night not with the rational, clear-thinking Tally that he knew and loved, but with a sensitive young woman who had just been through a shattering experience. Her nerves must have been rasped to threads, and the consuming embrace they had shared, as well as their declaration of love for each other had no doubt led to an understandable seesaw of emotions.

How could he, an acknowledged wordsmith whose experience with women was wide and invariably empathetic, have blundered so crudely?

Well, he thought fiercely, he had been granted a reprieve, and by the Lord Harry he would make the most of it. He would make Tally realize that she was more precious to him than anything else in the world, and if she wished to make a paying career of dancing in tights on the stage of the Pantheon Theater, so be it.

Thus, his first instinct as he saw her waiting for him in the mist, was to greet her with arms open and ready to envelop her in a welcoming embrace. He stopped short, however, on observing her definitely unloverlike mien, contenting himself with grasping both her cold hands in his.

Tally withdrew them hurriedly and brushed away from her cheek the feather that drooped disconsolately from her riding hat.

"I appreciate your meeting me so early, my lord. I have a matter of import to discuss with you which requires more privacy than we might be accorded at Richard and Cat's home."

Jonathan gazed down at her and smiled despite himself. "I take it I am still in your black books if I have once more been reduced to the status of 'my lord.'"

Tally flushed, but returned his gaze steadily.

"I have not asked you here to discuss our—our personal relationship—Jonathan. I'm afraid I have some very bad news."

As the two slowly paced the damp sweep of lawn, Tally told Jonathan of Crawshay's visit, and of his demands. At the end of her recitation, she turned to him and observed in dismay that his face had hardened, and the muscles in his lean jaw were tense.

"I cannot say that I am surprised," he said harshly, "I doubt that there is any form of perfidy to which Crawshay would not stoop. I just wish that I had impressed on him a little more thoroughly the unwisdom of his despicable little stratagems. How dare he threaten you! I believe I must have another little session with him."

"Jonathan!" cried Tally in consternation. "You're not—you must not punish him! It wouldn't take him five minutes to put two and two together. Then we would both be at his mercy!"

A taut silence stretched between them, until Tally saw with relief that the fire had faded from Jonathan's eyes. She continued in a calm voice.

"I have told you this only because I wish to assure you that, although my own name will become known as having been involved in the creation of *Town Bronze*, your own need not be revealed. I intend to remove myself from London, and thus will not be available for the prying and poking of the gossip mongers."

For a long moment, Jonathan stood silent, regarding her with his heart in his eyes. Then he reached very slowly to touch her cheek with one gloved finger.

"Oh, my little darling, what an ordeal you have been through."

Tally quivered at his touch and at the tenderness in his voice, but she forced herself to step away from him. She lowered her eyes lest he perceive the longing in them.

"Please," she murmured, almost panting with the effort it took not to lift her arms to him. "It is an ordeal that will soon be over."

She moved toward the place where she had left her little mare, Blossom, tethered. "I must go home now. I hope to catch Richard before he leaves for Whitehall. He must be apprised of Miles Crawshay's intentions."

She found her way blocked as Jonathan stepped lithely in front of her.

"We will go together, Tally, but I think we can take a moment to discuss you and me first."

He placed his hands lightly on her shoulders. "I was wrong, my darling," he said softly. "I will not ask you to give up what has become a brightly promising career. I see that to have asked such a thing of you was inexcusable."

Tally's eyes filled with tears, but she held herself rigid in his grasp. "I fear, my lord," she said in a controlled voice, "that I rather mistook my own emotions on the— the occasion of our last meeting. I must confess the events of the evening quite overset me, and I allowed myself to—that is, I behaved in a manner totally foreign to my nature. I would greatly appreciate it if you could contrive to forget what happened."

It had taken her hours last night to perfect that little speech, and now, regarding Jonathan, she was not at all sure it had met with success. She was quite sure that it had not, when instead of retreating in stoic acceptance as any gentleman of sensibility should have, he pulled her to him.

"Foreign to your nature, Lady Talitha?" he murmured, his breath warm on her cheek. "Would you have me believe that you are a milk and water miss?"

He brought his mouth down on hers in a kiss that spread a slow fire throughout her body. All her resolutions fled as though they had never been, and she pressed against him, reveling in the feel of his muscled hardness. Her arms wound around him, and her lips moved beneath his, opening in welcome acquiescence.

It was only when the sounds of an approaching group of riders sounded through the fog that Tally came to a sense of her surroundings. She stiffened in Jonathan's embrace, and he released her immediately. He retained her hands in his grasp, however, and stood smiling down into her eyes.

"Tell me again," he said unsteadily, "about your mistaken emotions. Tell me that you do not love me."

Tally's gaze, as she met his, was luminous. She shook her head, and tried to speak through the tears that gathered in her throat.

"I cannot—for I love you with all my heart, Jonathan, and that is precisely why I am leaving London. I cannot be with you—you must not be with me—when all the world turns its back on me."

Jonathan's expression grew stern. "Is that what this is all about?" he asked harshly. "Do you think I would be unwilling to face the consequences of Crawshay's poison? Don't you know that you mean more to me than the good will of what is so absurdly called the Polite World?"

"But, Jonathan . . ." began Tally.

"But, my love . . ." Jonathan drew a long breath, and suddenly assumed a more cheerful mien.

"As you were saying, we must intercept Richard before he leaves for Whitehall. We shall put him in possession of the facts, and then put our heads together in order to come up with something to spike Miles Crawshay's guns."

"No!" Tally put a hand against Jonathan's chest, as though to physically restrain him. "I will not have you involved in this. This is my problem, and I shall see it through myself."

As though she had not spoken, Jonathan swept the restraining hand into his own and planted a hurried kiss on the corner of her mouth.

"But, I am involved. You are mine now, to protect and cherish, and I intend to do both to the utmost of my ability. Besides, I am partly responsible for your predicament, you know. Yes, I am," he continued in response to her look of startled inquiry. "For if I had not convinced Mapes that you were the very person needed to bring Clifford and Clive to life, you would never have embroiled yourself in so much trouble by inflicting Granny Posey on an unsuspecting public."

With that, he swung a temporarily speechless Tally into her saddle and sprang to the back of his own mount.

Gathering up her reins, he led the way from the Park, a bewildered Jem bringing up the far rear.

Richard, intercepted as he was about to leave home, listened to their news with all the attention they could have wished. At the end of their stirring acocunt, however, his reaction was not in the least what they might have expected.

The three were ensconced in Richard's study. Richard sat at his desk, fingers steepled before him, gazing abstractedly into the empty air, as Tally and Jonathan watched him in growing puzzlement. At last, he raised his eyes, and, to their astonishment, broke into a peal of delighted laughter.

"Richard!" gasped Tally indignantly. "Have you gone mad—or did you not understand what we have just told you?"

"On the contrary, my dear," he replied. "You have just brought me the best news I have heard for many months."

His guests simply gaped at him in stunned incomprehension. Richard rose and began to pace slowly in the space behind his desk.

"It goes without saying, that what I am about to tell you must remain in this room." He continued after observing their assenting nods. "We at the Foreign Office have been interested for quite some time in Miles Crawshay's activities. He came to our attention some three years ago, after his return from the Peninsula. One began hearing of his heroic activities in the Battle of Corunna, which was odd, because the fellow was cashiered at the time for cowardice under fire. His unit came under heavy artillery fire and suffered severe casualties, while our lad himself was seen scuttling to the rear, leaving his men to face the enemy."

"But, he said he caught a ball in his shoulder!" exclaimed Tally.

"He did, indeed. In the back."

"But how could he have the effrontery to proclaim himself a hero?" asked Jonathan in a hard voice.

"That's just it, he never did. He would somehow manage to work the subject of his wound into conversation, always in modest but completely false terms. He is considered to be of good *ton*, of course, and who would doubt his word? It was his beautiful cousin, however, who seems to have actually spread the word of his supposed heroism."

Jonathan stiffened, and Tally could not forbear a small gasp.

"Clea!" she cried. "She will be devastated when she discovers that Miles is a traitor. She is—quite fond of him, I believe."

Jonathan snorted. Richard smiled faintly and glanced sharply at Jonathan.

"Cat pointed out to me an article in the *Morning Post* declaring your betrothal to Lady Bellewood at an end. I hope you will forgive me, old man, if I tell you that we are not particularly sorry to hear it, nor do you seem particularly brokenhearted over the split."

"No," replied Jonathan shortly. "The breakup was not precisely amicable, and, since, over the past several weeks, I have come to count you my friend, I will tell you that my—infatuation for Lady Belle died an unmourned death some time before the actual termination of the engagement."

"I see." Richard gave an odd little sigh. "I, too, have had some dealings with the lady and can understand your, er, disillusionment." He shot a minatory glare at Tally and hastily turned the subject.

"Getting back to Crawshay. While we were quite sure that he was acting as an agent for the French, we were unable to discover the identity of his contact, until, that is, a certain talented, but uncautious artist delivered him to us on a silver platter, or, rather, on a grimy sheet of drawing paper."

Tally leaped to her feet.

"My sketch of Miles and the man he was with at Limmer's!"

"Yes. The stranger was recognized as one Carlos Mendoza, supposedly the son of a Spanish nobleman. He runs a small import business based near Dover. We keep a routine surveillance on all such foreign merchants, but up till now, had never found reason to suspect him of anything beyond some very small-time smuggling. Your little sketch created quite a stir in our department, Tally."

"But why did you ask me to include it in my illustration?"

"Because I knew it would cause Crawshay and his contact some consternation, to say the least. We now believe that Crawshay works for Mendoza, who must have been highly upset to see his connection with Crawshay, whom he no doubt realizes is already under suspicion, made so public."

"Well," sighed Tally, "I'm pleased that your little problem seems to be solved, and I'm certainly more than willing to take every bit of credit for it, even though I was completely unaware of Miles's activities at the time. I wish I could say that it makes my having to leave London worthwhile, but"—her eyes brightned with unshed tears—"I'm afraid I just can't."

"Oh, but the problem is by no means solved," said Richard, startled. "What is all this about leaving town?"

"I told you, Richard. Once Miles discovers that I am not going to procure the information he wants, he will lose no time in broadcasting my dark secret all over town. I suppose I should have the fortitude to face down the snickers and the cuts direct, but I'm afraid I'm not made of such stern stuff."

"But your part in this is not over, Tally. Now that we know the target of Mendoza's current operation, we'll need your help to scoop the two of them up. We cannot arrest him until he accepts the papers from you, so you will have to meet him at the masquerade ball as ordered."

Chapter Twenty

Tally's startled gasp was covered by the sound of Jonathan's explosive "No!"

Richard turned a surprised gaze toward him, and Jonathan continued in a more reasonable tone.

"You cannot possibly be serious in proposing that Tally place herself in the hands of that bas—snake. I won't permit it."

Tally, who had been about to enter a strong caveat against Richard's proposal, suddenly found herself reversing her position. She lifted her brows and favored Jonathan with a frigid stare.

"I wish, my lord, that you would rid yourself of the notion that you have anything to do with the ordering of my life. Whether or not I choose to meet Miles Crawshay at Lady Crewell's ball is my decision."

Richard interrupted hastily as Jonathan frowned ominously and opened his mouth to speak.

"But you don't understand—either of you. Tally, you must know that I would never place you in any kind of jeopardy. When—that is, if, you appear on schedule at the ball, you will have lots of company. You will be surrounded by squads of government agents, and we will have more concealed in the area where you are to meet Miles. The moment you hand over the documents to him, he will be apprehended."

"But what if something goes wrong?" asked Jonathan, his dark brows still drawn together.

"We'll make sure that it doesn't. Not only will we have Tally surrounded, but we'll be watching Crawshay, as well. I think we can safely say that in a few days, Mr. Miles Crawshay will have been rendered a spent force."

"He will still be in a position to smear Tally's name

all over London. By the by, what information do these precious papers contain—if you can tell us?"

Richard sighed. "Only the names and locations of all the British agents in Austria, and the key to the codes currently being used by them in their dispatches."

"Whew!" whistled Jonathan softly. "What the French wouldn't give for that treasure trove!"

Richard grimaced. "Yes, Crawshay and Mendoza would be rich men if they could deliver it into the right hands. Ordinarily, I wouldn't keep such critical material at home, but recently I have been obliged to receive agents here at odd hours of the night, and I must have the list handy to verify their identities, and to decipher immediately the dispatches they bring."

After a moment of appalled silence, Jonathan continued briskly.

"At any rate, as I was saying, even after Crawshay is arrested, he will still be in a position to do Tally a great deal of damage. I should imagine that when he is brought down, he will lash out like the reptile he is."

"And don't you think," interposed Tally, "that Mendoza is also privy by now to my—artistic activities?"

"I wonder," mused Jonathan, "if it would not be possible to persuade those two gentlemen to forget what they know?"

"Are you suggesting violence to persons living on the King's mercy?" asked Richard in mock disapproval.

"Yes," Jonathan replied tersely.

"Oh, Jonathan," exclaimed Tally. "You must not, not for me. If you were to do such a thing, I don't think it would take Miles long to put two and two together and realize that you must be the author of *Town Bronze*."

Richard cleared his throat noisily.

"I hope you don't think I'm prying, but it seems to me there has been a pronounced scent of April and May in here since you two arrived into the room."

"Nothing gets by you Foreign Office chappies, does it?" Jonathan grinned. "You are right, of course, and you may wish us happy."

"No!" exclaimed Tally. "You may not! Jonathan, I cannot marry you while I have this—this cloud hanging over my head."

Jonathan's response to this was interrupted by the entrance of Cat, who swept into the room gowned in a walking dress. Observing the little group huddled in one corner of the study, her delicate brows rose in surprise.

"But what is this? Richard, I had thought you on your way out. Tally, why did you not tell me you had a visitor?" Her gaze dropped to where Tally's hand lay clasped in Jonathan's and her expression changed to one of gleeful surmise.

"Yes." Jonathan's grin widened. "You may wish us happy, Mrs. Thurston."

"Tally!" Cat squealed. "And you did not say anything?"

Tally snatched her hand away, and tears shone in her eyes.

"No, Cat—you are not to wish us happy." She twisted to face Jonathan, who reclaimed her slender fingers.

"Jonathan, I will not marry you. I cannot. I have explained this to you over and over."

Jonathan merely smiled and bent his smokey gaze to hers. His hand reached for hers, and he stroked the back of it with one finger, an activity that nearly destroyed the control Tally had been maintaining so rigidly.

"And I have explained to you over and over," Jonathan was saying, "that you are speaking nonsense. In a few short days, the man will no longer be a threat to you."

"Threat?" exclaimed Cat. "What in the world are you talking about?"

The three glanced at one another, and by unspoken consent, drew Cat into the room and apprised her of the circumstances at hand. It took her several moments of confused questions and infuriated animadversions on the character of Miles Crawshay before she settled in a chair to contribute her mite to the planning session.

"It seems to me," she commented, "that once Crawshay and his contact—Mendoza is it?—are arrested, you need only imprison them somewhere and keep them incommunicado. Unless they are possessed of magical powers, they will be effectively silenced."

Richard chuckled and said to Tally and Jonathan, "Did I not say she is a born conspirator?"

He drew his wife into the circle of his arm and planted a kiss on her cheek.

"There is just one problem with your otherwise eminently practical solution, my love," he continued. "We are not living in Spain or Russia. We civilized English do not keep our prisoners in isolated dungeons."

"More's the pity," muttered Jonathan.

Richard ignored the interruption.

"Crawshay will be allowed visits from counsel and assorted near and dear ones, allowing him ample opportunity to trumpet Tally's dark secret throughout the land, if he so chooses."

Tally had sat with her head bowed during this exchange, but at this, she lifted her eyes and spoke in a clear voice.

"We're talking treason here, and the first consideration must be the destruction of Miles's plans. Once he and his partner are brought to justice, we can return to the problem of my dark secret."

Three pairs of eyes swung to her with expressions varying from puzzlement to appreciation to glowering disapproval.

Cat opened her mouth to speak, but was forestalled by a heated outburst from Jonathan.

"Tally," he began angrily, "I can't let you—"

He stopped short as Tally raised her hand with calm authority.

"I appreciate your concern—all of you. But it is my decision, and you cannot gainsay the logic of my position. Crawshay must be stopped—no matter what the personal consequences to me."

The four sat for a long moment, gazing at each other in silence.

"Well, then," said Richard at last. "Let me get to Lord Whittaker about this and put our plan before him. Then we shall see."

Jonathan said nothing more, but a thoughtful expression crossed his lean features as he gazed at Tally.

Tally had often reflected that the behavior of the *beau monde* generally revealed its members to be a pack of bored, spoiled children, and nothing proved this theory more than a masquerade ball. She gazed around Lady Crewell's ballroom and watched as a portly Henry the Eighth preened himself before a sinuous Cleopatra. A

Chinese princess peered speculatively over her lacquered fan at a Roman centurion brandishing a pasteboard sword. Secure in their anonymity, and released from the rigid rules of propriety, a hundred pair of eyes conducted velvet flirtations through the slits of their masks.

Nowhere, however, amidst the fantastic assortment of plumed and glittering beings could Tally find the one figure she had been seeking since she had arrived over an hour ago.

She glanced at Jonathan, who stood close beside her. He had come to the ball dressed as a medieval knight, and in his close-fitting tunic and hose, his powerful frame showed to devastating advantage. He looked the very personification of heroic power and chivalry.

"I don't see Miles anywhere, do you?" she asked.

Jonathan turned an appreciative gaze to the diminutive figure before him. Tally was a tempting confection in layers of multicolored spangled gauze, which floated about her slim body in a dream representation of Titania. A silver filet had been threaded through her chestnut curls and fastened with a diamond crescent, borrowed from Cat. Her mask was a work of art, comprised of satin and brilliants curved in an upward sweep. Silver slippers, sprinkled with diamond dust completed the ensemble, and she shimmered with every movement, as though she had borrowed some of the fairy queen's magic as well as her name in order to flutter, suspended, among lesser mortals. She should not, thought Jonathan with savage tenderness, have to bear the burden of a nation of those slender shoulders.

"I would not be sorry if he didn't show up at all," he rasped. "Do you remember what you are to do?"

"I could scarcely have forgotten in the three minutes since the last time you asked me," Tally replied tartly. "I am not to allow myself to be alone with him until the time of the meeting. I am to notify you before I leave the ballroom to go to the meeting. I am not to enter the room until . . . oh!" Her face paled, and she dug her fingers into Jonathan's arm. "There he is! See? By the door? He must have just arrived."

Jonathan's eyes followed Tally's stricken gaze and came to rest on a tall, black-robed form at the other side of the ballroom. It was impossible to discern his features, for not only was he masked, but his face was almost entirely concealed in the shadow of his voluminous hood. He, too, glittered in the blaze from hundreds of candles, glancing in shafts from the silver symbols emblazoned on his cloak. But for all his magnificence, thought Tally, he was a creature of the dark.

Jonathan took her cold fingers in his own. "Are you sure you want to go through with this?"

Tally closed her eyes for a moment. "Of course, I don't want to go through with it! But, I must."

She shook herself and managed a shaky laugh.

"Just listen to me! You'd think I were going to fight a duel with him, when I simply have to hand him a few papers. Richard and his men will do the rest."

She glanced around the room, aware that not all the costumed and domino-clad guests strolling about the rooms were the bored party-goers they seemed. She thought of the men hidden even now in the small salon where she was to meet Miles in less than an hour. She knew there was no personal danger to her in the assignation that would take place shortly, but she could still look forward to it only with dread.

But, she thought wearily, what did it all matter? Despite Jonathan's insistence that they would face her exposure together, Tally had no intention of letting that happen. She had already suborned one of the Thurstons' footmen, a young man blushingly dedicated to her, into purchasing a ticket for her on the stage leaving for Cambridgeshire on the following day.

She had contracted with George Mapes to provide the illustrations for two upcoming publications, and after a great deal of sometimes acrimonious discussion, they had reached an agreement that Tally would conduct her dealings with the publisher via post.

Within a year or two, she reflected dismally, she would be financially independent. She could move out of Henry's household into her own establishment. Perhaps she would move to the Continent, as had other disgraced practitioners of the arts, such as Lord Byron. Perhaps . . . Her uncomfortable ruminations were cut short as she felt Jonathan stiffen beside her.

She looked up, startled, to find Merlin, in all his bewitching brilliance, standing before her.

He nodded silently to Jonathan and then turned to Tally. Even at this close range, she could not clearly discern his face, but the familiar mocking note in his voice identified him.

"How pleasant," purred Miles, "to find a fellow denizen of the enchanted realm. And such a charming representative, as well. May I have this waltz, Your Ethereal Majesty?"

Jonathan moved as though to intervene, and Tally hastily put out her hand to Miles.

"Of course, my lord Wizard," she said in a calm voice. The next instant she was whirling about the floor in the black velvet embrace of Miles Crawshay, leaving Jonathan watching uneasily from the perimeter.

For a time, there was little conversation between the two. Tally found that her distaste for her partner distracted her from the rhythm and beauty of the music, and several times Miles's soft chuckle sounded as she stumbled in a misstep.

"Really, my dear," he drawled. "I am not going to ravish you right here on Lady Crewell's dance floor, though the idea has a certain piquancy. Do you think you might relax just a fraction?"

Tally stiffened, and tried to keep the trembling that had started in the pit of her stomach from reaching her voice.

"I do not fear you, Mr. Crawshay."

"Do you not, my queen? How very unwise of you, for I assure you, I can be very dangerous. Do you have the papers with you?"

Tally had been conscious all night of the bulky packet that had been sewn into one of the lawyers of gauze that made up the skirt of her costume.

"Yes," she whispered through dry lips.

Tally sensed rather than saw the familiar, hateful smile that flickered in the hooded shadow before her.

"Very good. And you have not forgotten our little rendezvous upstairs later this evening?"

Unable to speak, Tally shook her head.

"Excellent. I shall see you there shortly. Do not fail me," he concluded dramatically.

As though Miles had planned it, the strains of the waltz

died away at that precise instant, and with a dazzling swirl of his enchanter's cloak, he was gone.

A moment later, Jonathan was at her side, and she pressed gratefully into the strength of his lean body.

"Are you all right, Tally?"

She raised her eyes to his and was warmed by the concern she found there. "Yes, yes of course. We spoke of the merest commonplaces. Except at the end," she added, forcing a laugh. "He became quite sinister as we finished our dance, implying doom and disaster to anyone trying to thwart his evil plans."

Jonathan instinctively rose to the balls of his feet in a boxer's stance, and his hands clenched into fists. He sent a savage glance after Crawshay and prevented himself with great difficulty from going after him. He felt utterly helpless at the moment. It was not an emotion with which he was familiar, and he found that he did not like it above half. He ached with the desire to protect this vital, vulnerable little creature who meant his life to him, and he could do nothing.

"Tally—my darling—it's not too late," he said urgently. "We can still slip away. Crawshay is not possessed of much physical courage, and I have little doubt I can persuade him of the unwisdom of smearing your name all over London. As far as putting an end to his little spy operation, now that Richard knows of his plans, he can surely figure out some other way to trap him."

The security of Jonathan's strength, and the temptation to accept his suggestion was almost overwhelming, but Tally steeled herself.

"No, Jonathan, it must be this way. Richard has been after Miles for too long to allow this chance to slip away. He must not be left at large for a second longer than necessary. Who knows what other irons he has in the fire right this minute? Just think of the damage he and that Mendoza person could inflict in even so much as a day."

At this point, a lanky pirate with drooping moustaches claimed her hand for the Boulanger, and Tally smiled brilliantly at Jonathan over her shoulder before floating off in a cloud of gauze on the pirate's bony arm.

The next half hour passed by in a blur, as Tally was claimed for one dance after another, until at last she found herself cast up from the sea of sporting merrymakers almost at the feet of Cat and Richard, garbed as gypsies, who were recouping their strength at the punch table.

"I saw you dancing with Miles Crawshay!" were Cat's first words, as she handed Tally an iced champagne cup. "What did he say? What did *you* say? Oh, Tally, are you sure you're up to this?"

Tally said nothing, merely shooting her friend a speaking glance. Cat drew a deep breath, glanced up at her husband, and laughed in self-deprecation.

"I must sound a perfect pea goose. Richard has assured me that you will be safer than houses when you go to meet Miles, but I must confess I am in a positive quake."

"And *I* must confess," replied Tally with a weak smile, "you've expressed my sentiments exactly."

She, too, raised her eyes to Richard's and that gentleman cleared his throat and put his hand to the gaudy scarf tied round his neck as though it had suddenly seen fit to strangle him.

"Both of you are being quite nonsensical," he said austerely. "We have had Miles under surveillance from the moment he left his lodgings this evening, and we have been watching Mendoza, as well. He has not left his house all day." He placed a hand lightly on Tally's shoulder, and his tone was serious. "You know I would not allow you to be placed in jeopardy." A twinkle suddenly appeared in his eye. "If anything were to happen to you, I shudder to think of the consequences to my marriage."

"How can you joke about such a thing?" asked Cat, her huge golden earrings atremble. "Now, tell me again, about the men who are watching Tally, and the others who will leap out and bring Miles Crawshay to justice. I do think—"

But Cat was forced to leave her sentence unfinished, as a tall gentleman in an olive green domino halted before the group and diffidently requested Tally's hand for the next dance.

Tally opened her mouth to refuse, but her gaze was caught by Miles's glittering black robes gliding silently through the throng on the other side of the room like a storm cloud intruding on a children's picnic. She shivered instinctively. No, she had a half an hour before she need confront Miles and his perfidy. Until then, she would try to enjoy herself.

She smiled a farewell to her friends and moved into the rhythm of a sprightly waltz on the arm of the green domino.

Try as she might, however, she could not quell the panic rising in her throat at the thought of the rendezvous that was drawing nearer by the second. Nothing could possibly go wrong, she assured herself. The next second she thought, but what if something goes wrong?

She was forced to smile at herself, and her partner bent his head questioningly. Guiltily, for she had not had two words to say to the gentleman in the green domino, she turned her smile on him and uttered an inconsequential remark about the quality of the orchestra. He mouthed an appropriate response, and as the music began to die away, she looked around for Jonathan. At that moment, to her astonishment, the tall gentleman, who had been holding her so respectfully during the dance, suddenly tightened his grip on her and moved swiftly into a small, dark corridor leading from the ballroom.

Tally went rigid with shock, and the next instant she began to struggle. She opened her mouth to scream, but instantly a hand was clamped over her mouth. She twisted so violently that her mask was torn from her face, to be trampled underfoot.

Swiftly, the man dragged her along the winding corridor, until he reached a door set deep into the wall. Wrenching it open, he thrust Tally inside a small, dark room.

Chapter Twenty-One

Miles Crawshay's eyes shone with mockery, and his laugh was cool and derisive as he turned the key in the lock behind him.

"I hope you don't mind, my dear. I rescheduled our appointment. I apologize for startling you, but, you see, I have grown wary over the years, and, while I am sure you would not betray my innocent trust, I feel it is better—much better—to be safe than sorry. I do so want this little interview to be strictly *entre nous.*"

He removed his hand from her mouth, and Tally wiped it vigorously to remove the musky taste of him. The room in which they stood was small and bare, except for a few pieces of discarded furniture, obviously left there for storage. A single candle burned feebly on an old commode set in one corner. Tally's first instinct was to flee, but she was still held in Crawshay's grip. In the next instant, she realized with a sickening lurch of her heart, that it would ruin everything if she were to make an effort to escape. Crawshay would perceive immediately that he had been betrayed, and all the plans that had been so carefully laid would come to naught.

"But . . . but . . ." she quavered. "I saw you—just now—across the room! That is . . ."

His fingers slid caressingly over her hand as he released her, and his lips drew back in a pleased smile.

"I am a man of some agility, but, of course I cannot be in two places at once. In order to assure any, er, interested observers that I was still safely moored to the dance floor, I merely passed my very noticeable costume along to a gentleman hired specifically for the purpose. No doubt even the perspicacious Lord Chelmsford believes that I am at this moment sipping punch in full view of the assembled merrymakers."

Tally's forehead creased worriedly as she considered this to be probably all too true. How in the world was she to convey to Jonathan that everything had gone terribly awry? And Richard! He had probably already made his way upstairs to that little salon at the other end of the house. How would . . . ."

Her panicky ruminations were interrupted as Miles laid his hand on her arm. She jerked away instinctively from his touch, and his eyes glittered dangerously.

"The papers," he said softly. "Where are they?"

Silently, Tally tore the little packet from their loosely stitched hiding place in her skirt and handed them to Miles. She prayed she was not making a terrible mistake in turning over documents of such importance to him. There was no one to stop Crawshay from simply walking away with them. She must manage to raise an alarm— but how? She could not escape from a locked room, and there was little likelihood of the servants' coming to this remote section of the great town house. All would be occupied among the noise and the revelry far away. She began to look around surreptitiously for a weapon.

Crawshay reached eagerly for the papers, and his smile broadened as he examined them.

"Excellent, my dear," he breathed exultantly. "These will bring me a fortune. You have done well—and in such an excellent hand, even though you were obviously hurrying at your work."

He bent on her that feral smile which she had grown to hate, and she assumed an expression which she hoped combined outrage with sullen fear.

"Of course, I was in a hurry. I was terrified the whole time that someone in the household would catch me at my work. It was cold in Richard's study, too," she added peevishly. "Now you have what you wanted. Please let me go, for I should not want anyone to find us together. Being seen alone in your company would ruin me."

She turned toward the door, but to her dismay, Crawshay maintained his grip on her arm.

"I do like a female with spirit. How fortunate that we are to have opportunity to become better acquainted."

Tally stared at him coldly.

"I cannot conceive what you are talking about. If you think I shall ever—"

She stopped abruptly as a soft knock sounded on the door. Miles released her and strode to admit a female figure muffled in a cloak of deep red silk. She slid into the room and turned to Crawshay, one hand fluttering up to touch his cheek.

"Oh, Miles, I couldn't wait any longer. Is it done? Can we leave now?"

Tally stared in puzzlement as the woman moved into a pool of candlelight. It was the Chinese princess she had seen earlier in the evening! As Tally watched in growing confusion, slender fingers reached up to remove mask and dark wig.

Tally drew in a sharp breath. "Lady Belle!" she cried, in stunned disbelief.

Clea Bellewood whirled at the sound, looking equally astonished, and none too pleased. "Miles!" she gasped. "What on earth is this—this creature doing here? You were supposed to return her to the ballroom once she gave you the documents, were you not?"

Miles dropped a kiss on her rouged cheek.

"Patience, my love," he murmured soothingly. "I shall explain all."

"But, I don't understand!" Tally cried. "Lady Bellewood, you cannot be—that is—are *you* part of this—wickedness?"

Clea's wide blue gaze was cold and steady as an alpine wind.

"Wickedness is a relative term, don't you agree? One does what is necessary."

"But, this is treason! Surely, you would not . . ."

But Clea had already turned back to Crawshay, and it was as though Tally had ceased to exist.

"You see," continued Crawshay, "Mendoza feels it would be better if we take our little conspirator"—he nodded at Tally—"away with us, so there will be no chance of her raising an alarm. That is why I brought her to this room on the ground floor. As you will observe"—he moved to draw aside a curtain—"there is a door here, which leads directly outside to a side street, where I have a coach waiting."

He glanced around expansively, as though expecting applause for the cleverness of his arrangements.

Suddenly cold, Tally glanced fearfully first at Clea,

then at Miles. "What do you mean, take me away? Where are you going? And why must I go with you?"

Almost simultaneously, Clea spoke in a rasping tone. "But I do not wish her to accompany us! Whoever heard of taking a chaperon on an elopement?"

"Elopement!" gasped Tally.

By now, a somewhat harassed expression had settled on Miles's features. He moved to a nearby table, evidently a refugee from the school room, for it was covered with old slates and chalk. Brushing these aside, he set the documents down and lifted his hands in a placating gesture to both women.

"If I could have a moment, ladies."

He turned to Tally. "It's very simple, my dear—that is, Lady Talitha," he hastily corrected himself at the sound of a hissing intake of breath from Clea. "Lady Bellewood and I have decided to elope to the Continent."

Clea preened, while Tally simply gaped at the pair.

"You see," he continued, an edge creeping into his voice, "it has become obvious that my, er, covert activities have come to the attention of the authorities. Now, with the appearance of your clever little sketch in that clever little book, I fear the connection between myself and my partner, a certain Señor Mendoza, has been discovered. Mendoza feels that our operation is now in such jeopardy that it must be discontinued.

"Meanwhile, the love of my life"—he indicated Clea with an ironic gesture—"has decided that England no longer holds any charms for her. It does, however, contain an increasingly vocal set of creditors. Thus, our decision to take up life abroad. In a few moments, we shall depart for Dover, where Mendoza will meet us aboard one of his boats. We shall then all three sail for Calais."

Tally's heart dropped to the toes of her silver slippers at these words. She assumed an expression of petulant dismay. "But what has all this got to do with me?" she whined.

"Yes, I think I'd like to hear about that, too," Clea chimed in, her blue eyes blazing incongruously in their painted Oriental delineation.

"Mendoza feels that Lady Talitha is a threat; that she must not be allowed to go free until we are well away. I do apologize, my dear." Crawshay bent a bland gaze on Tally. "The plan is to bring you along to our rendez-vous point. We will leave you on the remote stretch of beach from which we shall embark."

Tally listened to this recital in growing horror. The picture was growing more disastrous by the moment. Once more she tried to collect her whirling thoughts into a coherent strategy.

"Surely you don't believe you can get away with this?" she gasped.

She was startled by the sound of Clea's silvery laugh.

"But, of course we will. We are going to sail away on Carlos Mendoza's lovely yacht, and when we get to Calais, we will be met by a coach and four."

She turned to Miles and favored him with a winsome smile.

"And with the money we get for the documents, Miles is going to buy us a chateau, aren't you, darling?"

Miles bowed. "Where we will live happily ever after, my princess, in a castle filled with servants and silk settees—and trinkets to replace the ones you were forced to sell."

Tally stared, appalled. "How can you talk of castles and chateaux," she cried. "You have both betrayed your country!"

There was an uncomfortable silence, as Clea's gaze fell to her embroidered silk slippers, and Miles shrugged awkwardly. He straightened then, and scooped up the papers once more.

"We have wasted enough time," he growled. He reached once again for Tally and drew from his waistcoat a small, silver pistol.

"My apologies once again, little Mouse, but you must see that at this point I can take no chances. Please be assured," he continued with murderous softness, "that if you so much as open your enchanting little mouth before we reach the carriage, I shall not hesitate to use this."

He gestured with the pistol and drew her toward the door leading to the outside. He ushered Clea outside and then turned to push Tally ahead of him.

Again, Tally knew a moment of panic. There seemed to be no hope now of alerting Jonathan or Richard or any of the agents who were lurking about in all the wrong places. Her mind raced in ever narrowing circles as she considered her options. There was to be no miracle; no Jonathan rushing to her rescue; no government agents bursting onto the scene. England was about to lose a critical phase in the war with Napoleon, and there seemed to be nothing she could do.

She peered into the gloom ahead of her, where Clea was making her way to the street. Crawshay's fingers bit deep into the flesh of her arm.

Tally arranged her features in an expression of abject submission. She caught at his sleeve, causing some of the chalk pieces on the schoolroom table to fall to the floor.

"Please, Miles!" she sobbed. "I did everything you asked, and you know I wish only to keep my secret safe. I am not a threat to you. Please!"

She shuffled her feet in agitation, leaving a small pile of crumbled chalk where she stood. In a swift motion, she slipped her little pearl ring from her finger and dropped it to the floor, where it lay gleaming atop the soft white particles.

Miles chuckled. "There, there, sweetheart. Despite your tribulations, you can take comfort in the knowledge that when you do return to London, your reputation as a proper young lady will be untarnished, for soon I shall be out of gossip range. No one will ever know of your scandalous artistic endeavors."

He pushed her unceremoniously into the street. Ahead, Clea uttered a contemptuous sniff.

"We shall see about her reputation when she comes limping home tomorrow in a torn masquerade costume on the back of a drover's cart. Not that there can be much left of her supposed virtue after weeks of traipsing through the back alleys of London, dressed in filthy rags, plying her disgraceful trade!"

Crawshay snickered again and bent to whisper moistly in Tally's ear. "She has a point, love; perhaps you should come to Calais with us. A *ménage à trois* might have its possibilities, don't you think?"

Instantly, Clea was upon them. She whirled on Crawshay and caught his sleeve in fingers that curled like rakes. "Leave her alone, Miles!" she screeched. "I have not bartered my soul and endangered my neck to share you with this scrawny little drab!"

Crawshay smiled insultingly.

"It rankles, does it, pet? The possibility of having two men stolen out from under your lovely nose in the space of a fortnight by the same little charmer? No, no, my dear." He waved the packet of documents admonishingly. "You have treated us to enough of your temper for one evening."

Clea stood for a moment in wordless fury before turning abruptly.

Crawshay's lips curved in a thin smile as, still with those appallingly critical papers tucked casually under his arm, he brushed Tally's cheek with the barrel of the pistol and drew her through the door.

The carriage stood waiting in the lamplight, and the coachman had already taken his place, with reins in hand. With a murmured word of instruction to make haste, Miles bundled Tally inside the coach. In the next instant, the vehicle sprang into motion, and with a clatter of harness and a snap of the whip, they were underway.

Upstairs, Jonathan prowled the dance floor in growing uneasiness. It had been a good five minutes since he had seen Tally, and now he searched in vain for her gauzes and shining filet. His glance flicked across the room to a dark, glistening figure, deep in conversation with a sprightly Columbine.

A moment later, he spied Richard entering the ballroom from an ornate doorway that led to the upper corridors of the house. In answer to his signal, Richard approached quickly.

"What is it?" he asked anxiously. "Where's Tally?"

"That's exactly what I was going to ask you. She danced off with some fellow in a green domino, and I lost sight of her. Now, I can't find her."

"Is Crawshay—"

"He's still here. He's over there flitting about like a diamond-studded bat, so there's—" Jonathan stopped abruptly, his eyes narrowed. "Wait a minute!"

He strode across the floor, a puzzled Richard in his wake. Upon reaching the gentleman in the spangled cloak, Jonathan spun him around, causing the man's hood to fall to his shoulders. He stood thus revealed as a dark-haired stranger.

Gripping his arm, Jonathan wrenched the man into

one of the many alcoves lining the ballroom. "Where is Crawshay?" he growled.

The make-believe wizard studied the pair with a carefully blank expression. "Who?" he inquired politely.

"Miles Crawshay," repeated Jonathan, his stance acquiring a menacing aspect. "Tell me where he is, you bastard, or . . ."

The imposter yawned and studied his fingertips. "Don't know any Miles Crawshay, and I—aagh!"

This last came as Jonathan grappled the stranger around the neck and twisted his arm.

"It would give me a great deal of pleasure to break your neck," panted Jonathan softly.

"I think I'd take him seriously if I were you," added Richard meditatively. "Fellow has a deuce of temper. Better tell him what he wants to know."

One more upward thrust on his arm convinced the imposter of the benefits of cooperation.

"I d-don't know anything," he choked. "I've done odd jobs for Crawshay before—nothing anyone could take exception to, of course—and this time I was told just to weasel into the house, meet up with Crawshay at eleven-thirty, and exchange my green domino for his mask and cloak and hood."

"But what's he up to?" grated Jonathan, increasing the pressure on the man's arm.

As Crawshay's confederate increased the volume of his protest, Richard lay an admonishing hand on Jonathan's arm.

"Leave be, Chelmsford. He can tell us nothing more, and we're wasting time."

At this, Jonathan released the man's arm with a suddenness that caused that gentleman to lose his balance. They left him sprawled on the floor of the little alcove, gasping and massaging the offended appendage.

"I last saw Tally over there," said Jonathan urgently. "Over there by that door. She and—oh, God, if I'd only known—she and Crawshay were dancing, and as I watched, another couple moved into my line of sight. When I looked again, they were both gone."

They had by now reached the door pointed out by Jonathan. Opening it, they found nothing beyond but darkness. Wrenching a candle from a nearby wall sconce, Jonathan led the way into the corridor.

"Look!" he gasped, pointing.

There, on the floor, lay a mask, made all of silver satin and encrusted with brilliants.

"There must have been a struggle," said Richard quietly.

Jonathan did not respond, but picked up the mask and simply stared at it, as though it might speak.

"But, why?" continued Richard. "Why would Crawshay go to all this trouble to abduct Tally from the dance floor, when he was due to meet her in half an hour?"

"Because," whispered Jonathan through stiff lips, "he possesses a great deal more cunning than any of us gave him any credit for. Come." He darted down the corridor. "Pray God we're not too late. If he's taken her away . . ."

Richard started and plunged after him. "Wait! Chelmsford, wait! There's something I must tell you. Something you must know!"

Chapter Twenty-Two

For several minutes after the coach lurched into action, Tally remained motionless, crouched in the corner where she had been flung by Miles. She could not seem to think beyond the cloud of despair that surrounded her. She had failed in preventing Miles from leaving Crewell House with the papers, and now he was on his way to the Continent with them.

Her glance flicked to Clea, sitting motionless, her eyes closed and her head resting against the squabs of the carriage. She looked as perfect as a marble sculpture, and, thought Tally, she was surely as coldhearted. There would be no help from that quarter.

The speed at which the carriage raced through the darkened streets did not make for a comfortable ride, and Tally's head throbbed with the beginning of a motion-induced headache. To divert her mind, she thought back to the little ring she had left on the pile of chalk rubble and smiled bitterly. What had made her think that anyone seeing it—assuming anyone was liable to find it at all—would be reminded of the chalk cliffs of Dover? She shrugged her shoulders wearily. It had been an idea born of desperation, and was no doubt, as most such inspirations must be, doomed to failure.

The coach, having clattered across London Bridge, was already passing through the outskirts of Southwark. In a few minutes more, they had reached open country. Their speed increased, and Tally watched dismally as moon-silvered fields flashed past her view from the window.

She turned her head and cast a surreptitious glance at Crawshay. He had apparently fallen into a light doze, his head rocking to the motion of the speeding coach. In his lap lay the packet of papers, and the silver pistol drooped from his fingers.

Hope surged in Tally's breast, and she lifted her hand toward the little pistol. Crawshay did not turn his head, but his grip on the gun tightened, and his voice sounded in a lazy chuckle. "Not a good idea, Mouse. As I told you before, you will have to content yourself with the thought that soon you will be returning to your home in London, your anonymity intact."

Clea suddenly jerked to life, and she uttered a burst of high, shrill laughter. "I think not, my lady!"

Tally stared at her in consternation. Clea settled back against the squabs and returned her gaze with a spiteful glare.

"When you return to London, Lady Talitha Burnside, on the back of that drover's cart, you will find yourself rejected by anyone with any pretension to gentility. You will be the butt of coarse jokes and the subject for gossiping tattlemongers, because, you see," she finished in a burst of venom, "by this time next week, your shoddy little secret will be spread all over London!"

"What?!"

Tally's voice trembled with the force of the shock she had sustained. She felt physically bruised by Clea's tirade and cast an anguished glance at Miles.

"You promised me! How could you . . . ?"

Crawshay turned to Clea, his eyes glittering in amusement. "What have you done, wicked one?"

Clea tossed her head in malicious pleasure. "Just before I left my lovely house for the last time, I sat down and wrote a note to—" she cast a sidelong glance at Miles—"to one of my dearest friends, describing how our charming, witty little Lady Talitha has betrayed all her friends in the Polite World by holding them up to ridicule in that filthy piece of trash, *Town Bronze*."

She leaned forward, her beautiful face contorted with rage.

"Jonathan will repudiate you utterly, you sneaking little bitch. Did you really think you could appropriate my fiancé?"

She breathed deeply and settled back into her seat. "My only regret is that I will not be around to help him pick up the pieces, for surely you know that I have only to beckon and he will come running to my side."

Such were the emotions churning inside Tally as Clea's

lips curled in a satisfied smile, that for several moments she could not speak. To be sure, her own problems were trivial compared to the catastrophe that was about to overtake the British Foreign Office, but as she considered the ruins of her life, a small sob escaped her.

Silence settled upon the occupants of the carriage, and for the next several miles, all that was to be heard was the sound of horses' hooves at full gallop, the raucous jingling of harnesses, and the increasingly loud creak of strained leather as the vehicle bowled along the road.

Tally's thoughts tumbled in frantic chaos. She could see no way out of her predicament. There was no possibility of rescue; she knew that now. Nor could she hope that an opportunity would arise for escape with or without the papers before she found herself stranded in sandy isolation on some remote shore.

She peered out the window, but in the thin light of a clouded moon, she could perceive nothing beyond the fact that the coach was fairly flying along the Dover Road, sometimes veering dangerously close to the ditches bordering the thoroughfare.

She nudged a somnolent Crawshay and pointed out this fact to him, but received only a cold chuckle for her trouble.

"The coach travels in haste at my orders, Mouse. We must reach our destination before the tide goes out, and I whiled away too much time at Crewell House. Be assured, my coachman knows what he is about."

He yawned and closed his eyes once more. Tally's eyes were drawn to the packet of papers resting on his lap. If only . . .

As though at last heeding her prayers, Providence chose that moment to intervene. The coach careened around a curve, and passengers were thrown violently against its side. Clea screeched, and Miles cursed as he scrambled for purchase against the vehicle's upholstery, clutching the packet against his chest.

The next moment, the coach jarred to a wrenching stop, and the scream of panicked horses filled the night. The coach tilted crazily, so that Tally found herself lying on her back, pinned against the door by a hysterical Clea, while Crawshay's curses mounted in violence. A slap sounded, and a yelp from Clea.

"Miles!" she cried out in a sobbing gasp. "You struck me!"

Crawshay vouchsafed no reply, but grunted and swore himself to an upright position. He waved the pistol threateningly at Tally as he made his way past her to the door on the other side of the carriage, now open to the sky.

"Stay here, and don't move," he snarled, "while I see what's toward."

Tally observed, to her dismay, that he maintained his grasp on the documents as he scrambled from the coach. In a moment, she heard voices as Crawshay berated his coachman. She glanced at Clea, who still lay crumpled in an awkward heap at the bottom of the coach.

Cautiously, Tally peered through the door from which Crawshay had just made his exit. She could see him wildly gesticulating as he continued to vent his spleen on the hapless driver.

There!

Crawshay set the papers down on a rock—probably the one which had precipitated the wreck—and he moved to assist the coachman. Apparently, the carriage was undamaged. Two wheels remained in the road, while those on the other side had settled in the ditch. The horses strained mightily at the coachman's command, and it appeared that the vehicle would be shortly righted. The only light on the scene was provided by the coach lamps and by the dim rays of the lantern held by the coachman on the other side of the carriage. Another sidelong glance at Clea indicated that the countess had fallen into a half swoon, for she had neither spoken beyond a crying whimper, nor attempted to right herself.

Gathering up the tattered remnants of her gauze skirts, Tally lifted herself silently through the coach door. Without a sound she dropped to the ground and made her way swiftly to where the packet of documents lay on the rock. She could not believe her good fortune! Crawshay's attention was still concentrated wholly on the struggling horses.

In another second, she had the documents in her hand and was racing across the road to the cover of a nearby spinney.

"Dear Lord," she prayed silently as she ran. "Please don't let him notice! Just another few seconds—please!"

But Providence had apparently withdrawn its hand. A sudden shout sounded behind her, and a thundering exhortation to stop. Her heart felt as though it would explode as she attempted to run faster.

Suddenly, a shot cracked through the night air, and a spurt of flame made itself felt along Tally's shoulder. She staggered with the shock and pain of it and fell to the ground. She heard the sound of running feet and tried to rise, but could not summon the strength. Trembling, she waited for what was to come.

What came was an unexpected grunt from Crawshay. Dazed, Tally looked up to see a dark figure standing in the road. At his feet lay a second form, motionless in the dust.

"Tally! Tally, are you all right?"

The sound of Jonathan's voice was the most beautiful music she had ever heard, and she cried out in relief. "Yes! That is—yes, mostly. Oh, Jonathan, I knew you'd come. But, watch out—Miles has a gun!"

"Not anymore," was the terse reply, and then Jonathan was bending over her. She winced as he gathered her into his arms.

"You *are* hurt! My God, the bastard shot you! Where—?"

"Hush, love. I think the bullet barely grazed me. See, there's not even any blood to speak of, although I fear Queen Titania has made her last appearance, at least in this costume."

Jonathan drew her gently to her feet.

"And see," she continued excitedly. "I have the papers! I was just trying to figure out how to burn them in the coachman's lantern when you came. Oh, Jonathan, I was so frightened!"

"Ah, yes, the papers," murmured the viscount softly. He took them from her, then handed her the little pistol, which she received as though she had been given a live firecracker. He led her back to where a groaning Miles Crawshay lurched to his feet.

From his pocket, Jonathan drew a pistol, somewhat larger than the one Crawshay had carried. He leveled it at the befuddled creature before him, and Tally gasped.

"Jonathan! No! You must not! He is not worth it!"

He paused, and after a heartstopping moment, he spoke in a voice Tally had never heard before.

"No, most definitely not worth swinging for—but, by God a bullet between the eyes is a much kinder fate than he deserves."

Crawshay uttered a wordless whimper and dropped to the ground again. Jonathan nudged him ungently with the toe of one boot and urged him once more to his feet. In a moment, the incongruous trio had made its way back to the carriage.

The horses had brought the carriage out of the ditch, and the coachman now stood at their heads with his mouth open. Jonathan, his back to the open coach door, gestured curtly with the pistol, and the coachman leaped to stand beside Crawshay, his hands in the air.

"Jonathan!" called Tally, intending to warn him of Clea's presence in the coach. Even as she spoke, however, Lady Belle appeared in the doorway, a heavy, ornate dressing case lifted in her hands.

Before Tally could form a warning, the countess brought the case crashing down on Jonathan's head, and with a groan, he crumpled to the ground and lay still.

The next few moments passed in a blur of confusion for Tally. Crawshay uttered a shrill cry of triumph and bent to snatch the papers from the unconscious figure. In a single movement, he scooped up the pistol Jonathan had dropped as he fell.

Tally cried out in horror as Crawshay pointed the gun at Jonathan's head, and at the sound, Crawshay jerked spasmodically. Clea had sunk back in another swoon, her handkerchief pressed against her lips. Without thinking, Tally lifted the hand in which she still carried the pistol Jonathan had given her.

Crawshay relaxed and allowed a faint smile to cross his lips. "Put that down, Mouse, before you hurt yourself."

His smile phased into a contemptuous smirk, and he turned his attention once more to Jonathan. Once again, he leveled the pistol at the unconscious man before him.

For Tally, the universe seemed to shrink to the circle of reflected moonlight from the barrel of the gun. In an almost reflexive gesture, she fired, and with a howl,

Crawshay grabbed his shoulder, dropping the gun in a spasm of agony.

The coachman, suddenly galvanized to action, ran instinctively for his perch atop the carriage. Crawshay, after a single, fulminating glance at Tally, hurled an oath and leaped for the coach. He slammed the door as the vehicle surged into motion.

Tally sank to the ground at Jonathan's side. She scarcely noticed when the carriage rattled away and was soon lost to sight.

She lifted Jonathan against her breast and cradled his head in her arms, murmuring words of endearment which she realized were perfectly useless. To her vast relief, he began to stir within a few moments.

His first action when he at last opened his eyes was to draw Tally's head down to his for a long, blissful kiss, and it was only with the noisy approach of a group of horsemen that she freed herself from his dizzying embrace.

Richard's voice called out, and thankfully, she turned back to the man on the ground.

"Jonathan!" she gasped. "Are you really all right? I was afraid she had split your skull!"

Reluctantly, Jonathan released her and struggled to a sitting position. He probed the back of his head gingerly. "Well, I think I'll wait a few more days before engaging in any sparring matches, but I believe I'll survive. I only wish I had the opportunity to do just a little more damage to Crawshay."

He peered into the darkness into the direction taken by the departed coach, and, with a groan, Tally jumped to her feet.

"Oh, no!" she wailed. "How could I have forgotten? Jonathan, they have the papers! They've gotten away with them!"

Chapter Twenty-three

Tally whirled and ran to where the men were dismounting from their horses.

"No!" she cried wildly to Richard. "Do not dismount! Miles Crawshay—and Clea—have escaped, and they have the papers—all of them. You must go after them!"

To her anguished frustration, Richard paid no attention, but ran toward her with outstretched arms.

"Tally! Good God, are you all right? And Jonathan?"

"Yes!" She wriggled impatiently from his embrace. "Didn't you hear what I said? They've stolen the documents!"

To her outraged astonishment, Richard merely clucked at her and drew her over to where Jonathan had now regained his feet. The two men shook hands awkwardly.

"A near thing, I take it," murmured Richard.

"As near as I'd care to see it," Jonathan replied with a rueful chuckle. "I suppose I should come up with something clever like 'All's well that end's well', but my aching head doesn't quite agree with that statement. Have you any idea what it takes to maintain a civil conversation with a person who wishes you nothing but ill, all the while knowing that any second you are going to be knocked senseless from behind?"

Tally's eyes widened.

"You knew Clea was in the carriage?" she gasped.

"I knew."

"But—but, I don't understand!" Tally exploded, fairly dancing in her wrath. "What's the matter with you two? Don't you . . ."

The eyes of the two met over Tally's head, and a rueful glance flashed between them.

"Tally," interrupted Jonathan. "It's all right. They don't have the documents."

"Yes, they do!" she cried, wringing her hands and fingering the place where her ring should have been. "I gave Miles the papers! I tried to take them back, but I failed!"

She gave a despairing sob, and her shoulders slumped.

Jonathan grasped her and shook her gently. "Tally—my darling, listen to me. They do not have the real papers."

"Real papers?" she echoed stupidly.

Richard drew close to them.

"The papers taken by Crawshay and Mendoza were plants, Tally. They were false from top to bottom."

Tally's gaze swung between the two men in growing bewilderment. "But—but Miles told me he would be able to tell if I tried to fool him."

"And so he would have," responded Richard cheerfully, "if *you* had tried to falsify the code key. However, I am a little more familiar with the material than you, and the documents I created for his perusal were skewed just enough to make them completely useless to the other side, while still appearing to be the real thing. More than that," he added in satisfaction, "they could be downright disastrous if the Frenchies try to put any of their shiny new information to use."

"That's why," interjected Jonathan, "I was forced to allow my ex-beloved to bludgeon me from behind. We had to get the papers back into Crawshay's hands."

"But why didn't you tell me?" The question was fairly ripped from Tally's lips.

This time the glances exchanged by Richard and Jonathan were sheepish, and they shuffled uneasily.

"Jonathan didn't know," said Richard, "until to-night—after you disappeared. It was for your own good," added Richard hastily, as Tally rounded on them furiously.

"My own good! I was nearly k-killed trying to retrieve those stupid papers. I—I nearly killed a man because of them!"

The two men stared, appalled, at the little whirlwind raging before them.

Richard put his hand on her arm in a placating gesture, but she shook it off angrily. After a moment, however, when some of the shock had worn off, Tally said gruffly, "Well, what?"

He sighed and shifted uncomfortably. "We—at the Foreign Office—were concerned that something might go wrong, and we were trying for some sort of contingency plan. We—that is, I thought that it would be better if you did not know, so that you would not inadvertently give the plan away. In—in the heat of the action, so to speak," he finished in a perspiring rush of words.

"Of course," said Tally in a voice of studied calm. "You could not be expected to place your reliance on a poor, weak female, who as everyone knows, might tend to sink into an attack of the vapors at some critical moment."

"Richard meant well, Tally," said Jonathan quietly. "He was acting from a typical male viewpoint—as I have done myself in my misguided past. He believed he was protecting you."

"And," pointed out Richard, "if all had gone according to plan, you would have been none the wiser. Not," he added hastily, "that makes my actions any less, er, regrettable."

Tally looked from one to the other of them and sighed heavily. "I am still angry—very angry, but I am too tired to continue this discussion. Please"—she lifted her arms to Jonathan—"take me home."

He lifted her tenderly into the saddle of one of the horses tethered nearby and swung himself up behind her. Richard also mounted, and the party started at a leisurely pace back to London. Tally's eyes closed, and she allowed herself the supreme luxury of leaning back into Jonathan's arms. Despite herself, she reveled in the security and warmth she felt there. The steady thud of his heart sounded in her ears, and she curled contentedly into his embrace.

In a few moments, her curiosity got the better of her, and she lifted her head. "But how did you know where to find me?" she asked.

Jonathan chuckled deep in his throat. "Your stratagems were successful, my darling. We puzzled over that pile of chalk dust for some time. We knew you must be trying to tell us something, but it took awhile to make the leap from slate boards to the white cliffs of Dover.

Oh, yes"—he paused, fishing in his waistcoat pocket.
"Your ring, madame."

"Oh, Jonathan. Thank you! I thought I'd never see it
again."

She lifted her hand so that he could place it on her
finger.

Richard now took up the thread. "You see, we had
no idea that Crawshay planned to leave the country after
stealing the papers, since his usual pattern was apparently to pass information along to Mendoza, who then
carried it abroad. However, one of my men hurried in
to report that Mendoza had left his home in a traveling
carriage, heading at a smart pace toward London Bridge.
It was then that we realized a sea voyage must be in the
offing. Thanks to your clever message, we realized the
embarkation point must be Dover."

"It did not take us long," Jonathan continued, "to
catch up with Crawshay's coach, but we dared not approach for fear of endangering you further."

"Our first piece of luck came when the coach went off
the road." Richard smiled. "When you came tumbling
out, we couldn't contain Jonathan. Before I could stop
him, he was loping off cross-country, pistol in hand like
a bandit of Señor Mendoza's native land. If he had been
spotted, Crawshay could have picked him off like a
spring turkey."

Tally tightened her grip on Jonathan's coat sleeve and
smiled mistily at him. Then she straightened abruptly as
a thought struck her.

"But tell me how you knew about Clea?"

"Ah, yes, the lovely Lady Belle," mused Jonathan.
"That was the hard part. I knew she was inside the
carriage, and I was certain that she would not let the
fact that for years she has been proclaiming her undying affection for me sway her from removing me from
her path."

"We have been monitoring Lady Bellewood's activities
for some time," Richard put in dryly. "We knew she was
part of your little entourage tonight."

"I had," continued Jonathan, "to allow them an opportunity to escape with the false documents, and she
was the only one among those present in a position to
render me inoperable."

"But what if she'd had a gun?" Tally felt herself grow cold.

"That thought did disturb my serenity somewhat," Jonathan replied cheerfully. "But I was pretty sure that even if the lovely Clea were possessed of such a weapon, an extremely unlikely contingency, she would not be able to bring herself to actually fire it." He glanced down at Tally. "She being, of course, one of those weak females who tend to fall apart in a crisis. She is, on the other hand," he continued, ignoring the sharp dig in his ribs administered by his love, "quite adept at hitting and throwing, and I had every confidence in her ability to fell me with a single blow."

He lifted an arm away from Tally's shoulders to rub the back of his head, and Tally reached up to touch the bruise with gentle fingers.

"My only concern at that point," he went on, pulling her hand around to press a kiss on it, "was that with me out of commission, you would once more be at the mercy of our treacherous friend, Crawshay, which is why I turned over that pistol to you. I have every confidence in the marksmanship of Richard and his stalwarts, but at a hundred yards, under a cloudy moon, I hesitated to take the chance. Besides"—he twinkled—"I know you to be a female who can keep her head in a crisis."

Jonathan's arms tightened around her, and Tally twisted about to look at Richard once more.

"But how did you know about Clea?" she asked. Her eyes widened. "Richard! All that time you were making such a cake of yourself over her, you were . . ."

"Yes," he answered with a heartfelt sigh. "We have been aware for some time that Lady Belle has been, er, assisting Crawshay in his treasonable little sideline."

He sighed again.

"It is a truly lowering reflection," he mused aloud, "that we males can be so easily duped by a beautiful face. And," his voice sharpened, "that we persistently underrate the intelligence of the fair sex. I shudder to think of the number of men who, possessed of the utmost discretion in their dealings with other men, become babbling idiots in the presence of their ladies.

They boast, they muse aloud, they leave important papers about.

"Clea Bellewood, since her marriage to the earl, has moved in the best of circles. She has had as lovers"—he shot a quick glance at Jonathan, who merely shrugged—"men in the highest levels of government, as well as others less well placed. Last year, she ensnared a young fellow in our department, Daniel Ridgeway. He knew little of importance himself, but he had access to some extremely sensitive material, even if it did mean nothing less than breaking into the offices of his superiors. He was the young man, who, apparently torn between loyalty to his country and his infatuation with the lovely Lady Belle, hanged himself last year."

"Oh, dear lord!" Tally pressed a hand to her lips. "How awful!"

"You see," Richard continued, "Clea, though she was left a very wealthy widow, has extremely expensive habits—the clothes, the carriages . . ."

"The gambling," finished Jonathan tiredly.

"Yes, above all the gambling. When Crawshay began his treason, it did not take him long to realize that in Clea, he had his perfect tool. In fact, we believe that it was his cousin's advantageous position in the *haut ton* that gave him the idea for his scheme."

"Good Lord." Jonathan laughed shortly. "And here I thought it was Clea who was making use of Crawshay."

"Well, it was most likely a partnership of mutual benefit. At any rate, we were not sure about Clea's activities until—until she chose me to replace the young clerk as her conduit for stolen secrets." He stopped abruptly, and a slow flush spread to his cheeks.

"Oh, Richard," breathed Tally, her eyes wide. "The night Cat and I came upon the two of you at Lady Talgarth's ball . . ."

"Yes, he interrupted hastily. "I reported her, er, interest in me to Lord Whittaker. It was decided that I would appear to respond to her lures, at least until she incriminated herself thoroughly. And we hoped she might lead us to Crawshay's contact. At that time, of course, we were still trying to ferret out his identity."

"Do you mean," interjected Tally indignantly, "that Lord Whittaker actually asked you to place your mar-

riage in jeopardy by making love to that . . . that . . ."
She dropped her eyes. "Lady Bellewood?"

"Yes—well, I did meet with Clea several times, and
it was not long before she made the suggestion that I
could be extremely useful to her if I chose to do so.
Unfortunately, it became obvious that she wouldn't go
into specifics until our relationship had reached a
more, ah, physical level. At that point, I informed
Lord Whittaker that, while I was prepared to go to
almost any lengths to serve God and country, I regretted that my devotion does not stretch to ruining my
marriage." He smiled suddenly. "Whittaker replied
with the merest twitch of his lips that I should indeed
not be called upon to make such a sacrifice, and gave
me permission to end my so-far harmless relationship
with Lady Belle."

He bowed his head for a moment, then lifted it with
a hunted expression on his face.

"That was the evening I returned home to find that
my bride had discovered all."

"Poor Richard." Tally giggled. "You should be given a
medal for such selfless immolation on the altar of duty."

"Mmph. I'm not so sure Cat would agree with you.
At any rate," continued Richard, striving for a businesslike tone, "when my grand passion for Lady Belle cooled
so rapidly, Crawshay must have cast about for another
route to the papers which, as he had learned from our
clerk, I kept in my study at home."

"I wish I could have been there to watch him scan
those documents." Jonathan chuckled. "And I wish even
more that I could be a fly on the wall when the French
authorities realize they've been gammoned."

"I very much fear," added Richard laconically, "that
the future for Mendoza and Crawshay and Lady Bellewood
will not include castles and chateaux. They'll be lucky if
they escape the guillotine for this night's work."

There was a moment of silence before Jonathan said
with soft savagery, "For the crime they committed—and
for what they put Tally through, I'd be delighted to pull
the cord."

Tally shivered, then, still held securely in Jonathan's
arms, related the events that had taken place after her
precipitous departure from the masquerade ball. She

omitted any mention of Clea's note. She kept that bit of news tucked away in a corner of her mind, where it lodged like a steel splinter. There would be time to consider it later, when she was alone. Alone to make her plans to leave London—and Jonathan—forever.

Chapter Twenty-Four

When the little cavalcade reached London, the group of agents who accompanied the main players in the drama that had unfolded during the night drifted off to their respective homes, and dawn was beginning to lighten the shadows of Half Moon Street when three weary travelers pulled up to the front door of the Thurston home.

Scarcely had Jonathan lifted Tally from the saddle, when Cat flew out to greet them. She flung her arms about her husband, who quite lifted her off her slippered feet in an exuberant hug. Next Cat turned her attention to Tally, and the two friends joined in a tearful embrace.

"Oh, Tally," bubbled Cat. "I have been sitting by the window for simply *hours*! Are you all right? Tell me everything that happened this instant!"

"Oh, best of my friends." Tally laughed shakily. "Yes, I'm fine, although for a moment, the issue surely hung by a thread."

"Tell me everything," repeated Cat, ushering the group indoors. "But first, you must all be starved. I have had a nuncheon set out for you."

Over a splendid spread of ham and sirloin for the gentlemen, and kippers, eggs, and Tally's favorite muffins, the three took turns relating their night's adventures. Cat was the most appreciative audience any spinner of tales could hope for, and interjected the tale with gasps and oohs and shudders in appropriate places.

At one point her eyes grew wide, and her delicate brows rose almost into her hairline. "Clea Bellewood a spy!" she gasped. Then she smiled slyly. "Not that I did not always believe that she was, despite those melting blue eyes, and the most outrageously expensive clothes, capable of anything!"

Soon after, Jonathan rose to go, and Tally saw him to

the door. With his hand on the latch, he gazed down at her for a long moment, and Tally cast her lashes over her cheeks in confusion. He cupped her chin up toward him.

"This is not the time, my dearest love, but we have much to discuss."

His head was so close to hers that she could feel the warmth of his breath caress her cheek.

"You must rest now," he continued softly, "but I shall return this evening. Until then . . ."

His lips brushed hers, and she felt the familiar tingle start from her toes to spread through all her secret places. She held back the tears that were lodged in her throat, for she knew that by this evening she would be gone.

"Of course, Jonathan." She dipped her head to hide her eyes. "Until this evening."

She raised her mouth for one, last precious kiss, and then he was gone. She sagged against the closed door, suddenly weary beyond words. She returned to the breakfast room to find that Richard had also departed and was on his way to his own well-earned rest upstairs. Cat sat smiling among the cups and invited Tally to join her for more coffee.

"No, thanks, Cat. I simply can't hold my eyes open for another moment."

"Of course, dearest. Up you go, then, and I'll see you later this afternoon, if you have roused by then." She paused, suddenly alert. "Tally, what is it?"

Tally sighed. Trust Cat to know when something was amiss with her.

"Nothing. I'm just tired, I'll be . . ." But at the sight of her friend's loving concern, the tears at long last spilled over. Cat rose precipitously from the table.

"Tally! Oh, my dear girl!"

Cat threw her arms around Tally and led her from the dining room, while Tally, utterly undone, sobbed despairingly.

Upstairs, Tally sat down on her bed, gratefully accepting the lawn handkerchief proffered by Cat.

"I'm so sorry," she hiccuped. "I don't know what's the matter with me—I've never turned into such a watering pot."

"Well," replied Cat briskly, "you've never worn yourself to a thread chasing about the country with spies—at gun point, for Heaven's sake. That sort of thing tends to make a person edgy. Now," she commanded, "tell Mother what's bothering you. You'll feel much better when you do."

Blowing her nose fiercely, Tally related the tale of Clea's perfidy, at the end of which, Cat was suitably outraged.

"So, you see . . ." Tally found it necessary to apply Cat's handkerchief to her eyes once more. "Clea's friend—probably that wretched Laleham creature who dyes her hair—must have received the note by now, and the story is no doubt spreading about London right now, like some sort of foul miasma. By tomorrow, I'll be an outcast, and—oh, Cat, I wouldn't mind so much for myself—I can always seek haven at Summerhill—but it means I must leave Jonathan!"

Cat's only response was a blank stare.

"Don't you see?" Tally continued. "He cannot be expected to marry a social pariah! I would ruin his life! I cannot even remain his friend!"

Cat drew a long breath.

"Tally, this is fatigue talking, for you are refining on this too much. Richard and I count ourselves very much your friends, and we certainly don't intend to repudiate you. Nor, I am sure, will Jonathan."

"No, but . . ."

"What you are going to do right now, Tally Burnside, is have a bath and lie down on this bed and get some sleep. No one will disturb you until you ring your bell, and later, when you are refreshed, we will talk more."

While Tally's maid filled the tub, Cat helped her friend remove the ragged remnants of Titania's gauzes, and a little while later, tucked her in beneath a thick feather quilt. She moved to close the curtains in the room, and, turning at the door for one last glance, she observed with satisfaction that Tally's eyes were closed, and her breathing had already deepened.

When Tally opened her eyes again, dusk was giving way to darkness. She tensed for an instant, believing herself to be still in the confines of the dark carriage with her captors, but as her eyes became accustomed to the gloom, she recognized her surroundings and relaxed.

She lay motionless for some time, thinking. Cat was mistaken; a long rest had done nothing to restore her spirits. She imagined the gossip that must be taking place in a hundred drawing rooms and boudoirs right this minute. Had the talk reached Jonathan?

In a swift motion, she threw aside the coverlet and stood for a moment in her underclothes, poised for action. Jonathan had said he would return this evening, and she was determined to spare both of them the painful scene she knew must come. She must be gone by the time he arrived.

The coach on which her faithful footman had purchased her ticket was due to leave at nine o'clock. It lacked almost two hours to that now.

The inn lay some two miles from the Thurston home. She could easily walk that distance in the necessary time, for she would carry only a small bag, containing the essentials for an overnight trip. She would send for the remainder of her things later. However, her walk would take her through some of London's seediest neighborhoods, and her travels through the metropolis at night had taught her the danger in such a passage for an elegantly gowned female of gentle birth. And that was to say nothing of the unwanted attentions she would receive when stopping at the various coaching accommodations along the way.

She snapped her fingers—of course! She raced to the wardrobe in her dressing room and flung open its doors. Surely, Lettie would not yet have thrown away . . . Yes, here it was!

Some two hours later, a small, shabbily dressed old woman clambered breathlessly aboard the stage preparing to depart momentarily from the Swan With Two Necks. Her cracked straw bonnet sat askew on a head of greasy gray curls, and her skirts appeared to have been ingrained with the grime of centuries.

Her fellow-passengers, who included a plump farm wife with two toddlers on her lap, and a bespectacled clerk whose disapproving expression seemed permanently curved in the lines on his face, drew aside in dismay after receiving a whiff of the woman's gamy odor.

"The coach is already full," complained the clerk to the coachman. "If you do not remove this person, I shall report you to the authorities."

"Belt up," bellowed that worthy cheerfully and slammed the door of the vehicle.

"I paid fer me ticket, right 'n proper," croaked the old lady, "so you c'n get yerself stuffed, cully."

The next moment, the coach lumbered through the gateway of the coaching inn into the narrow confines of Lad Lane, and it was not long before the chimney pots of London had been left behind.

Tally peered at the fields flashing by the window. She was determined to shed no more tears, but she was forced to blink them back more than once as she considered all that she had left behind.

Oh, Jonathan! The words seem to echo in her mind like organ chords in a great cathedral. She had been happy before at Summerhill; surely she could be so again, even given the wretched state of affairs between her and Henry—and Henry's disagreeable wife. At least she had her own money now, and the means of earning more. In a year or two, if things didn't work out at Summerhill, she could move out and set up her own establishment in a location of her own choosing. A sparse cottage on a windswept moor, perhaps, or in craggy isolation on a mountaintop in Wales.

A tantalizing odor reached her nostrils, and she turned to discover that the farm wife had unwrapped a large meat pie, which she was apportioning to her children. Tally's stomach produced an audible complaint to verify the fact she had eaten nothing for a very long time.

Startled, the farm wife swung about, her hands still full of pie. Observing the expression on Tally's face, she broke off a piece of the aromatic pastry and handed it reluctantly to her, being careful not to touch her as she did so.

Beyond pride, Tally reached greedily, but before she had a chance to bring the morsel to her lips, a sudden shout and a clatter of horses' hooves brought the coach to a shuddering standstill.

"Mercy!" screamed the farm wife.

"Highwaymen!" screeched the clerk.

The next moment the coach door had been wrenched open and a dark head and a pair of muscular shoulders were thrust through the aperture. Gray eyes anxiously scanned the interior of the coach before coming to rest on the small, filthy form cringing in the corner. Anxiety turned to laughter, and the gentleman addréssed the frightened passengers.

"I am so terribly sorry to have disturbed you all, but I have been searching everywhere for this lady. She's my grandmother, you see. She has these spells"—he tapped the side of his head significantly. "Forgets who she is and dresses in rags."

In one, swift motion, he gathered the little old woman into his arms and prepared to lift her from the coach.

"No!" she screamed. "Jonathan, no!" She turned for succor to her fellow travelers. "Help me—he—he's kidnapping me!"

Jonathan merely clicked his tongue.

"Terribly sad," he said mournfully, and his audience nodded, spellbound. Tally continued her vociferous struggles, but since she had forgotten to maintain her street accent, and since neither the coachman nor his passengers were about to gainsay the doings of such an obvious swell, her pleadings went unheaded.

The coach, minus one insignificant passenger, rattled off into the darkness, and Tally found herself alone under the stars with the Viscount Chelmsford.

He carried her a few yards away to where his curricle waited and set her gently on her feet.

"Now then, Lady Talitha, as I recall saying earlier, we have something of importance to discuss."

Tally was determined not to cry again, nor to be swayed by anything Jonathan might have to say. The fact that her bones had turned to molten fire when he lifted her in his arms and pressed her against his chest did not make her decision any easier, and she was finding it difficult to think with the clean, masculine scent of him filling her senses.

"Jonathan, please let me go. I expect you are wondering at my odd behavior, but . . ."

"I ceased sometime ago to wonder at your odd behavior, my independent little love. Why didn't you tell me about Clea's last little burst of venom?"

"How—did Cat tell you?" she asked indignantly. "How dare she blather about things that I told her in confidence. Just wait till I get my hands on her!"

"You'll have that opportunity very soon, love, for I am taking you back there momentarily—as soon as we get a few things settled. What made you think that I would be willing to let you escape from my life just because you might become the target of a parcel of gossip-mongering cloth heads whose opinion doesn't mean a damn to me?"

"But, Jonathan . . ."

"Did it ever occur to you that I wish nothing more than to protect you against such calumny? I love you, and you have given me cause to believe you love me. A wedding usually follows such declarations, and believe me, I shall cut up very stiff if you play me false." He became serious, and he gazed at her for a heart-stopping moment. "*Do* you love me, Tally?"

"Yes," she replied simply. "With all my heart, Jonathan, but . . ."

His mouth came down on hers, and her resolutions flew away on the sweet scented night breeze. She melted against him and returned his kiss with an abandon that shocked her. Her arms lifted around him, and she wound her fingers in the dark thatch at the base of his neck, pressing him even closer. His hands moved along the curve of her back, and she reveled in the controlled strength she felt in them.

His lips left hers, and she felt momentarily bereft before they began a slow path along her cheek, her throat, and finally to the hollow at the base of her neck. His fingers worked deftly for a few minutes at the collar buttons of Granny Posey's old bombazine bodice, and Tally gasped aloud as his mouth moved along the curve of her breast.

It took every ounce of strength she possessed, but in one wrenching thrust, she pushed Jonathan away and stood back, panting.

After a single, compulsive gesture toward her, Jonathan remained where he was, only the banked fires visible behind the smoke of his eyes indicating the depths to which he had been stirred.

"You cannot deny that we belong together," he breathed.

"I can deny nothing," she replied brokenly, "but I must leave. I cannot bear that you should be the victim of my petty wish to make a career for myself. Clea has had the last laugh, after all, Jonathan. She has destroyed me."

"Ah, yes, Clea," said Jonathan, his voice oddly cheerful. "Did I tell you that I heard from her today?"

"What?" gasped Tally. "Surely, even she could not have the effrontery to write to you . . ." She stopped, puzzled. "But, she could not have had time to . . ."

"No, of course not. It was a note she wrote just before her flight with Crawshay. I cannot tell you how shocked I was by its contents."

"What on earth . . . ?"

"Yes, you see she revealed to me that she has discovered the identify of the illustrator of *Town Bronze*."

Tally stood staring as the implication of his words sank in.

"Jonathan," she said slowly, unbelievingly, "do you mean to tell me that the 'friend' to whom Clea fired off that poisonous little note was you?"

Jonathan nodded. His eyes were alight, but his mouth was twisted into an expression of mock outrage.

"She related with much relish that *you*, Lady Talitha Burnside, daughter of a belted earl, are the person responsible for those 'filthy, scurrilous scratchings.' " He eyed her wickedly. "And now that I am cognizant of your guilty secret, you are completely in my power."

He advanced on her purposely, and she retreated until she found herself backed up against the curricle.

"Now, Jonathan," she quavered, as he placed his hands on her shoulders.

"Not to worry, my sweet," he said, and his smile curled into an exaggerated leer. "As long as you agree to a lifelong collaboration with the author of that scandalous piece of trash, your secret is safe with me."

"You have me at your mercy, sir," she whispered, just before she found herself swept into another dizzying embrace.

Much later, Tally sat beside Jonathan in the curricle cantering slowly back to London.

"I wonder," mused Jonathan aloud.

Tally glanced at him quizzically.

"I wonder if we should not consider simply announcing our guilty secret to the world. If we were to face the public together, we would survive pretty much intact, I think—and, somehow, becoming known as 'one of those writing coves' doesn't seem to me the stigma that it was before. In fact, I begin to realize that I have been pretty stupid about the whole thing." He turned to face Tally squarely. "I know the dust raised would be much worse for a woman, so if you would rather, we'll keep our nefarious occupation a secret, but—it's something to think about, isn't it?"

Tally cocked her head thoughtfully. "Yes, it's something to think about. But not now."

She drew closer to Jonathan and laid her head on his shoulder. Her hands stroked his sleeve, and his own loosed the reins for a moment to cover them. Tally sighed contentedly.

"I'm afraid it will be the middle of the night—again, when we arrive at Cat and Richard's, but I don't think they'll mind being roused."

"If I know your meddlesome friend, Cat, she will be standing at the door waiting for us—again."

"Mmp," Tally growled. "Just wait till I get my hands on her!"

"You're not going to chastise her?" Jonathan asked in surprise.

"No." Tally snuggled further into Jonathan's shoulder. "I'm going to hug her until her ribs crack."